THE ADVENTURES OF

1

IZZY ADAMS

Jessica Lee Sheppard

DESCENDING
INTO
DARKNESS

JESSICA LEE SHEPPARD

SHEPLEN
PRESS
PUBLISHING COMPANY

Book One of The Adventures of Izzy Adams series.

Copyright © 2023 Jessica Lee Sheppard

First Edition November 2023

Sheplen Press Publishing Company

ISBN (ebook): 978-1-7380280-1-6
ISBN (print, paperback): 978-1-7380280-0-9
ISBN (print, hardcover): 978-1-7380280-2-3
ISBN (audio): 978-1-7380280-3-0

Book Cover Design by ebooklaunch.com

To my husband and soulmate, for your unwavering love, support, and belief in me every step of the way. And to my four beautiful children, who bring so much joy and purpose to my life.

CONTENTS

Author's Note

Please note, as a Canadian author, the spelling throughout this book adheres to Canadian English conventions, which may differ slightly from American or British English.

CHAPTER ONE

ECHOES OF THE PAST

The embalming room was dimly lit, with a single bulb swaying gently from a wire overhead. Shadows danced on the walls, animated by its wavering light and the chilly drafts from the ceiling vents. A white curtain sectioned off the room, hiding the bodies waiting to be prepared from the one on the table.

Nestled against the curtain's edge, a stainless-steel surface supported the weight of the room's current centrepiece. A slender woman with golden, chaotic hair bent over the table, focusing on the lifeless form beneath her.

The woman leaned closer toward the skeletal corpse. As her hair parted, it revealed the college sweater she wore. It was faded and worn down from frequent use. She sighed, the sound echoing in the room as her fingers grazed the icy, waxen arm of the deceased. The cold touch awakened a memory, taking her back to a hot summer afternoon of her childhood.

The warm air hummed with the symphony of lawnmowers as seasonal enthusiasts took to their yard work. From the vantage point of a bird in flight, the neighbourhood presented a sea of newly constructed townhomes, each nestled on impeccably manicured lawns.

One lawn stood out amid all the rest: wild thistles and towering grasses that reached almost to the knees of a young girl. She wrestled with a stubborn push mower, simmering with quiet resentment toward her father, who insisted she help their irritable neighbour—a woman who rarely left her home except to threaten neighbourhood children.

The large bay windows of the home overlooked the front yard. Their heavy curtains briefly parted to reveal a shadowed figure lurking within. The curtains draped shut again, and moments later, the front door swung open. A woman emerged onto the front steps, the sunlight catching her silver-streaked hair. She waved her arms wildly, managing to catch the attention of the labouring child.

As the young girl released the handle, the lawnmower's roar subsided to a gentle purr before stopping. She regarded the older woman with a glimmer of hope. Silently, she prayed that a cool bottle of water might magically manifest from within the folds of the woman's wrinkled skirt.

"Everything okay, Ms. Penny?" Sweat trickled down her forehead, seeping into the creases of her eyes and blurring her vision. She ran her tongue over her parched lips, wincing slightly at the salty taste.

"Isabelle Adams! You have gone and destroyed my garden beds!" Ms. Penny's thick finger jabbed down toward a patch of dirt alongside the front of the house. It was overrun with weeds and wilted flowers.

Isabelle's gaze followed the pointed finger, landing on the drooping petunias swaying gently in the breeze. She blinked, glancing between the flowers and Ms. Penny with a puzzled expression. After a long, drawn-out moment, she said, "I don't see what I've done wrong."

Ms. Penny's eyes widened, her arm swinging again in a wild arc, pointing toward the flowerbed. "The mulch girl! You've scattered grass all over it!"

Isabelle shrugged, her face indifferent. "Well, that's not my fault! I can't control where the lawnmower shoots out the grass, can I?"

Ms. Penny clutched the metal railing. "Not your fault? You're cutting the grass from the wrong direction, girl. Of course it's your fault! Where on earth is your father? What would he think about this?" She raised a gnarled hand, shielding her eyes from the sun as she squinted past Isabelle, scanning the area for any sign of her father.

Isabelle turned her head as if to examine the mulch again. She then rolled her eyes before responding with a practised calm. "He would say that I tried my best, and my kindness will earn me another step toward heaven, ma'am." Her voice held an edge of polite sarcasm, and she bit her lower lip to keep from grinning. "And I prefer to be called Izzy," she added, straightening her back as she met the older woman's gaze head-on.

This, of course, sent Ms. Penny into an overexcited rant. Izzy shifted away from her neighbour as she continued her tirade of yelling. Scowling at the mulch, Izzy muttered, "Maybe if you'd spent less time yelling at kids and more time watering your flowers, they wouldn't look so dead." She inhaled deeply, finding comfort in the scent of the freshly mown grass.

"The lack of respect given to seniors!" Ms. Penny continued, her voice rising in octaves. She placed her hand dramatically on her chest and said, "At my age, I shouldn't be expected to bend down and remove bits of grass from my mulch!" Her eyes then swivelled back to Izzy, a cunning glint flickering within them.

An awkward moment of silence hung in the air. Finally, almost reluctantly, Izzy said, "I'm sorry, Ms. Penny. I'll pick out the grass when I'm done mowing." She reached up and snatched at a piece of her hair and yanked on it, twisting it between her fingers. Her eyes glistened, and she bit the inside of her cheek, trying not to let the tears fall.

Ms. Penny nodded at her triumphally. "Apology accepted, dear. It's quite understandable that you wouldn't know the ins and outs of such a mature task." She gestured dismissively toward the blue-shuttered townhouse standing adjacent to hers. "Your poor father, always immersed in his undertaker affairs, scarcely has time to teach you much of anything, does he?"

She turned as if to re-enter her house, only to pause and look at Izzy again. "Oh, and *Isabelle*, while you're at it, be a dear and do some weeding. I expect that much shouldn't be too difficult for you to figure out." With a dismissive wave, she pivoted and disappeared back into her house. Izzy stood alone, pulling furiously at her hair, glaring at the retreating figure of her neighbour.

Slowly, the warm haze of her memory faded away. The comforting touch of the sun gave way to the cool feel of the arm under her fingertips. The faint, sterile smell of formaldehyde hung in the air, mingling with the metallic tang of the embalming room. Izzy opened her eyes and peered at Ms. Penny's corpse as if trying to pierce through the shroud of death.

"You were always such a miserable old bat," she said, her eyes hardening. "Not a single 'thank you' passed your lips in all those years. And yet, even in death, I still have to run errands for you."

Izzy held a pair of red socks in the air, her words steeped in exasperation. The mystery of why Ms. Penny would choose Adams Funeral Home as her final resting place was something she couldn't fathom. After all, the old woman had seldom shown anything but disdain for Izzy's family.

She took in Ms. Penny's emaciated frame and hollowed-out face, studying every detail. A wave of heaviness settled on her chest as her eyebrows knitted together. "I am sorry that you went the way you did, though. Cancer is a nasty way to die." She gently patted the corpse's shoulder, a silent apology hanging in the air. "You had your good moments too. I'm sure someone will miss you."

As she pulled her hand away, a bristly black spider scurried from underneath the body. Recoiling in alarm, she stumbled backward into a tray behind her, sending cotton swabs and blush palettes tumbling to the floor.

Panic surged through her, twisting her gut into a knot. The spider shot across Ms. Penny's chest, then back onto the embalming table, vanishing once more beneath the body.

Seeing it cross the table triggered unwanted thoughts in Izzy's mind. She was reminded of her childhood fear of spiders and the countless nights she'd crawled into her older sister's bed, having awoken from a nightmare about one.

"Deep breaths, Iz. It's only a spider. Just a tiny, eight-legged embodiment of every horror movie ever made," she muttered.

The curtain shook as if laughing at her, which Izzy attributed to the sudden blast of freezing air from the vent overhead. Shivering, she bent down to pick up the fallen items, placing them back onto the tray.

Izzy tossed the socks near Ms. Penny's feet, carefully avoiding touching the table. "Kate can manage the rest," she said, backing up to the door.

A soft click sounded behind the room divider. An eerie stillness enveloped the room as Izzy moved toward the exit. The slow drip of the sink vanished, replaced by the sound of heavy breathing.

She hesitated, fingers trembling near the doorknob. Slowly, she turned to look toward Ms. Penny's body, desperately searching for the rise and fall that would betray any flicker of life. Finding the chest unmoving, Izzy sighed and reached again for the doorknob.

The room was once again wrapped in silence. And then, a raspy breath cut through the stillness, sounding louder than before. Each echo was a cool whisper against her skin, filling her with dread. Her mind replayed all the old ghost stories she'd heard as a child huddled around the campfire.

"This isn't happening," she said, her voice wavering and sounding small. "I'm just tired. It was a long drive." She shook her head as if to cast off the lingering terror that clung to her soul. "Still, I should just make sure . . ." She took a deep breath and then strode toward the lifeless figure on the table. She leaned down again and touched the arm.

The skin felt reassuringly frigid and marble-like beneath her fingers. "Definitely dead. Sorry, Ms. Penny," she said, laughing nervously. "There's a tiny, rather inappropriate part of me—the part that's watched too many zombie movies—that's a bit relieved you're not planning a surprise comeback tour."

Without warning, the body beneath her hand recoiled from her touch. Izzy's face paled, and she was once again frozen in place. With another twitch, the arm jolted forcefully. It struck the edge of the table, knocking Izzy's hand away.

A scream grew in her throat. It emerged as a feeble croak, drowned out by the adrenaline coursing through her body. Pivoting fast, she collided with the tray of cosmetics once more, sending it crashing to the ground along with her.

She scrambled backward in blind terror, a flurry of cotton swabs scattered in her wake like tiny ghosts. Her back crashed against the door. She frantically tried to rise to her feet, but her legs—reduced to a quivering mass of nerves—refused to respond.

In desperation, she grabbed at her hair. Yanking hard on a blond lock, she tried to focus on the sharp pain to drown out the overwhelming fear that surged through her. A deep laugh rolled through the room. It bore no resemblance to Ms. Penny's yet was strikingly familiar nonetheless.

"Eddie!" Izzy said, her mouth twisting into a snarl. Her eyes were icy blue and ablaze with fury. They fixated on the black dress shoes poking out from beneath the white curtain near the table.

CHAPTER TWO

GHOSTS IN THE DARK

Adrenaline pumping through her veins, Izzy leaped to her feet. The spider that had set her heart racing was forgotten as she strode toward the table. Leaning over the body, she gripped the fabric of the curtain. With an unceremonious yank, she drew it aside. A man, not much older than herself, stood there, bathed in the harsh glow of the light.

His charcoal grey suit, sharply tailored and impeccably pressed, appeared out of place in the morgue. Taken by surprise, he stumbled back into the empty table behind him. "Ow!" He gingerly rubbed at his side, wincing. An amused grin played across his face as he looked up at Izzy.

She crossed her arms and pressed her lips into a thin line. "Eddie! The dark humour isn't appreciated."

"Aw, come on, Iz, it was pretty funny," Eddie said, smoothing out his dress shirt.

"No, it wasn't. It was morbid!" Izzy's hands moved instinctively to her hair, bunching it up into a messy ponytail, only to let it fall back down. The scent of roses filled the air around them. "Did Lyssa know about your prank?"

Crimson bloomed across Eddie's cheeks, a stark contrast to his strawberry-blond hair. He started to fiddle with his bolo tie. "Yeah, she knew." The words tumbled out as he tugged harshly on one string. "She called my joke 'poor taste.' She didn't seem so happy when I left the house."

Izzy's gaze fell on the tie, concern etching lines on her forehead. "You're going to break that," she warned. "It was Dad's, wasn't it?"

Eddie nodded, the string bouncing back into place as he let it go. "Yeah, it was with some other stuff that Mom wanted to donate. Lyssa recognized it when she was dropping the box off."

Izzy's eyes welled up at the news, and she bit down on her lip. "She gave away Dad's things?" A muffled sob slipped past her lips.

Eddie's eyes widened, and he quickly circled the table to comfort his sister. "No, Iz. Crap, I'm sorry. I didn't mean to upset you!"

He opened his arms like a protective cocoon, and she stepped into the warmth, immersing herself in the familiar, spicy scent of their father's cologne. It now clung to her brother like a nostalgic ghost.

"It was caught in the sleeve of one of Dad's old shirts. I didn't want it. The shirt was too big." He patted Izzy gently on the back, continuing, "Mom kept the important stuff. When we're ready, we'll all go through it together, okay?"

Izzy sniffed, her face nestling into the fabric of her brother's shoulder. "I don't think I'll ever be ready." Hot tears rolled down her cheeks, soaking into the material of his suit. "I miss him."

Eddie tightened his embrace, tears welling up in his coffee-coloured eyes. "Me too," he confessed, his voice breaking. Time halted momentarily as they stood there in their shared grief.

Izzy pulled back from her brother, her gaze falling on the bolo tie. She traced the engraved maple leaf, a tentative smile beginning to tug at her lips.

"Do you remember the charity gala Mom organized, the one where Dad's belt broke?" Her smile widened at the memory. "Dad just fastened this bolo tie around his waist and strutted around the rest of the evening like he'd invented a new fashion trend."

Eddie chuckled, "Yeah, and he wore it all the time after that. He called it his 'Backup Belt Buddy.'"

"Dad was so funny." Izzy sighed, her hand releasing the tie. "And his laugh . . . Remember his laugh?"

"Mortifyingly loud but contagious," Eddie said as he carefully adjusted the tie.

"I miss that laugh," Izzy said, her gaze dropping to the socks near Ms. Penny's feet. She picked them up, her mind shifting gears to the task. Carefully, she unravelled the fabric before pulling the first sock onto the deceased woman's foot.

"Yeah, me too," he said, sidling closer to the table. "What's with the socks?"

"Kate called me on my way into the city. She said she forgot to put them on. Ms. Penny specified it in her funeral plan—had some concern about her feet becoming cold." Izzy picked up the matching sock and slipped it onto the other foot.

"Or she was more concerned about people seeing her ugly feet," Eddie said, his gaze wandering off to a desk nearby. "Ugly feet to go with an ugly personality. What a horrible person that woman was. I never liked her!"

He walked over to the desk and leaned against it. The radio perched on the corner crackled to life. A screeching sound filled the room, making Eddie wince and cover his ears. As the noise gradually tuned into a song of questionable tempo, the lyrics floated out:

> *Young lad, best mind your words,*
> *Time's a river. Fast it surges.*
> *In its wake, we all turn old.*
> *And beauty fades in its bold hold.*

Izzy looked at Eddie, a perplexed expression crossing her face as the haunting melody continued, its volume increasing with each line.

> *In your prime, you jest and jeer,*
> *But remember, your twilight's near.*

Izzy's hands flew to her ears. "Shut it off!" The song continued. Its volume now cranked to the highest the radio could go:

> *When your time comes, as it will,*
> *You won't be smirking when you're*
> *laying so still.*

Izzy watched as Eddie fumbled with the buttons. At last, the room fell silent except for the dripping from the nearby faucet. Recovering, she lowered her hands, shooting her brother a surprised look. "I think you upset Ms. Penny," she said, glancing at the body on the table.

Eddie frowned at the radio and stepped away from it. "Yeah, that was . . . weird." He approached the embalming table and fiddled with Ms. Penny's arms.

"I wasn't kidding. It sounded just like Ms.—Hey, what are you doing?" Izzy squinted, peering over his shoulder. She caught sight of the fishing wire he extracted from the deceased woman's sleeve and gasped. Eddie wound it up and stowed it in his pocket.

With a sheepish grin, he said, "Can't let Kate find this. She would lose her mind if she knew I used it to move Ms. Penny's arm." His voice trailed off as the air conditioner hummed back to life.

"I think it's gotten colder," Izzy muttered, pulling the strings of her hooded sweater tighter around herself. "Kate must have tinkered with the thermostat again." She jammed her hands into the pockets of her jeans, trying to warm them.

Eddie shot her a knowing glance before striding over to the sink to silence the dripping tap. "A frosty room to match her frosty attitude."

Izzy chuckled, watching Eddie return to the table. He stretched his back with a crack, jostling Ms. Penny's body. The radio blared back to life, this time with a more sombre melody:

> *Don't you know that I'm hurting over here*
> *Have a little respect for me, my dear.*

"Jeepers!" Izzy quickly covered her ears again, her heartbeat hammering against her ribs as an eerie sensation tingled up her spine.

> *Would it harm you to shed just one sincere tear?*
> *Invisible I may be, yet I'm standing right here!*

As the radio screeched out its last note, Eddie rushed to it again, his fingers slipping over the dials as he tried to shut it off. Izzy bolted to the wall and yanked the power cord from the outlet. The radio fell silent.

She looked at Eddie, her pale face making her small scattering of freckles jump out. "Do you think . . . Could she be here, listening to us?" Izzy's voice came out in a whisper as if afraid Ms. Penny might hear.

Eddie's gaze softened, and he shook his head. "You've been reading too many of your spiritualism books, Iz," he said, chuckling lightly. "The radio's just old. There's nothing supernatural going on here."

"Don't make fun of my books," Izzy snapped. After a moment's pause, she said, "They make me feel closer to Dad. It gives me a better understanding of where he might be now."

"Sorry, Iz," Eddie said, his voice quivering. "If those books make you happy, that's all that matters. Just . . . don't bring them up around Mom. You know how she feels about the whole spiritualism thing."

He strode to the embalming table, reaching over Ms. Penny to close the curtain. "We should get going. We'll never hear the end of it if we're late for dinner."

A sigh tumbled from Izzy, and her face grew shadowy with weariness. "These Saturday dinners are turning into an ordeal. The drive from Belleville to Toronto is exhausting."

Eddie walked over to the overturned tray, righted it, and gathered the broken blush palettes and cotton swaps Izzy had knocked over. As he gestured for her to toss him a towel, he said, "It's her way of grieving. It gives her control to have us all safe under one roof. Saturdays are hard for her now . . . You know that."

Izzy turned away, her vision blurring as tears swelled up once again. "I'm just tired," she said, focusing on a small crack in the wall. "I suppose if I leave early, the drive won't be so crappy . . . A couple hours tops? I can manage that . . . at least for now."

Eddie nodded and rose to his feet with the grime-smeared cloth in his hand. "It won't be forever. It's almost been a year, you know. I'm sure things will go back to normal soon."

Things will never be normal, Izzy thought, her gaze drifting to her brother as he attempted to lob the dirty towel into a hamper across the room. It sailed through the air, missed the mark entirely, and slapped Ms. Penny's face.

A strange tension hung in the air, sending a trail of goosebumps marching up her spine. Suddenly, the overhead bulb burst with an ear-splitting crack. Glass shattered down like rain, plunging the room into darkness.

CHAPTER THREE

SHATTERED DREAMS

In the absence of light, the room took on an even eerier quality. It was as if an unseen entity were there with them, chilling the air and sucking out all the warmth.

Eddie and Izzy fumbled for the door in unison, their shoulders colliding as they each scrambled to be the first one out. Being the quicker of the two, Izzy reached the door first, grasping at the handle with clammy hands. With a hard yank, she pulled it ajar.

A wedge of light sliced through the darkness, casting long shadows in the room. The siblings staggered into the hallway, leaning heavily against the cool wall as the door closed with a thud behind them.

Eddie's head lolled back against the wall; his eyes squeezed shut while his breaths came in gasps. "Do you think Lyssa . . . do you think she caused this?"

Izzy looked at her brother in disbelief, hugging her knees to her chest as her heart resumed its natural rhythm. "Yes, Eddie. She blew out the light with her magical powers."

Annoyance flickered across Eddie's face as he opened his eyes and turned to look at her. "But she knew we were in there!"

Izzy climbed to her knees and gestured for him to remain still. She gingerly picked out tiny slivers of glass glittering in his hair. "We could have been hurt. She wouldn't have done that."

Eddie's frown softened as he nodded. "Yeah, you're right. Must've been a power surge or something like that?"

"Sure, or something . . . Now quit moving around," she muttered, her hands meticulously working through his hair. Once satisfied that his head was clean of glass, she stood up and used her sneaker to push the shards up against the wall. "We'll worry about the mess later. We really should get going."

Eddie followed his sister up the steep staircase, his grumbles echoing through the dimly lit space. "Taking the elevator would've been much easier."

"Cramming into a metal box suspended by only a cable is the last thing I want to be doing right now," Izzy replied as she arrived at the top landing. She looked down at her brother, a small smile dancing on her lips. He slowly made his way up the stairs, his face flushed with exertion.

"Yeah, good point."

The landing opened into the rear section of the funeral home. It was wrapped in shadows as the establishment remained closed for the afternoon. To Izzy, the absence of activity painted the space with an uncomfortable stillness.

Faint rays of sunlight struggled through the skylight overhead, revealing a delicate ballet of dust motes in the air. As they walked through the room, their footsteps were muffled by the plush carpet. Izzy trailed her fingers along the edge of one of the carved caskets on display, feeling the intricate details etched into the wood.

"Have you sensed anything odd around here lately?" she asked, pausing to readjust the artificial flowers atop one casket lid.

Eddie's steps faltered. "Sensed anything? You mean like ghosts?" he said, fluttering his hands spookily, accentuating the word *ghost*.

Izzy's narrowed gaze pierced through the dim light, her mouth tensing with irritation. "Not ghosts," she said. "I mean more like a presence . . . or just a strange, unsettling feeling you get when you're working." She held Eddie's gaze, searching for a hint of understanding.

He paused again, his face growing thoughtful, before responding, "Well, there was this one time when I was setting up chairs for a service . . . I could have sworn I felt a sudden chill." He shuddered dramatically, a mischievous twinkle glinting in his eye.

Izzy leaned closer toward her brother. Her voice softened to a whisper as she asked, "Really? What happened next?"

Eddie lowered his voice another octave. "And then . . . I noticed that the window was open," he said, unable to contain his laughter. Izzy's face crumpled at her brother's joke. She instantly wished she hadn't initiated the conversation.

"Have you . . . felt anything?" he asked.

She hesitated, unsure if she wanted to share her thoughts with her brother now. Her eyes darted around the room as if searching for a way to escape, but Eddie's gaze kept her anchored in place.

"Well, it's just some little things, really," Izzy began. Her voice was soft and thoughtful. "A few weeks ago, shortly before Mrs. Rose's funeral, someone kept placing a red rose behind her ear. I thought it was you, but then you showed up late . . . And her sisters saw it and started to cry. Apparently, she liked wearing one on special occasions."

Eddie's brows furrowed. "Yeah, I remember that day. The tire blew out on my truck."

Izzy wrapped a strand of hair around her finger, gently tugging at it as she continued, "And then there was Mr. Brightfoot's funeral. The one where only two people showed up."

Eddie laughed. "Yeah, one of them only came to make sure that he was actually dead."

"At that funeral, something strange happened," Izzy continued. "I had to keep stepping outside because I felt overwhelmed by feelings of intense hatred. I literally felt sick to my stomach." She shivered, wrapping her arms around herself as she thought about that moment.

A hushed silence hung in the air. Eddie finally spoke. "Have you . . . you know, seen a doctor?"

Izzy's breath caught in her throat. She clenched her fists at her sides, a stinging sensation prickling at her eyes as tears welled up and threatened to spill down her cheeks. "You think I've lost my mind?" she asked, her voice trembling with hurt.

A sigh escaped his lips. "No, but . . . you have been struggling with school and Dad . . . and you sometimes seem distant from us."

Izzy's gaze dropped to the carpet, her eyes fixating on a small coffee stain. "Just forget I said anything."

Eddie moved to step near her. Sensing his approach, Izzy's anger flared, her piercing blue eyes freezing him in place. "I'm not crazy," she said, brushing past him and pushing forcefully against the double doors. They swung open with a resounding crack against the wall.

A tall, formidable woman stood at the entrance to the foyer, her eyes widening in surprise. As she fell back a step, her arm brushed against a porcelain vase, setting it teetering on the edge of the table. She caught it just in time, placing it back into position.

A frown marred her smooth ebony complexion as she turned her attention to Eddie, who trailed behind Izzy as she crossed the room. Her voice had a hint of a Southern drawl as she spoke, "I reckon your brother's little prank didn't quite hit the mark, did it?"

Eddie's cheeks turned a deep shade of crimson as he sidestepped Izzy and approached the woman. "Yeah, Lyssa, you were right. It was a stupid prank," he admitted, tilting his head upward to kiss her lips.

Lyssa bent her head slightly, returning his kiss. And then she broke away, her dark eyes sparkling playfully. Casting a glance at Izzy, she caught the younger girl's sullen expression and paused. "Chèr, I reckon I'll ride along with your sister to the restaurant," she said, handing the truck keys to Eddie. He took them and sent a final, apologetic glance Izzy's way.

Izzy felt a pang in her chest at the sight of his regret before he pushed open the entrance doors and disappeared into the parking lot. Lyssa turned back toward Izzy, her dark tresses falling across her face. "Shall we, darlin'?" she suggested, nodding toward the exit.

After locking up, they went outside and were met by a crisp wind that caressed their skin and carried the bittersweet scent of decaying leaves. Izzy led the way to her blue Honda Civic, her feet crunching under the scattering of fallen leaves covering the parking lot.

She settled into the driver's seat, slamming the car closed with more force than necessary, causing the vehicle to shudder.

Lyssa slid in beside Izzy and fastened her seatbelt, turning to her with an expectant gaze. "Well . . . ?" she prompted.

Tears fell down Izzy's face as she bowed her head. Each one felt like a tiny betrayal to herself, a physical manifestation of her confusion and fear.

Lyssa unbuckled her seatbelt and leaned over to Izzy, pulling her into a hug that carried the scent of oranges. "Oh, darlin', I am so sorry. I warned that fool not to go through with his prank! He couldn't resist when he found out you were stopping here first."

Izzy sniffed, wiping her tear-streaked face with the sleeve of her sweater. "It's not that, Lyssa. I . . . well, lately, I've been feeling . . . different." Lyssa tightened her embrace, a silent encouragement for Izzy to continue.

Izzy recounted her conversation with her brother, her hands gripping the steering wheel for support. "I'm not crazy!" she insisted, a trace of anger mingling with her words. She broke away from the embrace to lean back against her seat, doubt growing in her belly.

Lyssa gently brushed back strands of Izzy's unruly hair. "Of course, you aren't."

"You believe me?"

Lyssa smiled at her. "Yes, I do. You've been seeking a connection with your father these past few months. It's not a far stretch to say that you've opened yourself up spiritually. It could be that you are more attuned to the energy left behind by those who pass on."

Turning to Lyssa, a grateful smile tugged at the corners of Izzy's lips. "I wish my family were as open-minded as you," she said, brushing away the remnants of a tear that clung stubbornly to her chin.

Lyssa's laugh was infectious, a bubbling melody in the confines of the car. "Oh, honey, your family's resistance to anything different is stiffer than a stale bagel."

Izzy's laughter joined Lyssa's. "I don't know how you put up with us," she said, grinning at her friend.

"Love ain't easy, darling—it involves work, and sometimes that work isn't just with your partner; it's with their family." Lyssa's voice was dreamy as she added, "And when you find the perfect partner, the work doesn't seem as bad."

Izzy couldn't help herself. She rolled her eyes at the mention of her brother being "perfect." The thought was utterly laughable to her. She started the Honda and pulled out of the parking lot, merging into the traffic flow. The surrounding neighbourhood was dressed in autumn hues. A dazzling array of fiery reds, warm oranges, and earthy browns painted a breathtaking picture outside her car window.

She could see the well-groomed lawns with their towering oak trees, the branches swaying in the wind. Bats and ghosts hung from the houses, lending a festive atmosphere that added to her anticipation for Halloween. Tapping her fingers to the rhythm of the song playing on the radio, she asked, "Where exactly are we headed?"

"Oh, the Artisan's Banquet, hon. Just make a left onto St. Clair. The restaurant is just past Spadina." Lyssa instructed.

Heat rose in Izzy's cheeks as she glanced down at her college sweater. "The Artisan's Banquet? Isn't formal attire required there?"

Lyssa looked over at Izzy, her brow furrowing. "Darling, formal attire is not required, but most folks will probably be dressed up," she replied, reaching down into her bag as she spoke.

"Why wouldn't my mom or Eddie have told me? I just assumed he was wearing his work clothes!" She glanced at her outfit again, cringing inwardly. She knew that her mother and older sister would be far from pleased with her evening attire.

"Oh, hun, don't worry on it. Eddie probably assumed you knew. You do have a preference for wearing . . . comfy clothes," she teased, a grin softening her words. She held out an elegant, navy-blue cardigan and a hairbrush. "You can wear this, chère. I brought it in case it got chilly later in the evening. It'll look lovely with your jeans. And use this to tame that hair of yours. You'll look just fine."

Izzy's eyes softened, and she let out a slow breath, her shoulders dropping slightly. "Thank you, Lys. I don't know what my brother did to win you over, but I'm sure glad he did."

She turned left onto St. Clair Avenue, passing a grand stone church that loomed over the road. They continued their journey silently, the city's evening energy unfolding around them.

As the twinkling lights of the Artisan's Banquet came into view, Lyssa shifted in her seat to look at Izzy. "Have you given more thought to our last discussion? Tonight might be the perfect opportunity to tell your mother . . ." Her words trailed off as she watched Izzy's face tense.

Uncertainty flickered in Izzy's eyes. "I don't know, Lys. It's always been an expectation that I go into the family business. Kate did. Eddie did. I should too . . ." A rising tide of anxiety wrapped around her like a chilling wind. Visions of her mother's potential reaction to her true aspirations filled her mind, and Izzy tried to blink them away.

She guided her car into the parking lot of the Artisan's Banquet. The elegant brick building was bathed in a warm glow by the old-fashioned lanterns adorning its walls. As Izzy pulled into an empty spot adjacent to Eddie's red Ford F-150, Lyssa cleared her throat as if preparing to make a speech. "Izzy," she began. "Life is too short. You should be chasing your own dreams, not someone—"

"My great-grandparents started the funeral home, and it's always been passed down in the family. It's tradition. I can't walk away from that."

"But is that what you want, darlin'? What about pursuing advocacy and human rights? University could be your pathway to that!"

"University was never part of the plan for me, Lys. Besides, my mom and Kate would never understand, and it would just cause conflict," Izzy said, her voice laced with defeat.

She pulled off her sweater, exchanging it for Lyssa's cardigan. With a few brushstrokes, she attempted to tame her hair, contemplating a ponytail before allowing the locks to fall around her shoulders, framing her round face.

"Well, to hell with what your m—" A sudden rap at Lyssa's window cut through the air, startling both women. "Oh, my lord, Eddie. You nearly scared me to death," she said, her manicured hand pressed against her chest.

Eddie swung the car door open, extending his hand to assist his fiancé in getting out. Their lighthearted banter filled the air as Izzy slid out of the vehicle, her ears greeted by the laughter and soft melodies spilling from the restaurant.

As she trailed behind them, her thoughts drifted to her older sister, a familiar knot tightening in her stomach. Since their father's death, Kate had undergone a disconcerting transformation—growing colder, crueller, and increasingly challenging to be around.

Izzy found herself hoping that she wouldn't be seated next to Kate. She tightened Lyssa's cardigan around her slight frame as the cool autumn breeze rustled the leaves around her.

Her eyes were drawn to a massive raven. It was perched atop one of the wall lamps, observing her intently. Frowning, Izzy paused, captivated by the intelligent gleam in the bird's dark eye. A chill ran down her back. It prompted her to jog to Eddie, who patiently waited by the entrance with an apologetic expression, holding the door open for her.

Izzy ignored him, feigning interest in the sprawling ivy that cascaded over the lobby walls. Its green tendrils reached toward the ceiling. The air was infused with the tantalizing aroma of baked bread with the subtle fragrances of herbs and spices.

She moved to join Lyssa, who had approached the reception desk to announce their arrival. Within moments, a young woman greeted them with a warm smile. Gesturing for them to follow, she led them through the softly lit dining room to a corner table.

Izzy sighed, her shoulders dropping as Eddie and Lyssa took their seats first. She silently reproached herself for not moving more swiftly. Left with no alternative, she reluctantly took her place next to Kate, who greeted her with a twisted scowl etched upon her face.

"Where's Mom?" Eddie inquired as he tore into the loaf of bread placed in the table's centre.

"She stepped outside to take a phone call," Kate said, recoiling as she watched Eddie rip off a slice of bread. "Manners, Eddie," she said, neatly unfolding her white napkin and placing it on her lap. As Eddie flushed a deep crimson, her gaze shifted to Izzy. "Are you wearing . . . jeans, *Isabelle?*"

Izzy shifted uncomfortably in her seat, the denim suddenly feeling rough against her skin. Childishly, she wished she could slink under the table.

"No one told her about the venue, Kate," Lyssa said, attempting to divert Kate's withering gaze from Izzy.

Kate regarded Lyssa with a disinterested glance. "I believe I told her," she said. Turning back to her siblings, she continued, "Mother's charity event is next Saturday. I expect that you will all be in attendance."

Izzy's eyebrows knitted together in a frown. "You mean that fundraiser for raccoons? That's next Saturday?"

"Yes," Kate's voice bore an icy edge, her lips pressed into a thin line. "Mother is being presented an award for her commitment to protecting the well-being of raccoons."

Izzy snorted. "Mom's only getting the award because she wrote a hefty cheque after she was caught throwing bottles at a raccoon outside our house. Who would have guessed that our neighbours were such hardcore animal lovers?"

Kate glared at Izzy, her eyes hardening. "That never happened."

"It did. I was there," Izzy replied, reaching for the loaf of bread. "Anyways, I can't come. I have my own charity event." She slathered a generous amount of butter onto her bread.

Interest flared in Lyssa's eyes. "Your own charity event, darlin'? Why haven't you mentioned it before now?"

A blush warmed Izzy's cheeks. "It's a fundraising walk for the Belleville food bank. They've been struggling with donations this year. It's not a big deal, Lys."

"If it is not a big deal, then you won't mind missing it," Kate said. Her words were punctuated by the sharp thud of her menu hitting the table.

"I meant that it's not a big deal that I organized it," Izzy said, raising her eyes to meet Kate's. She felt a sudden surge of defiance, and her hands clenched under the table. She always allowed her family to make her decisions, but this was different somehow. It wasn't just about her.

"You're not missing Mom's charity event, Isabelle. They can find a replacement for your . . . little race."

Izzy flushed, the heat of suppressed anger spreading through her. Izzy's gaze lingered on her sister, the corners of her mouth twitching slightly. "Do you realize that the highest users of food banks are kids, Kate? Child poverty is a thing in Canada, believe it or not. I'm sorry for the inconvenience, but prioritizing starving children over raccoons seems to be an easy choice."

She brought the cool glass of water to her lips, briefly quenching her rising anger. After taking a sip, she set the glass back on the table, her gaze hardening with determination.

"I'm not going to abandon my event."

Izzy watched as a furious hue of red swept across Kate's face. The clinking of cutlery against china and murmuring voices from neighbouring tables faded into the background as Izzy stared defiantly at her sister. Her brother moved to disrupt the silence, but a swift glare from their older sister stopped him.

Kate's voice rang out, reverberating off the walls and into the neighbouring table. "If Dad were here, he would have gone with Mom." Her words seemed to hang in the air. "But he isn't here, is he?" she said, her tone growing venomous. "He isn't here because you took him away from us."

A sickening feeling squirmed up from Izzy's belly. She pushed herself from the table so abruptly that her chair toppled over.

"I can't believe you would . . . I need to use the bathroom," Izzy managed, tears welling in her eyes. As she spun on her heels to leave, she could hear Lyssa's voice rising in her defence.

Navigating her way through the throng of servers balancing overloaded trays of food, Izzy found herself slipping into a bubble of her own grief, the noise of the restaurant receding into a distant hum.

A single tear fell from her eye, catching in her lashes. It carried the weight of her sister's cruel words—words that amplified a deep-seated guilt she'd harboured since her father's death. Hearing it vocalized felt like a raw wound being pried open. It also confirmed that she was the catalyst for the transformation in her sister's demeanour.

The bathroom door closed behind her with a soft click. Izzy was drawn to the gilded mirror hanging above the sink. The face reflected at her was barely recognizable. Her eyes were swollen, and her pale complexion stood out against the lush bathroom interior. Time seemed to stand still as she remained rooted to the spot, consumed by her dark thoughts.

The silence was sliced by the door whispering open, followed by the distinctive clacking of heels against the tiled floor. Lyssa came up beside Izzy, wrapping her up in a comforting embrace. They stood for several long moments before Lyssa spoke.

"You are not to blame for your father's death, chère. It was an accident," she said, gently pushing back tendrils of Izzy's hair from her tear-streaked face.

"An accident that I caused," Izzy replied, her words laced with self-loathing as she looked at herself darkly in the mirror.

Instead of responding, Lyssa twisted the faucet, allowing cool water to soak into a napkin. She wrung it out and began to dab it against Izzy's flushed cheeks.

Letting the napkin fall away, Lyssa placed her hand on Izzy's shoulder, her reflection meeting Izzy's in the mirror. "Unless I'm mistaken, darlin', you weren't grabbin' the wheel from your Daddy's hands."

Izzy rolled her eyes, turning to face her friend. "That's not what I meant," she said, folding her arms.

"No? Well, I don't see any other way that it could be your fault, darlin'," Lyssa drawled, stepping back to give Izzy space. "If you insist on shouldering the mistakes of others, you'll soon find yourself on a lonely, dark path."

Izzy's shoulders slumped. "I'm starving," she said, moving past Lyssa. "Let's just go back, okay?" Nodding reluctantly, Lyssa fell in step behind her as they left the bathroom.

As they re-entered the dining area, a lanky man with a mop of dishevelled brown hair stumbled into Izzy, knocking her off balance. Startled, she reached out, her fingers catching the edge of a nearby table for support.

"Sorry!" she said, glancing toward the family whose table she had grabbed. She was met with blank stares from the two adults, who immediately returned to their private conversation, their lips moving rapidly. Their son, however, gazed past Izzy, narrowing his eyes at the man who had bumped into her.

As if caught in an uncontrollable dance, the man stumbled again, colliding with a server. The quiet hum of the restaurant was suddenly riddled with a symphony of clattering dishes. The man, finding himself covered in hot soup, protested angrily, his voice carrying throughout the restaurant. He gestured at the server, swinging his arms in frustration.

Izzy's attention was drawn to the sound of the child snickering beside her, his bright green eyes sparkling mischievously. A pink mist danced across his hand, swirling between his outstretched fingertips. Alerted by his laughter, his mother leaned closer, scolding him quietly. When Izzy looked back at the small hand, she found the palm empty. It was marked only by smudges of dirt and remnants of the boy's dinner.

"Seems like he got what he deserved," Lyssa said, coming up behind her. "You alright, darlin'?"

Izzy nodded slowly, her eyes reluctantly leaving the child. She followed Lyssa back to the table, her thoughts buzzing with what she had just seen. She decided it was a trick of the light or an illusion. Or just plain exhaustion. She resolved to start going to bed earlier.

As they neared the table, Izzy's gaze landed on her mother, who had finally joined them. Michelle Adams sat at the head of the table, an outwardly charming figure with soft, brown eyes and an inviting smile.

She was often mistaken for being a warm and compassionate woman, which maybe she was when at the funeral home, a business where comfort and support were expected. A business inherited from her father. It demanded all her attention, leaving little time for maternal affection.

To Izzy, her mother was an authoritative figure, unrelenting in her need for control—especially over her children. When faced with the unexpected loss of her husband, Michelle's sense of control was shaken, leading to a new level of heightened anxiety.

The familiar scent of jasmine and honey permeated the air as Izzy approached her mother. She bent to kiss Michelle's cheek before straightening and returning to sit next to Kate. Her sister deliberately avoided her gaze, focusing instead on the flowered wallpaper behind their mother.

"Isabelle," Michelle began, "We were discussing the vacant lot for sale near your college. Are you familiar with it?"

Izzy's eyebrows furrowed as she glanced from her mother to the soup that had been ordered for her. Her eyes filled with uncertainty. She dipped her spoon into the creamy broth.

"There are a bunch of empty spots around the college, Mom."

Her mother nodded, swirling the wine around in her glass before taking a sip. "Yes, there are. But this particular lot is cleared and ready for construction." She set the glass down and turned to Izzy, tucking a loose strand of blond hair behind her ear. "I purchased it earlier this week."

Izzy paused, her spoon hovering midair. "You bought it?"

"Yes. Belleville is the perfect spot for our expansion. The area is growing. More people are leaving the city for the countryside—especially those looking to retire. And with your father's connections there, I knew we couldn't let this opportunity slip away."

Izzy stiffened. Her grip on her spoon slackened, and it splashed back into the bowl. "You . . . want to build a funeral home in Belleville?"

She glanced at Lyssa, her throat tightening, making it hard to swallow. A suffocating weight enveloped her, binding her to a future chosen by her mother. She had never voiced her dreams aloud, never found the courage to go after what she really wanted. And now it was too late.

The painful realization that she had let her dreams slip away without a fight sucked the air from her lungs. "Why?" she finally managed to choke out.

Michelle's eyebrows pinched together. "I already told you why. Belleville presents an opportunity we should—"

"No, I don't mean why Belleville. I mean, why expand at all? Isn't one funeral home enough?"

At this, Kate swung to face Izzy, her brown ponytail slicing through the air. "Because, you idiot, with the three of us joining the family business, it only makes sense to expand."

Her lips curled into a sneer aimed at Izzy. "Typical of you to act ungrateful. Mother could have gone with Orangeville, but she picked somewhere she thought you would be happy. Try showing her a little gratitude." As Kate lifted her glass to her lips, the amber liquid seemed to leap out, splattering down the front of her white dress.

As Kate let out a cry of dismay, Izzy turned around, drawn to the sound of a child's laughter behind her. It was the same boy from earlier, his green eyes gleaming happily as he watched Kate's reaction. Izzy glanced at his hand and found pink mist swirling again in his palm.

The boy's mother leaned toward him again, her voice low and urgent. Izzy swore she heard the word *magic* muttered. She glanced back at his fingers, but the mist had vanished, leaving her questioning if she had truly seen it at all.

CHAPTER FOUR

ILLUSIONS IN THE RAIN

Raindrops pelted the windshield relentlessly, splattering the glass as Izzy maneuvered her car onto the Wallbridge-Loyalist Road exit. The tires hissed across the slick surface of the highway, splashing through puddles. Ahead, the glow of traffic lights guided her toward the distant silhouette of the college.

Through the misty haze, she caught glimpses here and there of the foliage that still clung stubbornly to the trees, their fiery hues muted under the overcast sky. The woodsy scent of decaying leaves and damp earth—the unmistakable fragrance of autumn—wafted in through her cracked window. It stirred memories of past visits to the area as a child.

Despite her dour mood, nostalgia washed over Izzy. Memories surfaced of afternoons spent assisting her grandmother with piling wood, the rough bark chafing her hands. The smoky scent of burning wood mingled with the autumn smells, rising from the chimney in soft puffs of grey.

The echoes of Izzy's past, along with her smile, evaporated as swiftly as they'd appeared. Ahead, a jarring sight demanded her attention—a garish *Sold* sign stark against a barren patch of land. The plot her mother had purchased stood sombrely amid the surrounding autumn forest. It was an unyielding symbol of her irreversible future.

"So, this is it," she said softly, blinking back the salty tears brimming against her eyelashes.

The first sob seized her as she coasted through the initial set of traffic lights. A lofty stone pillar appeared before her; its surface was etched with the name *LOYALIST*. Proudly fronting a small, decorative stone wall, it announced the entrance to the college. Pressing onward, she watched the entrance recede in her rear-view mirror. Ahead, the parking lot unfolded like a tapestry, with parked cars and vacant spots playing hide-and-seek amid the scattered trees.

Soon, another signpost emerged in her view, its arrow directing her toward the college residence. Her hands moved with practised ease as she guided her car to the left. She eased her vehicle to a stop near a small cluster of residential buildings.

The rain, which had been lashing down moments before, dwindled to a soft spray, its droplets gently kissing the pavement. A wispy mist rose in response, weaving its way around the quiet buildings. It cloaked them in a hushed stillness.

Izzy remained motionless for several moments, her body shaking with sobs. The steady hum of the vehicle's heater reverberated in the quiet. Its warmth seeped through the vents, consoling her trembling form. Taking a deep breath, Izzy lifted her gaze to stare bleakly out the car window. The world outside was a watery blur.

"It's my own fault," she murmured. With a sigh, she closed her eyes. Lost in a labyrinth of what-ifs, she wondered how things might have been different. What if she had realized what she really wanted sooner? What if her father was still here to mediate and help her mother see reason.

Resigned that there was nothing to be done with it now, she opened her eyes to stare at the building in front of her. Drawing a deep breath, she grasped for a sliver of hope. If she could weather the storm of this final year of college, maybe, just maybe, things would brighten.

Her thoughts gravitated toward an assignment she had recently submitted. She shook her head once more in defeat. What was her mother thinking, believing she could succeed in the business and accounting program? It was almost comical. Bitter laughter bubbled up and burst out of her as the absurdity of the situation hit her.

Math, with its rigid laws and formulaic expressions, had always been a challenge. Kate and Eddie had effortlessly navigated through the program. On the other hand, Izzy constantly found herself drowning in a sea of equations and balance sheets. As each assignment landed on her desk, a familiar wave of anxiety would rush over her as she struggled to comprehend the concepts. The fact that she had scraped through the first year was a marvel.

If it weren't for her instructors' guidance and support, she had serious doubts that she would have survived. How could she run a mortuary business if she couldn't even navigate the challenges of school without constant support? Whether she remained or veered from this career path, she was bound to inevitably disappoint her mother. Looking at her residence, she questioned the point of even getting out of the car.

Thunder cracked overhead like a gunshot, making Izzy jump. Her thoughts, so focused on her failures and doubts, were scattered by the raw power of it. It struck her with clarity that she should seize the opportunity to run to her apartment before the rain resumed its downpour.

She silenced the engine and swung open the car door. Leaning across the passenger seat, she snatched up her duffle bag and a small stack of books. The vehicle door clanged shut as Izzy darted across the glistening pavement, clutching her books tightly to her chest.

As she approached the college, a persistent buzzing at her ear halted her steps. She turned, trying to dismiss the bug with a wave. Her gaze caught on a giant insect, its elongated body tapering into a plump abdomen. Its wings brushed against her cheek, prompting her to wrinkle her nose and swipe at the air to drive it away.

Her brows furrowed in disbelief at the sight of a mud wasp so late in the year. "Shouldn't you be in hibernation?" she muttered.

The deafening buzz amplified. Izzy let out a startled gasp as a swarm of mud wasps descended upon her. Her face turned pale, and the books she held slipped from her grasp, thudding into a puddle of water. Coming undone from its ponytail, her hair formed a wild halo around her face as she frantically swatted at the attacking insects.

Unbeknownst to Izzy, a stoic, black raven perched in the distance, its obsidian eyes fixated on the drama unfolding below.

In her panic, Izzy dashed back to the safety of her vehicle, her fingers clumsily searching for her car fob. It slipped from her grasp, clinking against the wet pavement. She stooped to retrieve it, her vision clouded by fear, making everything swirl and distort.

A primal scream erupted from her throat, harmonizing with the symphony of fluttering wings. Instinctively, she threw her hands up, forming a barrier over her head.

A weight pressed down on her shoulder, sending tremors through her frame. The relentless buzzing of the swarm faded from her ears, leaving behind a lingering hum. Through the haze, a muffled sound persisted, growing more insistent, cutting through the fog of her shock.

"Izzy!"

Lifting her head, her vision was momentarily obscured as strands of hair cascaded across her face. She brushed them away, finding herself peering into her roommate's deep blue eyes, which were framed by oversized glasses.

"Are you alright?" he asked, cautiously withdrawing his hand from her shoulder. His touch left a lingering warmth behind.

Pressing her palms into the pavement, she felt the sharp edges of small stones and debris digging into her skin. Closing her eyes, she let the painful sensation anchor her into the present moment. She took a deep breath and exhaled slowly, picking up her car fob as she stood up.

"Where did they go, Wally?" she whispered, her muscles taunt, braced for the swarm's return.

Wally's gaze shifted to where she was looking. "Where did what go?"

"The mud wasps." A tremor passed through her hand as she wiped the moisture from her forehead, smearing a mixture of water and cold sweat across her face.

An uneasy feeling churned in her stomach while she scanned the parking lot and the residences beyond. Her gaze caught on a shadow in a window, but she quickly refocused on Wally. "They were just here. Where did they go?" The wasps had vanished without a trace.

Wally ran his fingers through his poofy hair. "I . . . I didn't see any mud wasps. Did they sting you?"

A subtle flush crept up Izzy's neck as she murmured that she was okay. Wally reached out, his fingers brushing her cheek before abruptly withdrawing his hand, a rush of red colouring his face. Shifting his gaze downward, he scraped his shoe against the ground, splashing water onto his already-soaked sneaker.

"Well, I'm glad you're okay . . . because if you weren't, I'd take care of you," he blurted out. Realizing the awkwardness of his statement, he added, "I meant I'd get you help. Like a Band-Aid, or some ice . . ."

"Thanks, Wally," Izzy replied with a soft smile. Pushing away from the car, she retrieved her bag and waterlogged books. Wally hastened to assist her, bending down to pick up a textbook. Its pages were sodden and stuck together.

"I don't think this will be of much use to you now," he said, grimacing as he examined the ruined book. He tucked it under his arm and scooped up the rest, oblivious that his sweater was getting soaked.

"It never was of much use anyway," Izzy replied, reaching out to take the books from him. Their hands briefly brushed against each other, causing Wally's face to flush again.

"So . . . meditation books. That's cool," he said as he fell into step beside her.

They reached the building and stepped into the hallway. Wally quickened his pace, his long strides carrying him to their apartment first. Tugging at the handle, he wrestled with the door, his muttered complaints about its persistent sticking growing louder. The door finally relented, swinging open with a groan of protest.

Stepping inside, Izzy's eyebrows shot up at the sight that greeted her in the kitchen—the stove and countertops were a messy canvas encrusted with noodles and hardened splatters of spaghetti sauce.

"Freaking Arlo," Izzy said. The squishing sound of her sneakers was loud on the laminate floors as she entered the kitchen. "I'm not cleaning this up again!" Wally glanced at the disarray, his expression mirroring hers as he nodded in agreement.

"Lover's quarrel?" A young woman emerged from the small alcove serving as the dorm's common room. There was nothing remarkable about her appearance, from her dull brown hair that fell in a severe bob to her plain face and average height. A smirk danced across her lips as she eyed Wally. He looked away from her, focusing on a speck of red sauce staining the floor.

Izzy's shoulders drooped as she glanced at another one of her roommates. Emily's presence had been a constant source of tension since the beginning of the term. Her hostility grew more palpable as the months wore on. Relishing in Wally's infatuation with Izzy, Emily deliberately exploited it, trying to provoke her.

The college, once a sanctuary despite her reservations about the program, had lost its comforting embrace with the unwelcome addition of Emily. Every aspect of Izzy's life was slowly losing its warmth. It was as if a vacuum had sucked away all traces of joy or contentment—her dreams of university, her relationship with her sister, and now her safe haven.

Izzy's protective instincts kicked in as she noticed Wally's unease. She stepped in front of him, her arms crossed as she levelled Emily with an icy stare. "What do you want."

Emily's smirk widened, and her chin jutted forward. "From you? Nothing," she said, her tone dripping with contempt. She looked toward Wally again, a malicious glint in her eyes. "It's amusing seeing him follow you around like a devoted little puppy."

Wally's shoulders stiffened. Muttering a vague excuse about a forgotten item in his room, he turned and walked away. His damp shoes squelched with every footfall, leaving a water trail to the row of doors at the other end of the kitchen. Izzy watched him go, the slump in his shoulders and heaviness in his steps pulling at her heart. His door closed with a soft click behind him.

A surge of fury pulsed through Izzy's body, her chest tightening as she locked eyes with Emily. "You . . . you're sick!"

Emily turned her back on Izzy, striding purposefully toward her own room. Pursuing her, Izzy wedged her foot in the doorway before Emily could slam it shut. "There's something seriously wrong with you!" Izzy yelled.

Emily flung the door back open, her eyes darting from Izzy's foot to her unwavering expression. "You think something is wrong with me?" she asked, her voice dropping to a dangerously low whisper. Her fists tightened at her sides, and she took an intimidating step forward, forcing Izzy to retreat a step.

"You're one to talk with your sickening charade of a damsel in distress. 'Oh, Wally, help me with my math,'" she said, mimicking Izzy's voice in a childish sing-song tone. Her eyes darkened as she continued, "And that little spectacle in the parking lot tonight . . . do him a favour and stop stringing him along."

"I don't . . ." Izzy said, her voice quivering with outrage, "I don't sound like that. And, besides, I'm not the only one he's helped with math . . ." Her voice trailed off, and her gaze softened as a realization dawned on her. "You . . . you like him!"

The shock that swept over Emily's face swiftly turned into a tide of embarrassment. As she stumbled over her words, desperately seeking to deny the allegation, Izzy's attention was diverted by an abrupt movement just beyond Emily's body.

She leaned closer, trying to see beyond Emily's shoulder. Her eyes widened in disbelief as a small figure, nearly swallowed by shadows, peeked out from behind the neatly made bed. His wrinkled, grey skin was dotted with clusters of thick, black hair, giving him a weathered appearance.

Her brows drew together, creasing her forehead with confusion. As she blinked, the man seemed to dissolve into thin air, his presence replaced by a scruffy, undernourished cat. It was as if the man had been a trick of the light. The cat's yellow eyes bore into hers.

Recoiling in surprise, Izzy blinked. When she looked again, she was met with the same sight—an ugly cat. Izzy found herself grappling with the reality of what she had just witnessed. Had she just seen a miniature man in Emily's room? Or was it her mind playing some elaborate trick on her?

Shaking her head, she tried to dislodge the thoughts swirling in her mind. The weight of the last few weeks pressed down on her. The echo of Eddie's words drifted through her mind, weighing heavily on her heart. Maybe she was losing her mind.

Emily's gaze followed Izzy's, landing on the cat. He had moved from the floor to sprawl out on the bed and was licking his body. Glaring at Izzy with a new hatred, Emily shoved Izzy's foot aside with her own. "Don't you even think about reporting me," she said. At that, she slammed the door in Izzy's face, the noise bouncing off the walls.

Ensnared in the gloom of her own thoughts, Izzy made her way across the communal area to her own room. The pulsing rhythm of music bled through the cracks of Arlo's door as she ambled past. The spaghetti situation had receded to a mere ripple in her consciousness.

Yearning for the solace of her bed and the soft quilt her great-aunt had stitched for her, Izzy's fingers curled around her door handle. As she pushed the door ajar, it creaked softly, opening enough to reveal an unexpected sight.

A man lounged on her bed, decked out in worn jeans and a leather jacket. His boots—unlaced and streaked with mud—dangled off the bed's edge. Gazing out the window, his lips moved to a silent melody. Rooted to the spot, Izzy could only stare, her eyes locked on this unexpected guest. She drew a sharp breath that echoed through the room. Feeling her presence, he turned, fixing her with her green eyes. A slow smile played across his handsome features.

CHAPTER FIVE

A Choice Worth Making

"Kyler? How . . . how did you get in my room?"

Izzy's eyes were drawn to his tousled blonde hair resting against her pillow and then to his playful grin. Her breath quickened, causing her to sway slightly as if caught in a giddy breeze.

"Hey babe," he said, swinging his legs off the bed, leaving muddy footprints across the room's floor. Her eyes narrowed at the dirty splatters on the ground, but her annoyance dissipated once Kyler stood up. His tall stature overpowered the small room, his broad shoulders casting a harsh shadow against the dim light.

He bent down, his strong hand tenderly cradling Izzy's face. His touch sent a tingling sensation through her skin. The air seemed to crackle as his lips met hers in a lingering kiss.

Eagerly, she returned his kiss, letting her books fall to the ground. Her fingers entwined around his neck, drawing him closer. As she surrendered herself to the depth of her boyfriend's embrace, the turbulence in her mind began to still. The weight of her troubles momentarily lifted, overpowered by an overwhelming rush of desire that consumed her.

With practised ease, Kyler's fingers found their way beneath the hem of her sweater, gliding like silk over the smooth, warm expanse of her skin. Heat danced through her veins, electrifying her body. With it came conflicting panic that tightened her chest. She broke free from the embrace, her heart hammering against her ribs as she stepped backward.

The corners of Kyler's eyes flashed with a hint of annoyance. He swiftly masked it with a disarming smile as he settled onto her desk, sending several papers fluttering to the floor. She bent down to collect the scattered pieces and retrieved the books she had dropped earlier. She stacked them on the desk's edge near Kyler.

A damp, slightly deformed meditation book caught Kyler's attention. He gingerly picked it up, holding the warping pages away from him, a smirk forming on one corner of his mouth. "You really practise this crap?" he asked as he tossed the book back onto the pile with a thud.

Ignoring his mocking tone, Izzy moved past him, depositing her wet bag on a nearby chair. "Every night," she said, rifling through her backpack to find her phone.

Kyler responded with an indifferent shrug, already steering the conversation back toward himself. His chatter centred on his rock band and the festering friction with the lead singer, Lovepreet, filled the room. Izzy, in turn, continued her mission of unpacking her bag, nodding subtly as she listened.

Sitting down, she traded her wet sneakers for soft, black boots. As she zipped them up, the rich aroma of the leather filled her nostrils.

"Lovepreet is making us wear these ridiculous costumes for the set on Friday," Kyler complained. He leaned back against the wall, an arrogant smile on his face. "I should just start my own band."

Izzy paused, her hand still lingering on her boot. "The Gravediggers have a gig on Halloween?" A heavy dread settled in her stomach as she looked at Kyler. She knew he would expect her there, even though she had already volunteered to help the Children's Safe-T Town hand out candy. It was an event she had been looking forward to. Sighing inwardly, she once more felt herself tugged in two different directions.

"Yeah, babe. We scored a gig at the Shark Tank," he said, his voice tinged with a hint of self-importance. Catching her worried gaze, his brows came together briefly, and his lips pressed into a thin line. "You have to be there. It would look bad if my own girlfriend didn't show up for my big break," he said, crossing his arms.

Fatigue dimmed her blue eyes as she looked toward the streaked window. Outside, the rain had finally stopped, leaving behind traces of its presence. The dampened parking lot shimmered under the faint glow of the streetlights. At the same time, raindrops clung to windowpanes like glistening diamonds, silently reflecting the grey clouds that now retreated in the distance.

Izzy turned back toward Kyler, finding him staring at her expectantly. Sighing, she nodded her head. "All right, I'll be there." His features softened as he rose from the desk and drew her closer for another kiss.

Sharp rapping at the door interrupted the moment. Instinctively, Izzy pulled away from Kyler's embrace. The door swung open, revealing a woman with auburn hair. Her pale blue eyes widened at the sight of Izzy's flushed cheeks.

"Sorry, guys," she said, the rhythmic smacking of her gum filling the air. As she leaned into the room, her overly tight shirt displayed her generous cleavage, leaving little to the imagination.

"Melanie," Kyler said, flashing a charming smile that caused a subtle blush to tint Melanie's cheeks. His fingers traced a path along Izzy's hip, subtly pulling her closer toward him. "Melanie let me in," he explained, his lips brushing against the tender skin of Izzy's neck.

Melanie's gaze shifted away from Kyler. A fleeting glimmer of anger crossed her face so swiftly that it barely registered with Izzy. Stepping further into the room, her high heels punctuated her presence with sharp clicks against the floor. "I hope that's all right, Iz," she said, her attention momentarily captured by her reflection in the full-length mirror next to the desk. She fussed with a few flyaway strands of hair. "He was just going to wait outside for you, and the rain was pouring down." She turned back to Izzy, a fixed smile etched upon her face.

"It did catch me by surprise . . . but it's okay."

Extricating herself from Kyler's embrace, Izzy crossed the room to the far wall, where a row of coats hung from hooks. Her fingers grazed over the options, finally settling on a hip-length, dark blue tweed jacket. Its sturdy fabric promised protection from the elements. Sliding her arms into the sleeves, she settled the jacket snugly around her slender frame.

"Are you two heading out?" Melanie asked. "I was just coming to see if you wanted to grab something to eat."

"Actually, I'm meeting my great-aunt for dinner," Izzy explained. "I only came back to get my wallet. I left it here over the weekend." Retrieving it off the nightstand, she carefully slipped it into the jacket's deep pockets alongside her phone.

Kyler's expression shifted into a pout, his lips curving downward. "I wanted to take you out for dinner," he said, rubbing his hand through his already tousled hair.

"Sorry, Ky, but I'm not ditching my aunt. Let's go another night, okay?"

He opened his mouth to protest but, seeing the resolute expression on her face, thought better of it. Sighing, he nodded slowly. "All right, later this week then," he said, framing it as a statement rather than a question. Leaning down, he gently pressed his lips against hers while Melanie discreetly averted her eyes.

"I'll head out then," he said, winking at Melanie as he left.

Turning to Izzy, Melanie remarked, "I'm sorry for interrupting your little moment."

Izzy blinked, momentarily taken aback by her friend's lack of genuine remorse. However, she quickly dismissed the unsettling feeling, mistaking Melanie's apparent jealousy for embarrassment.

"It's okay, really," she said, shifting uncomfortably on her feet. Her gaze flickered toward the wall clock, its steady ticking reminding her that she would be late if she didn't leave soon. "I really do have to get going, though. I have to make a quick stop to pick up pizza first, so . . ." Her eyes subtly darted toward the door.

Finally catching on to the unspoken message, Melanie sighed. Mumbling something about having to approach Arlo for dinner, she reluctantly followed Izzy out of the room. Leaving Melanie with a sullen expression, Izzy returned to her car.

The chill in the air seeped through her bones, causing her to shiver involuntarily as she made her way back to her car. Trying to shield herself from the biting wind, she pulled her coat tighter. Each gust was a stark reminder that summer had officially surrendered to the onset of colder days.

Slipping into the driver's seat of her Honda, Izzy started the engine without delay. The familiar hum resonated through the vehicle, greeting her. She sighed as her icy hands sought the comforting flow of heat from the vents, mentally noting to pick up gloves sometime that week.

The cityscape shifted from dense forest to residential homes and businesses as she drove. Glimpses of the waterfront peeked through gaps between the buildings, a sparkling allure beneath the fading daylight. Izzy maneuvered through the familiar downtown streets. She stopped only once at a local pizzeria. Soon, the tantalizing aroma of bubbling cheese and rich tomato sauce swirled within the confines of her car.

Her journey ended at a parking lot beside a small apartment complex. Laughter filled the air as she exited the vehicle, hinting at the magnetic energy of a nearby theatre.

Izzy balanced the pizza box in one hand and crossed the pavement. She reached out, pulling open the building's glass door. Inside, she was greeted by the inviting foyer. A gentleman with tufts of grey hair beneath a tweed cap smiled at her. He held the inner door open, gesturing for her to enter first.

"Thanks, Mr. Smith," Izzy said, sliding past him. She nodded at the older women sitting by the flowering plants. Walking alongside Mr. Smith, they passed a room buzzing with the sounds of a lively game of bridge, the chatter and laughter drifting out into the hallway.

"Off to see your aunt, dear?" Mr. Smith asked, joining Izzy in the elevator. He pressed the button for the floor just above her aunt's, and with a muted buzz, the doors sealed shut.

Izzy nodded as she leaned against the mirrored wall behind her. A subtle crinkle formed on her nose as she caught a whiff of the lingering scent of damp fur emanating from the enclosed space.

Mr. Smith's smile widened. "Is the lunch meeting still on for Thursday afternoon?"

Mr. Smith's comment alluded to the much-anticipated monthly meet-up known as the Brunch Bunch, a community initiative co-founded by Izzy and her friend Rhylynn. Their goal was to knit the fabric of generations tighter, connecting the older residents of her great-aunt's building with the youth in the community. Each month, volunteers from the college would join the seniors for a communal meal at a local diner, which supported their cause with reduced prices.

"Yes, sir."

As the elevator reached her floor, the doors opened with a soft chime. "I'll be here at noon to pick you and Auntie A up," Izzy said, stepping out. With a wave, she turned to navigate the hallway, the carpet muffling her steps. A rich scent of rosemary filled the corridor, intensifying as she drew closer to her destination.

A knot of anxiety formed suddenly in her stomach, and she halted mid-step. A cold chill shivered up her spine. For a split second, she thought she glimpsed an eyeball on the door of her aunt's friend—its vibrant green pupil seeming to watch her.

Astonished, she blinked, and the eye vanished, replaced by a solid grey door adorned with a floral welcome sign bearing the name '*Rivers.*' Brushing aside the lingering unease, Izzy continued toward her aunt's apartment.

She rapped lightly on the door with her knuckles. As the door swung open, her great-aunt's face lit up with a radiant smile, illuminating the entire threshold. Despite her hunched and wiry frame, she enveloped Izzy in a firm embrace.

Laughter bubbled inside Izzy as she clung to the door frame, steadying herself to avoid stumbling. She returned her aunt's heartfelt hug with one arm and followed her inside the apartment. The brightness of the lights mirrored off the laminate flooring that Izzy's father had installed shortly before his passing.

The space radiated a feline charm. Izzy eyes landed on a porcelain kitten peeking out from behind a potted plant. Along the walls, framed photographs of white cats were interspersed with childhood snapshots of Izzy and her siblings.

Her aunt motioned toward the wooden table near her rocking chair in the far corner. Izzy carefully placed the pizza box down on the table's well-worn surface. As she lifted the lid, the enticing aroma of melted cheese wafted through the air.

Her aunt emerged from the kitchen, plates in one hand and a frosty glass of Pepsi in the other. The clink of ice cubes against the glass filled the room as she passed the drink to Izzy.

"So, tell me," her aunt said, sitting down. "How did the dinner go last night?"

Izzy summarized the previous evening, leaving out Kate's hurtful comment to avoid upsetting her aunt. When she reached the part about her mother's recent land purchase in Belleville, her aunt's hand froze, causing her pizza slice to thud on the table. Disbelief etched deep lines into her weathered face.

"If your mother thinks I'm going to use my connections in this city to further her ambitions, she's even more deluded than I thought."

Noticing Izzy's bemused expression, her aunt took a deep breath and straightened the white napkin draped over her shirt.

"I shouldn't speak ill of your mother, my dear. I suppose I should help her . . . Jamie would have wanted me to." Her eyes welled up as she mentioned Izzy's late father, her grief for her nephew still visible on her face.

Izzy gently took her aunt's hand, giving it a comforting squeeze. Her aunt patted Izzy's hand in return, then pushed her round glasses up to dab at her tears with a napkin. Despite her attempt at a brave smile, a trace of sadness remained in her eyes as she paused to take a sip of water.

Clearing her throat, she turned her gaze upon Izzy, who had resumed eating her slice of pizza. "So, what is this nonsense about giving up on your dreams?"

Setting her pizza slice back on the plate, Izzy's expression clouded with frustration. "It's not like I have a choice, Aunt Audrey," she said, tugging at a strand of her hair.

Reaching up, Audrey batted Izzy's hand down. "For goodness' sake, stop doing that. You're going to make yourself go bald!" Izzy nodded, her hand returning to rest on her lap as Audrey settled back in her seat. "And don't be ridiculous, dear. You always have a choice."

"Easier said than done," Izzy said, her voice barely above a whisper. Her eyes became fixed on the stained crochet placemat before her.

"I never said choices are easy," her aunt replied sharply. "In fact, the right choice rarely is. But that doesn't change the fact that you still have them." She abruptly rose from the table, crossing the room to a wooden cabinet against the opposite wall.

Izzy's curiosity was piqued as she watched her aunt rummaging through its contents. A soft stream of muttered words escaped Audrey's lips. Moments later, she emerged from the cabinet, her face lit up triumphantly, holding a thick manilla packet.

She returned to the table, a self-satisfied smile playing on her lips as she dropped the packet onto Izzy's lap.

"Open it!"

Izzy's hands trembled slightly as she carefully unsealed the envelope, the contents spilling forth in a colourful cascade of pamphlets and letters. The names of various universities danced before her eyes, each proudly showcasing an array of degree programs.

"You put this together for me?"

Audrey nodded, her eyes sparkling with excitement. "I've gone through them already. I think the social work program would suit you best, but there are other interesting options there, too."

Izzy's eyes softened, and she felt a tightness in her chest as she looked at her great-aunt. The corners of her mouth lifted into a smile. "Thank you, Auntie A . . . This is really thoughtful."

Hesitating, she searched for the right words to convey her thoughts without hurting her aunt's feelings. She took a deep breath and glanced at the pamphlets before meeting Audrey's gaze again. "But I already told you, I can't just walk away from the family business. Mom—"

"This is your life, Isabelle Adams, not your mother's. Follow your own path." Audrey reached out, her hands enveloping Izzy's in a firm grip. "Your father would not want this for you."

Izzy drew her hands away, her eyes welling up with unshed tears. "You don't know what my father would want."

Audrey sat in her chair, her gaze fixed intently on her niece's face. "No. But I knew your father well. He was a man of compassion, driven by a desire to make others happy," she said softly.

She paused to let her words sink in, then continued, "Do you honestly believe that your father would want his own child to sacrifice her happiness for the sake of her mother?"

Izzy's eyes fluttered closed. Her aunt, as usual, had hit the nail on the head. Jamie Adams had always been a pillar of support, attuned to his children's needs and willing to go to great lengths to see them thrive.

She opened her eyes and looked at her aunt, a sense of clarity washing over her. It was as if her father's spirit lingered in the room, nodding in agreement at Audrey's words. The pamphlets before her took on new meaning, and she could almost envision her dad pouring over them with her.

"You're right. Dad wouldn't have wanted this for me. He would have done exactly what you did." Leaning forward, she wrapped her arms around the older woman and kissed her cheek.

Izzy pulled the pamphlets closer, her fingers flipping through them until she pulled out one for York University. "You know," she said, a smile tugging at the corners of her mouth, "you could have just printed these off the internet."

Chuckling, Audrey waved off the suggestion. "Oh, that blasted machine," she said, gesturing toward the old computer gathering dust in the far corner. "There's too much happening on that tiny screen, and I can't seem to work the bloody keyboard." She dismissed the idea with a wave and added, "It was easier just to call and have them mail everything to me."

Smiling, Izzy squeezed her aunt's hand. "I appreciate it. We'll find you a better computer, Aunt A, something more user-friendly." As she leaned over to hug her aunt, the world seemed to tilt back into place again.

For the rest of the evening, Izzy and her great-aunt poured over the pamphlets once more. Excitement for the vast array of possibilities bubbled up within her. With each pamphlet, the notion of choice resonated more deeply, until a newfound certainty anchored itself deep within her.

CHAPTER SIX

RAVENS IN THE MOONLIGHT

The full moon reigned over the clear night. It cast a silver veil across the parking lot with its luminescent glow. Wet leaves clung to the ground, remnants of the day's storm. Each leaf glistened with the traces of raindrops, catching in the moonlight like tiny, sparkling gems.

A serene calm had settled over the area like a cozy blanket. The only sounds punctuating the silence were the occasional whispers of the wind caressing the naked trees and the distant drone of passing cars several streets over. And then, as if emerging from a canvas, Izzy materialized on the outskirts of the parking lot, her footsteps echoing in the silence.

She strode across the vacant lot, her steps light. Her mind was ablaze with dreams of university applications and the allure of lecture halls. She deliberately pushed aside the impending conversation she needed to have with her mother, refusing to let it cast a shadow over her sense of freedom at that moment.

Unbeknownst to Izzy, a shadowy figure appeared in the dark sky overhead. Gliding silently above her, a dishevelled raven descended to perch in a nearby tree. The branch quivered under its weight, setting the remaining autumn leaves into a jittery dance before they gracefully floated to the ground.

Izzy strolled past the tree, her boots sinking into the damp carpet of fallen leaves. Above her, the raven tilted its head curiously, its beady black eyes observing her every move.

She approached the Honda and unlocked it. The headlights flickered momentarily, casting flashes of light across the dimly lit parking lot. She settled into the driver's seat and shut the door with a soft thump. As her hand reached for the ignition, a sudden and unexpected chill permeated the vehicle, causing her to hesitate.

Frail tendrils of frost appeared on the windshield, expanding at an almost magical speed. Icy veins traced intricate patterns on the glass; their mesmerizing dance was beautiful and uncanny. Izzy gasped, her breath crystallizing in the frigid air, forming vapour clouds.

A chill swept through Izzy, sending her into a fit of shivers. She reached down and pressed the starter button of her car, the engine responding with a reassuring hum. Leaning closer, her fingers brushed against the seat warmer switch. Its glow illuminated the interior as warmth enveloped her.

At that moment, the radio sprang to life, belting out the opening chords of "Bad Moon Rising" by Creedence Clearwater Revival. Its infectious rhythm pulsated through the vehicle. As if caught up in the sudden burst of energy, the interior light flickered erratically, flashing intermittently in sync with the music's beat.

The music from the speakers washed over Izzy, compelling her to press her hands tightly over her ears. A grimace crossed her face, and her muttered curses were swallowed up by the relentless barrage of sound.

She desperately tried to silence the system, her fingers dancing over the radio controls. The volume seemed to amplify as if mocking her attempts. Around her, the vehicle's interior lights continued to stutter erratically, casting a haunting glow.

Leaving the radio, Izzy found the starter button and pushed it frantically. The engine, however, purred defiantly, growing louder. Fear shot through her—she no longer controlled the vehicle.

Abandoning any hope of regaining command, she reached for the door handle, only to be met with unyielding resistance. The door stubbornly refused to open. Amplified by the relentless beat of the music, panic swelled within her, her mind racing to make sense of the situation.

Driven by fear, Izzy made a final, desperate attempt to break free from the prison that her vehicle had become. Her body shifted sideways in her seat as she leaned against the armrest. With her feet together, she aimed for the driver's window, closing her eyes as she braced herself for the impact.

But the expected shattering never came. Instead, the ear-splitting music halted, leaving only the engine's soft purr. Izzy lunged from the car and hit the pavement hard. The coarse surface grazed her palms, sending sharp pains shooting up her arms.

As she scrambled backward, a harsh, guttural croak sounded out. Lifting her gaze upward, her eyes landed on an ancient oak tree beside her vehicle.

A majestic raven, its black feathers gleaming in the moonlight, descended toward the tree. With predatory grace, it swooped down on a dishevelled-looking bird perched on the nearest branch just above the hood of her Honda. The impact nearly sent the smaller bird tumbling. It pecked at the startled bird several times as if chiding it for a misdeed. The air filled with a symphony of squawking and flapping wings.

Captivated by the birds' altercation, time seemed to stand still for Izzy. Absurd questions whirled in her mind, each more outlandish than the last. Could these creatures somehow be connected to the strange happenings with her car?

As if sensing her silent query, the squabbling birds abruptly ceased arguing. They turned their heads toward Izzy in unison. A shudder convulsed through her, and she couldn't shake off the uncanny feeling that they could peer into her soul. An unspoken connection hung in the air, hinting at a hidden world beyond her understanding.

Izzy's trance was abruptly broken when firm hands gripped her from behind, hoisting her to her feet. A rush of adrenaline prompted her into action, and she spun around quickly, ready to face whatever threat had disturbed her. But rather than a supernatural threat, it was the warm brown eyes of her friend, Rhylynn Rivers, that she met.

The corners of Rhylynn's mouth stretched into a grin, which complemented the lively bounce in her curly brown hair as she stepped back from Izzy's clenched fists. Izzy marvelled at how such a petite figure had managed to lift her so easily. Her puzzlement soon gave way to relief. She was no longer alone in the parking lot.

"Hey, Izzy. Engaged in a bit of stargazing, were you?" Rhylynn asked, her words laced with a touch of dry humour. She examined Izzy over the rim of her glasses, which had casually slid down to rest on the end of her nose.

Brushing the dirt from her pants, Izzy grimaced when she felt the dampness from the puddle she'd landed in. Sighing softly, she looked around for something to wipe her mud-covered hands on. Finding nothing, she resorted to rubbing them on the sides of her jeans as she responded, "No, I . . . I tripped, getting into my car."

Rhylynn studied her, the corners of her mouth lifting in a polite smile, seemingly accepting the excuse. Yet, beneath the surface, Izzy sensed an unspoken doubt lingering in her eyes.

A cold breeze whisked across the parking lot, sending her wild hair into further disarray. Hugging herself for warmth, she glanced at the oak tree. The ravens had vanished.

Izzy's gaze returned to her friend. With her unconventional fashion choices, tenacious spirit, and odd quirks, Rhylynn had quickly become one of Izzy's closest companions. Their paths had first crossed through Izzy's great-aunt and Rhylynn's grandmother, Lila Rivers.

At first, Izzy had found Rhylynn's distinctiveness somewhat perplexing, but now she had grown fond of the spirited woman. In fact, it was Rhylynn's joke over lunch that had inspired the creation of the Brunch Bunch.

"How's your grandma doing, Rhylynn?"

"Oh, Gran's doing well," Rhylynn replied, her face lighting up. "She guided me through a new recipe tonight." Lifting her head triumphantly, she added, "I was actually able to replicate it this time."

A smile tugged at the corners of Izzy's lips. "Oh, really? That's awesome, Rhy!"

Yet a fleeting shadow marred her features, stirred by the recollection of rosemary wafting through the air on her way to her aunt's apartment. An unpleasant memory crashed into Izzy's thoughts—the haunting image of the vanishing eye on Mrs. Rivers's door.

Izzy shook her head, attempting to dislodge the image from her thoughts. "So, what did you make?" she asked, trembling as the wind whipped against her damp jeans.

"A pork roast. Gran is just relieved I didn't scorch her pot this time," Rhylynn said, pulling out a pair of orange knitted mitts from her jacket pocket and sliding them on.

"Anyways, I should head off before it gets too late. I just wanted to make sure you were okay."

Rhylynn reached over to hug Izzy. The distinctive fragrance of rosemary and sage wafted from her hair, wrapping Izzy in a soothing cloud of herbal scents. Rhylynn pulled away from the embrace and turned to leave.

Izzy's brow creased, a knot of worry forming in her stomach as her eyes scanned the vacant parking lot. Only now did she realize that her friend's truck was conspicuously absent. A surge of panic coursed through her veins as she grasped the truth—Rhylynn was walking home.

While charming and safe under the sun's warm embrace, the downtown core morphed into a shadowy labyrinth of potential dangers after dusk. Izzy's heart raced within her chest as her mind conjured up vivid images of the worst possible scenarios befalling her friend.

"Rhylynn Rivers, you're *not* walking home!" Izzy dashed toward Rhylynn, reached out to grab her arm, and halted her in her tracks.

Rhylynn turned her head, a bemused smile on her lips. "Izzy, I'll be fine."

Izzy released her grip on Rhylynn's arm, her fingers moving to the jabbing pain that now radiated from her side. She winced, feeling the discomfort pulsate through her. The thought of the gym sprang to mind—another daunting task looming on her ever-growing to-do list. Make a mental health appointment with her doctor, acquire gloves, and if still feeling motivated, perhaps use her dusty gym membership.

As the pain subsided, Izzy straightened up, refocusing on Rhylynn. "Where is your truck?" she asked, sweeping her hand around the empty parking lot.

"It's in the shop," Rhylynn said, sighing deeply. "It's leaking oil again. I should have it back in time for Thursday. Don't worry."

"Oh, well, that sucks! Let me drive you home."

Before Rhylynn could respond, Izzy's words spilled out in a rapid torrent. "You could be home in five minutes, Rhy Rhy," she said, giving her watch an exaggerated glance. "You'd be home in time to watch this week's episode of *The Laughaholics*. Think about it!"

The air seemed to dance with the sweet melody of Rhylynn's laughter. "All right," she said, holding her hands up for Izzy to stop. "You don't have to ask me twice."

A sense of relief washed over Izzy, dispelling the tension that had gripped her moments ago. Together, they made their way back to the Honda. A soft chime from the open driver's door greeted them, and a wedge of light from the interior gently illuminated the pavement.

Izzy settled into the heated seat and felt its warmth wrap around her like a comforting embrace. She moved the manila envelope to the backseat, clearing space for Rhylynn. Once her friend was comfortably seated beside her, Izzy guided the vehicle out of the parking lot, the shape of her aunt's apartment building receding in the distance.

As Izzy guided her car through the quiet streets of Belleville, Rhylynn's animated voice filled the small space. She regaled Izzy with a humorous account of her challenges in sharing a room with her younger sister.

"If I had to share a room with Kate right now, I'd go crazy," Izzy said, her smile fading at the mere thought of her sister.

"I couldn't imagine sharing a room with your sister. I ran into her once in the hallway when I was visiting Gran. Not exactly a cheerful person, is she?"

"No, she isn't."

"I couldn't live with your housemates either," Rhylynn continued. "Emily could possibly be insane. Seriously, there's something not right with that one." She paused, her face darkening. "And Melanie . . . I could do without her altogether."

Izzy's eyebrow arched upwards, a silent question lingering on her lips. What could Melanie have possibly done to upset Rhylynn, someone known for her laid-back nature? Despite her curiosity, she remained silent, sensing that her two friends had a complicated history. It was best, she thought, to not get involved. Fortunately, Rhylynn changed the conversation as if coming to the same conclusion, and the rest of the drive was filled with pleasant chatter.

Having bid Rhylynn farewell at her parents' modest ranch-style home, Izzy made her way back to campus. The highway stretched out before her, an unbroken path disappearing into the darkness of the night. Her headlights cast a narrow cone of illumination that pierced through the dark. Now and then, the ghostly figures of wildlife appeared on the road's edge. Their eyes would catch the light briefly before merging back into the black.

She spotted the familiar sign directing her toward her residence once again. Steering her car into the parking lot, she found a spot close to her building. She parked the Honda and stepped out. Taking a moment, she inhaled deeply, enjoying the brisk night air.

Away from the city centre, the rural night sky burst into a symphony of sounds. The distant howl of a coyote reverberated through the air. It was a visceral reminder of the wilderness beyond the campus. Her heart racing, Izzy hastened across the moonlit parking lot to her building. The main entrance groaned on its hinges as Izzy swung it open.

She walked down the hallway, only to find an unwelcome sight at her apartment. A low curse slipped past her lips when she saw the door ajar, most likely courtesy of her absentminded roommate, Arlo.

Izzy nudged it open, a swell of frustration bubbling within her as she prepared to air her grievances about safety. But before she could say anything, dirt showered her, pelting her lips and leaving her momentarily speechless.

CHAPTER SEVEN

WORMS AND DIRT

The dirt continued to rain down on Izzy as the laughter continued around her. A flush crept up her cheeks, spreading like wildfire from her throat. She fixed her gaze on the alcove where a group had gathered, some eagerly capturing the incident with their cameras. Melanie was among them.

Tentatively, Izzy inched into the room, brushing off dry remnants of earth that crumbled and fell from her body. As she moved, a damp sensation brushed against her forehead. Trembling, she raised her hand, her fingertips touching something cold and wriggling. A shiver of repulsion shook her body. She gingerly pinched her fingers around it, slowly bringing a worm down to her eye level.

Her jaw fell open, and she dropped both the squirming worm and her envelope onto the floor. Panic prickled her skin as she vigorously shook her body, trying to dislodge the mass of worms from the top of her head. Running her hands through her hair, she scattered dirt across the floor.

The room filled with an escalating roar of laughter. One voice pierced through the mirth, rising above the rest. At the water cooler stood a lanky young man, his body trembling uncontrollably from high-pitched giggles. Tears streamed down his thin face as he glanced up at Izzy, a wide grin stretching across his flushed complexion. Izzy's eyes narrowed as she recognized the person behind the revolting prank.

"Arlo!" Plucking the last worm from the creases of her jacket, she flung it at her roommate. Taken by surprise, he stumbled backward, colliding with the water cooler. A high-pitched squeal escaped his lips, mingling with the renewed chorus of laughter that echoed through the room. Arlo's attempts to steady the wobbling cooler only fueled the onlookers' amusement.

Bending down, Izzy retrieved her envelope from the floor. She shook it off gingerly, then straightened up. Smirking, she turned to Arlo and said, "Eight points for creativity." A triumphant grin spread across his face.

She let him bask in his moment of glory before continuing. "But you lose points 'caus' you could have used uglier worms, and the dirt wasn't dirty enough. Oh, and you know the rules—you pull the prank, you clean it up."

His expression morphed into dismay, his face falling as he surveyed the mess scattered across the floor. Izzy turned and made her way toward her room. Behind her, Arlo pleaded with their other roommates to lend him a hand cleaning up.

She entered her room and placed the envelope alongside the stack of damp books on her desk. The faint scent of mildew rose from their covers. She wrinkled her nose in response. Pausing briefly, she seized the most severely affected book. Its pages were clumped together from moisture. Peeling it open, she carefully positioned it near her portable heater to help it dry.

Removing her coat, she tossed it on a chair, along with her wet clothing. A subtle sigh of relief escaped her lips as she changed into dry clothing. Catching her reflection in the mirror, Izzy grimaced.

Her hair was a disaster—a tangled mess freckled with dirt. The sudden eruption of laughter outside her room served as a reminder of the company waiting for her. A shower would have to wait.

She hastily tied her hair into a messy bun and plugged her phone in to charge. Satisfied with her makeshift clean-up, Izzy left her room to join her friends.

To her surprise, she emerged to find a clean entranceway. The scent of scattered earth was gone, replaced by the enticing aroma of buttery popcorn that wafted through the air. A low growl emanated from her stomach. She grabbed a can of Pepsi from the fridge to accompany the popcorn.

"Hey, grab me one, too," Melanie's voice rang out.

Izzy obliged, her fingers wrapping around the second can. Returning to the alcove, she passed Melanie her drink and sat beside Vishvesh. His smile bore a silent apology as he glanced pointedly at the doorway. She returned the smile, grateful for his acknowledgement of Arlo's prank. While it might be a laughable memory someday, the shower of dirt hadn't been amusing in the moment.

"Where is Arlo?" Izzy asked, realizing that he wasn't in the room. She cast her eyes around the apartment, but nothing seemed out of the ordinary. The kitchen was spotless, much to her relief, especially compared to the earlier spaghetti disaster. Melanie must have coerced Arlo to clean his mess up, Izzy thought. She shot her friend a grateful smile.

Vishvesh shifted closer to his girlfriend, Tabby, who was nestled quietly against him on the couch. "Arlo's out disposing of the worms," he said, his dark eyes twinkling.

"Arlo *is* a worm," Melanie joked. She reached for the tab on the Pepsi, bringing the can closer to her face. As Melanie popped it open, a sudden eruption of liquid sprayed in all directions, drenching her face and foaming over her hands.

Shrieking, the can slipped from her grasp and landed on the table with a resounding clunk. The pop fizzed over, forming a brown puddle across the table.

Izzy jumped to her feet. "I swear I didn't shake your can. Maybe Arlo—"

Melanie shook her head, droplets from her nose splattering on the table. Grabbing the dishtowel from the kitchen, she wiped the sticky residue from her face.

"Arlo wouldn't waste a can of Pepsi," Melanie replied. "The guy practically survives on this stuff." She leaned over, using the cloth to clean the table. "I've just had a string of bad luck lately," she muttered, settling back into her seat.

The door banged open as Arlo strolled in. A wide grin adorned his face, radiating an infectious energy that seemed to fill the room.

Izzy smiled at her friend's cheerful disposition. Despite the lingering memory of the joke, a flicker of amusement danced in her eyes as she observed him. As their gazes met, Izzy's lips curved into a smile, silently acknowledging that there were no hard feelings.

He approached the table. His eyes widened at the sight of a dish towel on the table and the faint spattering of Pepsi on Melanie's shirt. He burst out laughing, clutching at his stomach. "Oh man, I wish I'd seen that!" he said between gasps.

"Just sit down," Melanie snapped, pointing at the vacant chair beside her. "We're running late. Let's just get this meeting over with."

Still chuckling, Arlo flopped in the seat and stretched his legs beneath the table. "All right, all right," he replied. Bringing his hand down with a thump on the armrest, he said, "I now call the meeting of the MonkeyShiners into session!" Izzy watched as Melanie rolled her eyes.

Vishvesh untangled himself from Tabby's embrace and leaned forward, producing a notebook from his sweater pocket. "Okay, let's discuss Arlo's latest prank. Izzy suggested eight points for creativity. Are we all in agreement?"

Everyone nodded except for Arlo, who chimed in, "Ten!" He playfully grumbled when he was promptly denied.

Vishvesh fell into silence. His pen glided across the pages of his notebook as he tallied the scores. Clearing his throat, he said, "With this latest prank, Arlo has moved into the lead. Izzy follows closely behind in a well-deserved second place."

Arlo leaped to his feet, a triumphant whoop bursting from his lips. Izzy, unable to resist teasing him, said, "Maybe we should have deducted more points for the mess you created."

Laughter filled the air as their banter carried on. Their voices rose in excitement as they dissected the intricacies of Arlo's latest prank and speculated on who might be the next target.

A bedroom door crashed open, sending a booming echo throughout the room as it collided with the wall. Izzy's eyes flicked toward the doorway as Emily emerged. The soft glow of the hallway lamp cast long shadows across her face.

"Do you know what time it is?" The words slithered from Emily's mouth, carrying a venomous sting that seemed to suck the air out of the room.

Izzy felt a chill creep up her spine as the entire room froze, the cheerfulness evaporating instantly. A devilish grin crept across Arlo's face as he leaned backward and met Emily's eyes. "Yeah, it's tool time!" he said, throwing out the reference to the old television show they had recently watched. His voice carried a carefree confidence of a man treading on thin ice—unconcerned about the risk.

The next moment was a blur—a look of surprise quickly replaced his triumphant smirk. The chair he had been balancing on fell backward with a clatter, sending him sprawling onto the ground.

Izzy found herself rooted to her spot. She watched as the scene unfolded, her pulse drumming a rapid beat in her ears. She stared at Emily, a confused look crossing her face as she tried to piece together what had just happened.

The timing seemed too perfect. Emily's lips curled into a smug smile, her eyes gleaming with satisfaction. A silent question began to form in Izzy's mind—could Emily have possibly . . . ? The thought stuttered to a halt as a painful groan from Arlo snatched her attention back.

She shifted her gaze from Emily to find Arlo cautiously sitting up, massaging the back of his head. Melanie reappeared from the kitchen with a bag of ice. He gratefully accepted it, cradling the bag against his head.

From the corner of her eye, she saw Emily's hands clenching the door frame. Her knuckles were turning a stark white against the polished wood. "It's ten o'clock at night!" she snapped. Turning on her heel, she disappeared back into her room. The door slammed shut behind her with such force that it shook the window behind Vishvesh.

"She's such a pill," Arlo grumbled.

Anger ignited within her as Izzy observed the flicker of pain across her friend's face. Emily's presence in their apartment was an unrelenting source of darkness. She cast a shadow of misery over everyone. Absurd as it may be, Izzy couldn't help but hold Emily partly responsible for Arlo's injury. Resolution crossed her features as she nodded to herself, coming to a decision.

Leaning forward in her chair, she stretched her hand out toward Vishvesh. She wordlessly made a *gimme* gesture, her fingers mimicking a typing motion. Sighing, Vishvesh handed over his phone. The device seemed to fuse with her fingers as she opened the browser, her touch on the screen fast and assured.

A few intense minutes passed as she feverishly keyed words into the search bar. Craning his neck, Vishvesh tried to peer over her shoulder at the screen.

"Hey! What are you doing? Don't search that stuff up on my phone." He moved in to take the phone back, but Izzy leaned away from him.

"What are you doing?" Arlo asked. He moved closer, attempting to see what Izzy was up to.

She batted Vishvesh's hand away. "Just giving Emily's inbox a surprise subscription to some intriguing mailing lists," she replied.

Vishvesh slouched in his seat, grumbling about the potential mess his algorithm would now face. "Oh, just take one for the team," Izzy said, an impish glimmer in her eyes as she finished and handed his phone back to him. "I wish I could see her face when she opens her email next."

Vishvesh pocketed his phone. "Well, you used her school email. It might be a while before she bothers opening it," he said, his eyes shifting to the notepad resting on the table. "But I think we should give you six points for your ingenious creativity."

"I don't know her personal email," Izzy admitted. "She'll stumble upon it eventually. Let's just relish the fact that at some time in the near future, Emily will have to waste her time weeding through an assortment of hilariously random emails." With a sly grin, she sipped her Pepsi, relishing the icy bubbles dancing down her throat.

Arlo lowered the melting bag of ice, his eyes fixed intently on Emily's door. "She deserves it," he muttered, his voice going cold.

As the minutes ticked by, the atmosphere in the room relaxed. The chatter of the friends became a low hum, carrying them deeper into the night. The impulsive prank Izzy had orchestrated on Emily gradually faded into the recesses of her mind.

Resting her head on her pillow several hours later, her thoughts replayed the conversation with her great-aunt from earlier that night. A sense of relief washed over her as she let out a long breath. It was as if a weight had been lifted off her shoulders, slowly dissipating into the night.

As she closed her eyes, a newfound lightness embraced her. It brought a sense of calmness and contentment that she hadn't felt in a long time.

CHAPTER EIGHT

A FUTURE OF SHADOWS

At the break of dawn, the sun emerged, piercing through the clouds and casting a warm glow upon the city. The remnants of the previous night's rainfall had been swept away. In the hushed embrace of morning, life stirred in a quiet neighbourhood.

A weathered glass door creaked open from a sleepy-looking building. Two young women emerged, laughter echoing in their wake as they walked across the narrow parking lot. A satisfying crunch accompanied each step as they walked over the fallen leaves. The autumn foliage swirled around them, creating a whimsical path to the blue Honda parked nearby.

"Izzy," a voice rang out, causing their steps to falter. A petite woman emerged from the building, her hair hastily gathered in a tousled bun, strands escaping to frame her face. A car fob dangled from her outstretched hand, its sleek surface catching the morning sunlight, winking brightly as she held it out.

Izzy's hand flew to her forehead in an exaggerated gesture. "Well, that would have been a long walk home," she said. She extended her hand, reaching out for her fob. "Thank you, Mrs. Lake!"

"No problem at all, Izzy." Mrs. Lake's smile remained steady as she acknowledged another car pulling into the parking lot.

"I'm really sorry I can't be there this Saturday to help with the walk."

"There's no need to apologize. We really appreciate all the effort you've put into organizing this event," Mrs. Lake said, patting Izzy gently on the arm. "Honestly, Izzy, your mother's recovery should come first. We'll manage just fine."

Mrs. Lake turned to leave, her voice floating over her shoulder. "Thank you for dropping off the signs and event preparations. We'll handle it from here. Don't worry!"

Returning to her car, Izzy slid into the driver's side. Melanie was already waiting in the passenger seat. "I didn't know your mom was scheduled for surgery."

Izzy's cheeks flushed as she leaned forward to start the car. "She isn't. It just didn't feel right to tell them I'm attending another charity event over theirs," she admitted. "Not that I want to," she added under her breath.

Melanie's eyebrow arched inquisitively. "Why are you doing it if you don't want to?"

Izzy tightened her grip on the steering wheel. "My mom's insisting on it." The memory of their after-dinner conversation clouded her thoughts, igniting a flicker of resentment. She swiftly repressed it, shame washing over her.

The neighbourhood seemed to come to life as they drove past a row of apartment buildings. Children, their backs hunched under heavy backpacks, plodded along the sidewalk, their parents trailing behind. Izzy eased the Honda to a halt as a crossing guard stepped onto the street. A procession of schoolchildren filed across the road. Their lively chatter and footsteps echoed across the asphalt.

With a decisive gesture, Melanie directed Izzy to turn left as the car picked up speed again. "Head toward the waterfront," she instructed, bouncing lightly in her seat.

Curiosity sparkled in Izzy's eyes as she steered in the indicated direction. She briefly recalled the gloves she had meant to pick up before class. But the memory dissolved as the water's shimmering surface came into view.

"Where exactly are we going?" Izzy asked, her gaze captivated by the silhouette of a bridge stretching across the bay.

Melanie motioned for her to turn left, right before reaching the bridge. The tires softly hissed against the road. Dominating the landscape before them stood a grand hotel, its position merely a stone's throw away from the harbour.

"A psychic convention," Melanie said, grinning as she popped a piece of gum into her mouth. The scent of mint wafted through the car, infusing the space with an unexpected freshness.

"A psychic convention?" Questions swirled in Izzy's mind. "Melanie, why on earth . . . ?"

Melanie's eyes softened as she turned to Izzy. "It's almost the anniversary of your dad's death, Iz," she said gently, her words hanging in the air. "You've been so caught up in those books on intuition lately . . ." A heavy silence fell. Clearing her throat, Melanie continued, "I just thought that this might cheer you up. Maybe you can connect with him or something."

For a moment, Izzy couldn't speak. The unexpected thoughtfulness stirred a whirlwind of emotions within her—surprise, gratitude, and a deep warmth that unfurled in her chest. It was as if a vibrant brushstroke had coloured outside the lines of Melanie's character.

A weighted silence stretched between them until Melanie finally shattered it by opening the car door. Sliding out onto the pavement, she gestured for Izzy to join her. "Come on. Let's go find out what this convention is all about."

Izzy nodded as she turned off the ignition. Melanie had already begun advancing toward the entrance to the hotel. Izzy got out of the Honda and quickly followed her. Despite the early hour, a stream of people flowed through the door. They formed an orderly queue that snaked along the far wall.

As Izzy drew closer to Melanie, the air was rich with aromas. The comforting scent of warm coffee intertwined with the fresh smell of conference materials. At the same time, a subtle hint of sage introduced an element of mystery.

Izzy's pulse quickened with anticipation as she took her place in the line. She expected to move at a crawl, but it surged forward. Paying her entrance fee, she stepped through the doorway, entering a vast room that hummed with energy.

Along the wall, vendors showcased their collections of charms, talismans, and amulets. Each mystical object was presented alongside a handwritten placard promising protection, luck, and spiritual enlightenment.

Izzy followed Melanie through the area, their path weaving through tables adorned with beautiful tarot cards. Sign-up sheets taped in seemingly every available space quickly filled with customers' signatures. Driven by curiosity and excitement, people eagerly inked their names in anticipation of having their futures unveiled.

Melanie stopped, her attention caught on a lavishly decorated table. Purple silks covered in golden stars twinkled in the light. An assortment of aquamarine and rose quartz crystals were scattered across the fabric, their extravagant price tags on full display.

Izzy's attention shifted to a towering cut-out. The figure depicted a handsome man, his tan complexion and unnaturally bright smile radiating confidence. Above the cut-out, a bold sign read:

Embark on a Journey with Master Xavier: Book a Reading.

Izzy's eyes landed on the swaying drapes concealing a corner beside the stall. Moments later, an older woman emerged, her cheeks flushed crimson. She leaned toward another woman, her excited whispers barely audible. Still, Izzy caught the words *handsome young man* among the soft chatter.

A graceful hand with manicured nails emerged from the shadowy drapes. It gestured theatrically, beckoning the next customer to come in. Melanie's gaze shifted to Izzy, her excitement palpable as she conveyed her intention to join the growing line for a reading with Master Xavier.

Izzy watched her friend wander off to the end of the line forming by the drapes and couldn't resist rolling her eyes. She knew Melanie's interest lay not in Master Xavier's self-proclaimed abilities. With a bemused shake of her head, Izzy continued toward the back of the room.

Lost in thought, she wandered through the room, observing the growing crowd. Amid the buzz of chatter, a serene tranquillity enveloped her. It guided her toward a table tucked away in the distant corner of the room.

Drawing nearer, Izzy noticed the psychic's minimalist setup. There were a few handwritten business cards and an empty sign-up sheet. Seated behind the table, seemingly unfazed by the throng engulfing the room, was a plump woman. Her grey head was bowed down as she counted her knitting stitches.

Looking up, the woman's blue eyes, comically magnified by thick, square glasses, met Izzy's. She wore a stained sweater decorated with an image of a kitten playfully entangled in a ball of yarn. Izzy was struck by the realization—the woman bore an uncanny resemblance to her great-aunt.

A surge of conviction overwhelmed her, leaving Izzy certain that her path had led her to this woman for a purpose. Lowering her head, she picked up a pen and scrawled her name on the sign-up sheet.

"That won't be necessary, sweetheart," the older woman said, a smile stretching across her lips to reveal a set of perfectly aligned dentures.

The woman motioned to the seat opposite her, inviting Izzy to sit. Squeezing herself into the tight space, Izzy perched on the wooden chair. She adjusted her position, discreetly leaning back to distance herself from the musty scent that clung to the other woman's clothing.

The knitting clattered on the table as the woman set it down. "Is this your first time seeking guidance from a psychic, m'dear?" she asked, her voice carrying the subtle lilt of a Newfoundland accent.

"Yes," Izzy confessed, her fingers tugging at her hair.

"Well, now, let me give you an overview of what I have in store for you today," the woman began. "First off, my name is Kathleen Burry." She paused, taking a moment to sip from her water bottle before continuing. "I offer a different style of psychic guidance. You won't find tarot cards or palmistry in my readings."

Izzy hung on Kathleen's every word, the rest of the room receding into mere background noise. "The information I receive can be both upliftin' and challenging. Are you prepared to hear the whole kit and caboodle, or are there certain things you would rather not know?"

A memory of her father's sudden passing flickered across Izzy's mind, leaving a lump in her throat. Taking a moment to compose herself, she swallowed hard and met Kathleen's gaze. "I want to know everything."

Kathleen nodded. "Very well," she murmured, absently scratching her cheek. "Please understand that the insights I provide are not set in stone. Life offers us numerous paths to navigate. I can only glimpse fragments of the one you are currently on." Shifting in her seat, she asked, "Before we begin, is there anything you're wantin' to know about what I do?"

"Can you . . . can you communicate with those who have passed away?"

Kathleen's gaze softened. "Yes, I'm both a psychic and a medium," she affirmed. "If I may ask, m'dear, who is it that you have lost?"

Izzy bit her lip, her eyes glistening. "My . . . my dad."

"I'm so sorry, sweet girl, it's a terrible loss." Kathleen paused, letting the silence sit between them before speaking again. "Your father, bless his kind soul. He had a big heart, didn't he?"

Izzy's breath caught in her chest as she nodded. Her eyes remained locked on Kathleen, waiting for her to continue.

Seeming to listen to something beyond Izzy's perception, Kathleen nodded and spoke with a quiet conviction. "Your father is still helpin' others on the other side. It's not a role you would expect, but he takes great joy in it."

A single tear traced a path down Izzy's cheek, her voice barely audible as she whispered, "Is he here right now?" Her eyes roamed the room as though searching for a glimpse of her father's presence.

"Yes, m'dear, he's right here with us. But you see, he can't stay for long. He's needed elsewhere."

Trembling, Izzy's voice barely rose above a whisper. "Dad?"

Reaching across the table, Kathleen pushed a tissue box closer to Izzy. Gratefully, Izzy accepted it, pressing the soft material against her damp eyes.

"Is he . . . is he mad at me?"

"Mad? Why on earth would your father be mad at you?"

Her question hung in the air as Izzy fell silent, her guilt forming a knot in her throat that kept her from responding. Izzy's mind drifted toward her father, consumed by questions she didn't dare vocalize. Did he hold her responsible for his death? More importantly, did he still love her? Her breath caught, her fingers drumming anxiously on the table at the thought of her father's rejection.

Kathleen leaned forward, her weathered hands cradling Izzy's soft palms. "Your father loves you. Nothing in this world would ever change that." Kathleen squeezed Izzy's hands before settling back into her seat.

"Over there," she said, flicking her eyes upward, "they lead different lives. Whatever happened with your father over here, he bears no ill will toward you in the place he's at now."

"Please tell him that I love him."

"He knows, sweet girl, he knows," Kathleen replied, a tender smile spreading across her face. "But he must be on his way. He wants you to know that he'll be checkin' in on you later."

Nodding, Izzy dabbed at her eyes with a crumpled tissue. She clenched it in her hand and then shoved it into the pocket of her jacket.

Kathleen cleared her throat. "Now, m'dear, we've come to the point of discussin' what lies ahead for you." She paused, her eyes slipping shut as if peering into a scene unfolding within her mind. Slowly, her eyelids fluttered open. Her once twinkling blue eyes now held a weighty seriousness.

Izzy listened intently as Kathleen's voice took on a grave tone. "Darkness follows you around like a shadow. All tangled up in your fate, it is." After a pause that seemed to stretch into eternity, a ripple of worry creased her brow.

"You have a roommate?" Without waiting for Izzy to respond, Kathleen pressed on. "Mind your step around her, now. She's got some wicked intentions aimed right at you."

Recalling the practical joke she'd played on Emily, an uneasy feeling crept over her. She quickly brushed it aside. After all, Emily wouldn't know that Izzy was behind it.

Kathleen continued the reading, oblivious to the thoughts consuming Izzy's mind. "But it's not just your roommate. Darkness lingers around your family. It haunts every path you take. I've never encountered a readin' quite like this before," she confessed. Kathleen stretched her hand across the table, grabbing her water bottle. As she raised it to her lips, Izzy noticed a faint tremor in her grip.

"Darkness may follow you, m'dear, but it does not own you. There are plenty of folks here . . . and *over there* that will help you stand against it. That is if you let them," she added, gently placing her water bottle on the table.

Izzy shifted uneasily in her seat, her palms damp. She absently traced the edge of her chair, eyes flitting to the other psychics around the room. Was Kathleen truly gifted, or was she just another phony amid the sea of frauds at the convention? So many of them were just putting on a show.

But deep down, Izzy desperately wanted to believe in the possibility of a real connection with her father. She craved for that brief moment of contact to be real. Yet the focus on darkness encircling her had smothered the excitement of the reading, casting a gloomy shadow over the room.

"My future can't really be that bad, can it? Don't you see more than just darkness?"

Kathleen's eyelids shut once more, and after a beat, she started muttering in a low tone that had Izzy straining her ears. "I see a long, treacherous trek ahead of you. By the end of it, you won't be the same soul, mark my words."

She opened her eyes, fixing her gaze on Izzy before speaking again. "Whether it be a blessin' or a curse, I can't rightly tell," she said, removing her glasses and polishing them against her sweater. "Your journey's going to be riddled with choices, not one of them comin' easy."

At the mention of hard choices, Izzy's thoughts gravitated toward the conversation she had shared with her great-aunt the night before. A wave of goosebumps danced along her arms, their touch sending a shiver through her body.

"Beware the foolhardy shepherd who doesn't tend to his sheep," Kathleen continued. "I'm also gettin' a whiff of an *M* name . . . They ain't who they claimin' to be." She stole a quick glance at the large wristwatch wrapped around her arm.

"I don't understand anything you just said," Izzy admitted, aware that her reading was ending. "Can't you be more specific? I'm not good with riddles."

I'm sorry, m'dear. I can only tell you what's shown to me. The riddles are a bit foggy to me as well."

Izzy exhaled deeply, her chest tightening with the sting of unmet expectations. The reading had hardly delivered on what she had yearned for—more precious time with her father, a peek into a brighter future, or even recognition of details unfolding in her current life.

She longed for concrete proof that life continued beyond death. She needed a glimmer of hope that her dad still existed somewhere, waiting for their paths to cross again. As she thought about it more, Izzy began to question whether the information provided by the psychic was truly accurate or just a result of guesswork.

Reluctantly, she dug into her coat pocket, pulling out two fresh twenty-dollar bills. She extended the money to Kathleen, who accepted it with a broad smile. Izzy watched as she carefully tucked the bills into the depths of her oversized purse.

"Thank you kindly," she said. "Remember, strength resides not only in our own two feet but in our heart's willingness to embrace the outstretched hands of those offerin' their help."

Nodding, Izzy murmured her thanks to Kathleen and went in search of Melanie. As she scanned the crowded room for her friend, the psychic's ominous warning pushed into her mind. *Darkness follows you around like a shadow . . . It haunts every path you take.*

That statement seemed chillingly accurate, considering her turbulent family life and the emotional chaos it caused. But what did the psychic truly mean? Was the darkness merely a metaphor, a recognition of emotional turmoil? Or was it a warning of a more serious threat?

A tremor of unease rippled through her. As her gaze darted around the room, shadows seemed to stretch and twist into grotesque forms.

She quickened her steps, her heart drumming in her chest. Fleeing the crowded room, she made her way outside. For now, the brilliance of the morning served as her sanctuary, a refuge from the consuming darkness the psychic had so cryptically mentioned.

CHAPTER NINE

THE UNFORGIVING EMAIL

The brief drive back to the college campus unfolded effortlessly. Lost in a labyrinth of her thoughts, Izzy only occasionally caught bits of Melanie's words as her friend delved into the details of her encounter with Master Xavier.

"So, then he told me that I was going to get my heart broken and that it would be my own fault! And the worst thing is that he laughed when I tried to give him my number! He said I have a curse on me."

"Yeah, a curse doesn't sound good," Izzy murmured. She guided her car into a vacant spot near the front of their residential building. The engine quieted to a gentle hum before dying completely as she switched it off.

Melanie flicked her hand dismissively at Izzy's response. "That's all just part of his charade," she said. "I've never had anyone refuse my number before!"

Ignoring Melanie, Izzy stepped out of her vehicle. She inhaled deeply; the fresh breeze filled her lungs, bringing the unmistakable scent of autumn's gentle decay.

Melanie's piercing shriek shattered the parking lot's tranquillity. Startled, Izzy turned, watching as the passenger door slammed shut with a resounding thud. Melanie distanced herself from the vehicle and furiously scraped the toe of her boot against the pavement.

"I'm going to kill whoever let their mutt crap all over the ground. These are Versace boots!"

Izzy's lips twitched uncontrollably as Melanie turned to look at her. "Maybe I really am cursed!"

"You're not cursed, Mel. It's just bad luck."

"What do you think bad luck is." Melanie's face twisted into a scowl as she spoke. Leaning against Izzy's car, she scrutinized her soiled boot. "I'll have to meet you in class. I need to go clean these off."

Izzy watched as Melanie stomped off toward their apartment, leaving her alone in the parking lot. She then turned and made her way toward the college, cutting a path behind the white sports dome.

Glancing at her wristwatch, she felt a flicker of urgency in her chest as she realized it was nearly ten o'clock. She quickened her pace and soon found herself sailing through the doors of her classroom with minutes to spare. Heading toward the back of the class, she settled into a theatre-style chair.

Izzy's gaze drifted toward the front of the room, settling on Emily. She was deep in conversation with their teacher. Izzy's heart sank as she realized it was the start of presentation week. Groaning, she slouched down in her chair. It was going to be a long class.

Emily stood near the podium, setting up her laptop. Izzy's eyes narrowed as she observed her roommate. The vision of Emily faltering during her presentation sprang to her mind. She quickly banished the thought, her cheeks burning with shame.

Leaning over her laptop, Emily called out, "I'm almost ready, sir." The school's login page filled the whiteboard behind her. Izzy observed Emily deftly navigating the digital landscape, quickly bringing up her email page. Time seemed to stretch as the screen sluggishly loaded. While she waited, Emily focused on arranging her handouts, standing with her back to the whiteboard.

A nagging sensation tugged at Izzy's consciousness, a whispering urge to remember something important. Yet, try as she might, she couldn't quite grasp the memory that danced just beyond her reach.

Soft laughter rippled throughout the room, yanking her back to the present moment. She turned to find its source—a young man, only a few seats down, nudging his friend and pointing toward the whiteboard.

A chill of apprehension descended upon Izzy, settling in the pit of her stomach as she slowly swivelled her eyes back to the front of the room. As if in slow motion, her gaze met the large screen that dominated the front wall.

Her face paled as the memory of the previous night's prank flooded back. Every muscle in her body tensed. She wanted to call out a warning to her roommate but found herself frozen in her seat. Helplessly, she watched Emily shuffle through her handouts, unaware of the email that had opened behind her.

The sniggering grew louder as more students looked up at the screen. Their gazes were fixed on Emily's account, now prominently displayed for all to see. Izzy's heart sank as a series of embarrassing emails—ones Izzy had never intended for public viewing—filled the screen.

She cringed as she read the first subject line:

Subject: Empowering Women's Incontinence Support Group: You're Not Alone, Emily!

Regret washed over Izzy as she realized the extent of her ill-conceived joke. At that moment, it lost its intended humour, revealing itself as a tasteless mistake. Her eyes reluctantly moved to the next subject line, her stomach twisting in a knot:

Special Invitation for Emily: Regain Your Confidence with Our Proven Yeast Infection Solutions

Each subsequent email was more embarrassing than the last. Izzy glanced over at Emily. The realization that she had orchestrated this public humiliation was unbearable. Slowly, she slumped further in her chair, attempting to shrink away from the scene unfolding before her. As the excited chatter and whispers in the classroom grew louder, it became painfully evident that Emily's lack of popularity in class only intensified the situation.

Emily raised her head to look at her classmates, her lips forming a tight line. Slowly, she turned around until she, too, was looking at the screen. The handouts she held slipped from her fingers, fluttering to the floor.

Snatching up the laptop, she slammed it shut, effectively cutting off the connection to the whiteboard. Izzy caught sight of tears glistening in Emily's eyes as she looked up. The snide laughter from the other students slowly subsided, giving way to an uneasy silence that settled over the room.

Without a word, Emily quickly collected her things. Clutching her books close to her chest, she hurried out of the room.

The class broke out in excited chatter, but Izzy didn't join in. Her eyes remained fixed on the empty doorway. She rose reluctantly, the scrape of her chair against the floor punctuating her decision. Hurrying, she set out to catch up with Emily.

The hallway unfurled before Izzy, a silent, deserted corridor. A warm, inviting scent of cinnamon drifted through the air from the nearby cafeteria. Meanwhile, the dim echoes of Emily's clunky dress shoes receded, bouncing off the tiled walls as she moved toward the building's main exit.

Izzy felt the urge to follow Emily and apologize, but a thick fog of uncertainty clouded her thoughts. Acknowledging the truth about her involvement felt like the right thing to do. Yet apprehension coursed through Izzy, awakening a swarm of worries about the possible repercussions that lay ahead.

Gathering her courage, she followed the sound of Emily's footsteps. The corridor turned, and Izzy's heart stuttered. There, amid the pale blue lockers, stood her roommate, her tear-stained face illuminated by the soft glow of the overhead lights.

Emily's trembling hand rose to swipe at her face, the fabric of her sleeve acting as a makeshift tissue. Sensing Izzy's approach, she raised her head sharply, her eyes locking with Izzy's.

"Emily, I am so sorry. I didn't think—"

"I knew it was you." Emily's words seethed with a venomous edge. She unravelled herself from the wall, closing the distance between them.

"I didn't know you would open it up in class. Honesty!" Izzy blurted out. "Since you moved in with us in September, you've . . . well, you've been distant, icy even. The joke was meant to annoy, not embarrass you," she confessed, her gaze faltering under the intensity of Emily's stare.

"Typical Izzy Adams, always making everything about herself," Emily said, her expression dissolving into raw, unmasked fury. "I'm the villain here? You humiliated me before our entire class because I didn't want to be your friend."

"I didn't mean to hurt you. It was supposed to be a harmless prank. But you're right. I messed up. Please, let me—"

"Let you do what?" Emily interjected sharply, her arms folding protectively over her chest as she loomed over Izzy. "What magical solution do you have in mind? Are you going to admit that it was you and risk expulsion for bullying?"

Silence hung in the air as Izzy's complexion drained of colour. Emily's cold laughter reverberated through the empty halls. "I didn't think so," she sneered. Her gaze drilled into Izzy, her eyes narrowing to deadly slits. "People like you never take responsibility for anything." She turned sharply on her heels, leaving Izzy standing there.

Desperation seizing her, Izzy lunged forward, fingers wrapping around her roommate's arm—a motion that brought Emily to a halt.

"Emily, I—" Izzy's words stumbled, cut short by a spreading warmth in her fingers. Her frown quickly gave way to a mask of agony, the growing heat consuming her hand as if it were caught in an invisible blaze.

A cry escaped her lips as she tried to pull her hand back, only to find it stubbornly glued to Emily's arm.

"What's happening?" Desperation contorted her features as she tugged frantically at her ensnared hand. A scream tore from her throat as fire seemed to race through her veins, igniting every nerve with unbearable heat.

Emerging from the shadows, a tiny figure darted forth, scuttling between Emily's legs and scaling her body. The grip on Izzy's hand vanished, and she stumbled backward, crashing into the lockers.

A bizarre sense of déjà vu enveloped her. She swore she had glimpsed the same tiny man in Emily's room yesterday. She watched as his elongated face appeared to contort and shift until it transformed into a malnourished cat.

Emily held the animal close to her chest. Its yellow eyes blinked at Izzy, conveying a silent warning that sent a tremor of unease twitching through her. The searing pain subsided from her hand, leaving only a tingly sensation prickling along her skin.

What had just transpired? Izzy's mind raced, heat flooding her chest as she fought to regain her composure. Seeking support, she leaned against the lockers, finding small comfort in the cool touch of the metal.

A heavy silence settled over the room before Emily spoke. "Your day will come. I will make sure of it."

Izzy stood rooted in place, watching Emily's retreating figure. This time, she made no move to intercept her.

Overwhelmed with emotions, she couldn't doubt the reality of what she had just experienced. However, it was inexplicable and defied any logical explanation, leading her to a chilling realization. If she wasn't spiralling into madness, then an undeniable supernatural force was at play, and Emily appeared to be the central figure in this enigma. The psychic's ominous prophecy echoed in her mind, casting a shadow of uncertainty over her future.

CHAPTER TEN

THE DOPPELGÄNGER'S GRIN

As the week wore on, Izzy found her days slipping back into their regular rhythm. The strange events of earlier in the week started to resemble distorted dreams more than reality as each subsequent day rolled by without further incident. Yet one irregularity lingered like an unwelcome spectre—a scruffy raven that seemed to follow her everywhere she went.

Take Wednesday, for example, when Izzy was dining with Kyler in the cafeteria. The raven appeared again, its dark head repeatedly thudding against the glass window. Its beady eyes fixated on her, competing with the noise of clattering trays for her attention. The raven was an unsettling reminder that her supposed normalcy was merely a fragile illusion.

For his part, Kyler was blissfully ignorant of the raven's theatrics. His main preoccupation was persuading Izzy to join him at his band's cluttered garage for a practise session. Much to her relief, she was able to turn down his invitation. Her looming midterm exam served as a perfect alibi.

Thursday soon rolled around, bringing with it the long-anticipated gathering of the Brunch Bunch. As Izzy guided her great-aunt across the uneven parking lot toward their chosen restaurant, she felt a familiar spectre make itself known. Perched atop a nearby garbage bin, the mangy raven peered down at her, its harsh squawks piercing the otherwise quiet afternoon.

The raven's seemingly unusual behaviour left a trail of chills down her back. Ignoring the bird, she quickened her pace, guiding her bewildered aunt toward the safety of the small building ahead.

"Slow down, Izzy," her aunt protested, her steps faltering as they approached the entrance. Mr. Smith, already at the doorway, gallantly held it open for them as they passed through.

"Sorry, Auntie A," Izzy said, slowing her pace to allow her aunt to regain her footing. The air inside the restaurant was infused with the rich, spicy aroma of Thai cuisine, which coaxed a rumble from the depths of Izzy's stomach. Her gaze swept over the tables in search of their reserved spot. Rhylynn's fluttering arm caught Izzy's attention and beckoned them over.

Guiding Audrey gently, Izzy maneuvered her to the table. Pausing beside Rhylynn's grandmother, Izzy bent down to hug her. Lila Rivers, a woman of considerable size, wrapped Izzy in her comforting embrace. The earthy scent of rosemary flooded Izzy's senses as her cheek nestled into the soft folds of the older woman's neck.

"You look well, my dear."

"Thanks," Izzy replied, sinking into the chair beside Rhylynn. A subtle smile curved her lips as she observed her aunt's skillful maneuvering, strategically placing herself between Mrs. Rivers and Mr. Smith.

Meeting Rhylynn's gaze, they shared a knowing look, silently acknowledging the unspoken rivalry that existed between Lila and Audrey. Despite their steadfast friendship, both women were notably competitive, particularly when matters of the heart were at stake. This was increasingly evident in their recent pursuit of Mr. Smith.

Lila leaned across the table. Her green eyes were accentuated by her dyed-red curls. Today, her hair was styled in an elaborate updo. "Did you catch the news this morning, Henry?" she asked, playfully batting her mascara-laden eyelashes. "They suspect they've unearthed the remains of that unfortunate girl. Frannie Davis, I believe that was her name."

Mr. Smith's eyes lifted from the menu. "Yes, Lila. His eyes dimmed, a shadow falling across his face. "She's been waiting fifty years for us to find her."

Audrey's eyes sparkled with curiosity as she leaned forward, eager for more information. "You were involved in the Dead Ringer case?" Her hand extended, gently resting on top of Mr. Smith's. The undercurrent of connection between them did not escape Lila's sharp notice. Her eyes narrowed.

Mr. Smith's face flushed under the sudden spotlight of attention. "Why, yes, I was," he replied, his voice conveying unease as he relived the memory.

Audrey released her grip on his hand to adjust her hearing aid. "Were you there when the police killed the lead suspect?"

"Adrian Mahoney," Mr. Smith said, the corners of his mouth subtly pulling downward. "Yes, I was there all right," he muttered. "What he did to those girls . . ." His voice wavered as he struggled to contain the emotions threatening to spill forth.

Rhylynn's long curls tumbled forward, brushing the tabletop as she leaned in. Her face was aglow with curiosity. "I had no idea you were a police officer, Mr. Smith!"

Lila's voice swelled with pride. "Our Henry was a highly esteemed member of the Toronto Police Services!"

A blush began to colour Mr. Smith's cheeks, tinging them with a rosy hue. His hand instinctively rose to scratch the side of his head, inadvertently nudging his tweed cap so that it perched at a slight tilt. "Well, Lila, I wouldn't go as far as to say that."

"Oh, don't be so modest," Lila replied, "The Dead Ringer claimed the lives of eight young women around your age, girls. He would kidnap them, bury them alive in remote locations, and attach a string to a bell above their graves. Those poor girls could ring that bell all they wanted, but no one was close enough to hear them."

"How did you catch him?" Rhylynn asked, brushing a curl behind her ear. The movement caused the llama earrings in her ears to sway, depicting the creatures with their tongues playfully outstretched.

Mr. Smith paused, taking a thoughtful sip of water before responding. "Well, dear, the department didn't actually apprehend him." Mr. Smith carefully placed his glass on the table.

He sighed. "You know, it wasn't enough for Adrian to go after regular girls. He had to target someone important, like the daughter of the premier of Ontario at the time. Pure stupidity." Mr. Smith shook his head. "Thankfully, the premier had stepped up his security due to some extremist threats, so Adrian never even got close to the girl." Izzy noticed a flicker of relief in Mr. Smith's eyes, the weight of the near-tragedy still lingering in his memory.

As his narrative unfolded, Izzy's attention began to waver, her thoughts returning to Emily. Her mind flashed to the moment she had returned home after their confrontation.

She had been rinsing out her coffee mug in the kitchen when the glass suddenly broke in her grasp. The sharp fragments pierced her skin. Startled, she jumped backward. A noise from the opposite end of the room drew her attention, and she turned around, clutching her injured hand.

Emily stood there, glaring at her. Her eyes were red, and her short brown hair was dishevelled, making her look like she had been crying. Izzy had stepped forward, intending to apologize, but Emily turned on her heel and slammed the door, cutting her off.

The flashback had taken her back to that awful day. Now, Izzy traced the edge of her bandaged palm, the weight of remorse settling heavily upon her. It was a foolish oversight to believe that Emily would only check her school email in the privacy of her room. Emily was nothing if not diligent, probably perpetually checking her emails. Shame washed over Izzy as she reflected on the damage that she had caused. Even Emily didn't deserve such treatment.

She sank further into her seat, feeling undeserving of her place at the table. Rhylynn cast a curious glance her way, but Izzy deliberately avoided her gaze. Instead, she focused on the server navigating her way toward them. She was balancing a tray loaded with drinks.

The young woman distributed the beverages with practised ease. She nodded at Rhylynn, leaving Izzy with an unmistakable impression that they knew each other.

Izzy's eyes strayed to the name tag pinned to the young woman's blouse. The inscription *Sydney* was etched in bold letters. Bending slightly, Sydney handed Izzy a drink, causing her long, dark ponytail to lightly brush against Izzy's shoulder. Their eyes met, Sydney's deep brown irises staring into Izzy's with a blend of intrigue and something else, something Izzy couldn't quite place.

A flicker of apprehension shadowed Sydney's expression, but it rapidly vanished, replaced by a slight sigh suggesting some decision had been made. She walked away, leaving Izzy to ponder the significance of their fleeting connection.

Rhylynn leaned in, her expression apologetic as she spoke. "I hope this is all right. I went ahead and ordered your drink for you. You always get Pepsi, right?"

Nodding, Izzy raised the cup to her lips and sipped the soda. The cool liquid slid down her throat, providing a refreshing sensation. Yet a subtle frown tugged at her features as a bitter aftertaste clung to her tongue.

"Thanks, Rhy Rhy," Izzy said, taking another sip. She puckered her lips slightly, detecting the strange taste again. "I think I'll ask for a new one. This one tastes a bit off," she remarked, wrinkling her nose as she set the glass down.

Leaning back in her seat, Izzy watched her aunt flirt with Mr. Smith. His words sparked a burst of laughter from Audrey. Lila rolled her eyes and turned toward Izzy and Rhylynn.

"Well, girls, what's new?"

"Nothing much, Mrs. Rivers. I have midterms to prepare for. That doesn't leave much time for anything else," Izzy replied. A peculiar sensation, akin to the delicate dance of butterfly wings, began to flutter within her stomach as she spoke. Instinctively, her hand moved to her abdomen, applying gentle pressure to alleviate the feeling.

"Oh, well, I'm sure you will do just fine, Izzy. Audrey tells me that you're a smart cookie."

Izzy smiled, her eyes darting over to her aunt with warm affection. "You know," she teased, "I'm not sure she's laid eyes on my transcript yet."

A laugh escaped Lila as she lifted her teacup to her lips.

Izzy's discomfort intensified as the unpleasant sensation wound its way from her belly to her throat. Before she could prevent it, a loud, repulsive burp escaped her lips. It carried with it an unpleasant odour of fish. Izzy's eyes widened in mortification, and she quickly covered her mouth.

Audrey turned to look at her. "Are you all right, Izzy?"

She forced a tight-lipped smile. "I'm all right, Auntie A." A mild discomfort tugged at her gut. "Just need a moment in the bathroom," she added, hastily rising from her seat.

A sea of tables occupied by other Brunch Bunch members stretched before her. With a dip of her head, Izzy averted her gaze, avoiding eye contact. The thought of rinsing her mouth in the sink consumed her mind and propelled her forward.

Once in the bathroom, she moved toward the sink and twisted the faucet. As the water streamed out, she leaned over to rinse her mouth. The cool sensation offered a brief respite from her current surroundings.

Memories of her cozy bed flooded her mind, and she longed to be there instead. Earlier this morning, she had felt a strong desire to cancel the lunch date but had ignored it. In retrospect, she realized the others wouldn't have been angry. She should have listened to her intuition.

She sighed and cupped her hands, allowing the cold water to splash against her face. Water droplets tumbled from her forehead, tracing a wet trail along her cheeks. In the mirror, her eyes, ringed with shadows, blinked back at her with a dull gaze.

A flushing toilet echoed through the restroom, interrupting Izzy's thoughts. Rattling stirred from the green stall behind her as someone wrestled with the stubborn lock. At last, the latch yielded, and the door swung open. A woman stepped out, her face concealed by a curtain of blond hair.

Izzy twisted the faucet knobs, shutting off the water, though the tap continued to release a faint trickle. She abandoned her futile efforts, turning her attention back to the mirror. A gasp caught in her throat as she noticed the woman's reflection. It was identical to hers. Another "Izzy" stood beside her, a strange smile on her face.

Panic gripped Izzy's body, its icy fingers stealing her breath away. Meanwhile, her doppelgänger maintained its unsettling smile. Its once-vibrant face withered away, the flesh decaying and sloughing off. In its place emerged a skull.

Adrenaline shot through Izzy's veins, jolting her into action. She frantically backpedalled from the sink, her body colliding with the stall door behind her. The door swung open, sending her sprawling to the ground in an ungraceful tumble. Agony radiated through Izzy's arm as her elbow collided with the edge of the toilet. The sharp pain brought tears to her eyes.

The doppelgänger turned to look at Izzy. A hiss echoed from the empty void where lips once were. It stepped toward her and bent down, its bony hand grasping Izzy's arm in its iron grip.

Izzy's bloodcurdling scream tore through the silence. Pushing off against the toilet, she sprang to her feet, shoving past the skeleton with such force that it toppled to the ground. Her heart hammered against her ears as she dashed to the bathroom door and threw it open. In her haste, she collided with a server just outside the door.

His tray teetered precariously before gravity took hold and launched its contents into a chaotic dance. Soup cascaded through the air, scattering droplets of vibrant colours before crashing down with a clatter upon the floor. A spray of the scalding liquid found its way onto Izzy's arm, burning her skin.

"I'm so sorry!" Izzy moved to assist the man in regaining his balance. Grumbling, he jerked away from her. As he bent to retrieve his tray, the bathroom door swung open. A woman burst forth, her short, dark hair framing her face, which was tight and contorted with anger.

"She's on drugs!" The woman flung her words toward the transfixed diners. Silence descended as curious eyes locked onto the unfolding scene.

"No, I'm not!" Izzy said, raising her arms in protest. "I just . . . Well, your face. There was something . . . wrong with your face. It was . . ." She stopped, realizing that continuing her explanation would only solidify the impression that she was under the influence of drugs.

"I'm sorry. I don't know what came over me. I just—" Izzy's apology hung in the air, but the woman shoved past her.

Izzy remained frozen on the spot. Fluttering waves of anxiety rose within her, causing her chest to tighten and her muscles to tense.

"Are you okay, Iz?" Rhylynn's voice floated to her.

Slowly, Izzy turned to face her friend. Her throat felt tight, and when she moved her lips, no sound came out. She looked at Rhylynn, desperation reflected in her eyes.

Moving toward her, Rhylynn gently pressed her palm against Izzy's neck. An unusual cooling sensation coursed through her body, dissolving the tension that had seized her. Izzy's racing thoughts gradually settled, allowing her to find her voice again.

Tears welling in her blue eyes, she poured out her confusion to Rhylynn in a whisper. "I don't understand . . . Something was wrong with that woman. She wore my face, and then she didn't."

A scornful chuckle resonated nearby. Startled, Izzy looked over, her pulse hitching as she found herself looking at Emily. She was seated in a nearby booth, a satisfied grin unfurling across her face.

"What is she doing here?" Izzy's pulse picked up, anxiety tightening its grip around her chest once more.

Rhylynn turned, her eyes widening in surprise at the sight of Emily. An expression of comprehension flickered across her face for a moment as if a missing puzzle piece had just fallen into place. Then, her lips pressed into a thin line, and her body seemed to emanate a crackling energy that Izzy felt in her bones.

Fatigue swept through Izzy, her steps faltering into a stagger. The remnants of her panic attack clung to her, siphoning away her strength. She placed a hand on Rhylynn's shoulder, redirecting her attention away from Emily. "Hey, Rhy, do you think you could give Auntie A and Mr. Smith a ride home? I need to get out of here."

"Are you okay? I can drive you home now and come back for the others later."

"No, I'm fine, Rhy. I just need to get out of here."

Rhylynn's face held a shadow of worry as she nodded. Turning away from her, Izzy made a beeline for the exit, hurrying to distance herself from the concerned eyes of her loved ones. Stepping outside, she closed the door on the chaos behind her. Alone with her pounding heart, a flurry of unanswered questions lingered, weighing heavily in the silence.

CHAPTER ELEVEN

THE UNEXPECTED VISITOR

The crisp autumn wind whispered through the air, resuscitating the fallen leaves into a kaleidoscope of colours. What was once the drab parking lot of her residence building now danced with a dynamic display of shifting hues. Nestled in the comfort of her car, Izzy's gaze remained transfixed on the performance.

Heat crept up her neck and settled on her cheeks as she recalled the incident in the restaurant. Closing her eyes, she leaned her head against the comforting warmth of her steering wheel. As if sensing her need to hide, Izzy's hair fell around her, providing a refuge from the world outside.

The terrifying idea that she might be losing her sanity was beginning to seem more likely. A cold dread seeped into her body. What was she going to do?

A rap on the window beside her sent Izzy's heart into a skittish dance, her body jerking upright. Her eyes flew open wide with alarm. Turning toward the source of the sound, she saw Melanie's face peering in through the glass. A knot twisted in Izzy's stomach as she observed her friend's nervous expression.

Melanie motioned for her to roll down the window. She reached for the control panel, her fingers fumbling before finding the switch. The glass pane whirred, descending slowly with a faint mechanical hum. The outside world immediately rushed in, carrying the sounds of rustling leaves.

"What's wrong, Mel?"

Melanie looked around, her fingers fidgeting with the hem of her shirt. "Your sister is here, Iz."

"Kate's here?" Izzy's shoulders tensed. Anxiety began to coil within her.

Melanie nodded, her voice sounding strained. "Yeah, she showed up about ten minutes ago. I tried calling you."

"My phone is on silent." Izzy's eyes darted toward their apartment as if anticipating her sister's sudden appearance.

She rolled the window back up and shut off the car. Melanie moved back as Izzy swung her door open, the thud of it closing echoing around them. As she walked toward her apartment, Izzy's stomach twisted in unease. Why would her sister unexpectedly show up at her college? A horrible notion crossed her mind—maybe something had happened to Eddie or their mother. Her pace quickened.

"So, your sister seems . . . nice."

Izzy nodded, her lips forming a grim line. "Did she say anything to you about why she's here?" she asked, stepping through the building's main entrance.

"Not really. I showed her to your room, and she slammed the door in my face." Melanie paused, a thoughtful expression crossing her features. "I think she would make a formidable match for Emily. It would be interesting to see those two meet for the first time."

Izzy shuddered, offering a half-smile to her friend. "I'll pass on that."

Melanie chuckled as Izzy opened the door to their apartment. Her laughter faded as they stepped through into the kitchen.

"Well, I should go study . . . Good luck," Melanie said, nodding toward Izzy's door.

As she watched Melanie walk away, Izzy's shoulders slumped. Sighing, she crossed through the opposite end of the kitchen, making her way toward her bedroom. Her hand hesitated on her doorknob a moment before finally gripping the cool metal and twisting it.

The door swung open, and Izzy's gaze was immediately drawn to the profile of her sister, Kate, as she stood staring out the window that overlooked the parking lot. Kate's chestnut hair, intricately braided into a French plait, gracefully fell down her back. Izzy stepped into the room. She let the door shut with a soft click behind her and leaned against its sturdy frame. At the sight of Izzy, Kate turned, her expression hardening. The manila envelope gripped in Kate's hands sent a twinge of unease through Izzy's gut.

"Is everything okay?"

Ignoring Izzy's question, Kate thrust the envelope into the air, her tight grip crumpling its edges. "What is this?"

"Why are you going through my stuff, Kate?"

Kate took a step forward, shaking the envelope aggressively. A flurry of colourful pamphlets and postcards spilled to the floor. Izzy's gaze darted from the fallen items to Kate, her eyebrows arching in silent shock. A whirlwind of thoughts and retorts swirled through Izzy's mind. Yet, she pressed her lips together, meeting her sister's gaze silently.

"Why do you have pamphlets on different universities, *Isabelle*."

"Aunt Audrey gave them to me," Izzy confessed, shifting her eyes away from her sister. Her focus drifted downward, landing on a pamphlet near her sneaker. The university's emblem stood out in bold red and white.

"Why would she do that?" Kate's eyes narrowed; the chill in her question hung between them.

Izzy inched toward her bed. Slipping off her shoes, she climbed onto the mattress. She drew the patchwork quilt—a handmade token from her aunt—around her shoulders as if seeking its familiar protection.

"She thinks that I should apply to university."

"Does she now," Kate said, her voice sharp with anger. "Well, that's a ridiculous idea." Her boot nudged one of the postcards, sending it skidding across the floor. "What a waste of time and materials."

Eyes clenched shut, Izzy scrambled for the words she'd rehearsed, now scattering like leaves in a storm. She wasn't ready to have this conversation. Her sister's unexpected presence threw her plans into disarray, knocking her off balance. Izzy drew in a deep breath. A mental image of her great-aunt flashed in her mind. Audrey's icy blue eyes—reminiscent of Izzy's and her father's—peered out from the depths and fixed upon Izzy as if reproaching her for remaining silent.

A tiny spark of courage ignited within Izzy. Opening her eyes, she met Kate's gaze with a glacial stare of her own. "It's not a waste of material, actually. I've . . . well, I've decided to apply to university. I'm not sure which ones yet, but I still have some time to figure it out."

Kate's jaw hung open in disbelief. "You are going to apply to university?"

Izzy nodded, her fingers tightening around the soft fabric of her quilt.

The lines on Kate's face hardened, and her eyes narrowed at Izzy once again. "You will do no such thing, Isabelle. That was never part of the plan."

"Well, it is now."

"No, it is not." Kate closed the gap between them, advancing on Izzy with her hands balled into tight fists. "You will graduate college and join Eddie and me in the family business."

"I don't want to, Kate. I want to make a difference in people's lives, not just take care of them after they've passed away. I was thinking maybe the social work—"

"Are you really that selfish, Isabelle?" Kate's words came out forcefully, specks of spittle punctuating her anger. "Mother is counting on us to run the funeral home. After all the money she has invested in your college program, you would dare throw that in her face now?"

"I will pay her back . . . eventually."

"You are not applying," Kate said, jabbing a finger at the pamphlets strewn around the floor. "This little pipe dream of yours is a waste of time," she sneered. "You have a *duty* to your family. You *owe* it to us."

Izzy shrank back, her shoulders hunching to shield herself from the sharp edge of Kate's words. "I . . . I think I would do well as a social worker, Kate. Dad would want it for me, too. He was always helping—"

"Dad would have expected you to put your family first," Kate retorted, her voice seething with resentment. "This isn't about your selfish ambitions! Mother's dream is to turn the business into a franchise. You've already taken Dad away from her. Are you really going to take this away too?"

Kate stormed to the desk, her movements sharp as she grabbed her purse and coat. Whirling to face Izzy, contempt twisted her face. "Mother is going to be so disappointed in you," she spat out. Slipping into her coat, she yanked it tight around her waist.

"But honestly, I'm not surprised. Your selfishness has always consumed you," she seethed, her words slicing through the air. "You make everything about yourself, regardless of who suffers because of it. First, Dad . . . and now our mother."

Izzy bit down on the inside of her cheek. With a tremulous effort, she lifted her gaze to meet her sister's.

She struggled to reconcile the memory of Kate's brown eyes—once warm and affectionate—with the cold stare that confronted her now. The stark contrast was like a harsh wind against her soul.

Kate's fingers clenched tightly around the door handle. With a vigorous wrench, she flung it open. "If you dare to proceed with this, Isabelle—mark my words—you'll be dead to me. I'll sever all ties with you if you hurt the only parent I have left." The door's slam sent a jolt through the air, the noise abrupt and final.

Surrendering to her sobs, Izzy clutched the quilt close. She buried her face in the plush comfort of her pillow, where the gentle fragrance of laundry detergent still lingered.

Her heart threatened to burst, tears flowing until exhaustion claimed her. Haunting dreams took hold: her mother's face was etched with grave disappointment, and her sister's, a mask of deep-seated hatred.

CHAPTER TWELVE

HALLOWEEN HORRORS

As Izzy wrestled with the emotional storm her sister had provoked inside her, the skies also released their fury. On Halloween morning, she woke and was greeted once again by steady rain and grey skies. The day progressed with a relentless downpour. By the time Izzy arrived for her volunteer assignment at the Children's Safe-T Town, it had tapered off into a fine mist.

Dressed in typical witch garb, Izzy weaved through the miniature cobblestone street toward her assignment: a festively decorated brick house. She adjusted her black wig, fastening it more securely as the wind picked up.

She smiled faintly at a young couple as she passed them. Their toddler—unfazed by Izzy's witchy guise—responded with a cheerful wave, her tiny hand fluttering in the air. The little girl then playfully pirouetted alongside her parents, her glittering princess attire billowing around her.

For the next two hours, Izzy kept her post, distributing chocolate bars and lollipops to a colourful procession of children. Despite her sombre mood, their presence brought her fleeting joy. The kids approached with infectious energy, eager smiles playing on their lips as they held their bags open wide.

Among the excited throng, some sported costumes lovingly crafted by their parents. The signs of last-minute creativity evident in mismatched fabrics and hastily applied face paint. Others wore well-tailored outfits, ranging from off-the-rack ensembles to homemade creations. From fantastical creatures to beloved characters, each child sported their chosen identity with confidence and pride.

As the night neared its end, the last remaining child was shepherded away by their fatigued parent. Yawning, Izzy started dismantling her station, only to be intercepted by another volunteer.

"Go and enjoy the rest of your night," she urged, waving Izzy away cheerfully.

Izzy sighed in relief, grateful for the opportunity to escape the mist that had saturated her wig, causing the strands to cling to her makeup. Her boots created ripples in the shallow puddles as she darted across the street to her parked car.

The drive back to campus took longer than usual. Izzy navigated cautiously through streets, now teeming with older children in sinister costumes. The extra time let her mind drift back to earlier that day when she had thrown the university pamphlets into her garbage can.

Reluctantly, Izzy faced the bitter truth she had been trying to ignore. Kate was right—the idea of applying to university was nothing more than an elusive fantasy. The weight of this realization pressed heavily upon her. Izzy knew how much her mother had suffered this past year and couldn't imagine hurting her even more than she already had. Emotions surged within Izzy, causing tears to well up, but she swiftly wiped them away.

A familiar weight settled on her shoulders, dragging her down as she neared the sign pointing toward the college apartments. She grudgingly acknowledged that staying in Belleville wasn't completely terrible—it kept her close to her great-aunt.

Maneuvering her vehicle into the parking lot, she killed the engine and stepped out into the damp evening. Her building loomed ahead, a towering outline against the night sky. A chorus of laughter echoed from a cluster of students garbed in pirate attire. One broke away to hold the door open for her, sending her a cheeky wink before darting off to rejoin his friends.

Once in her apartment, Izzy was met with an unexpected hush, a glaring contrast to its usual liveliness. She moved through the space toward her room, but as she passed the bathroom, the door creaked open. Melanie emerged, enveloped in a white towel with water beads glistening on her skin. Stepping into the communal area, she left a trail of wet footprints behind her.

"The shower went cold on me," she grumbled, her lower lip jutting out in a pout. "I was in the middle of shampooing!"

Izzy's shoulders slumped. Her fingers twitched toward her collar; the damp fabric clinging to her skin was a stark reminder of the hours she had spent in the rain. "I was hoping to freshen up before Kyler's gig."

"It'll probably be nice and hot for you. Everything seems to be going wrong for me lately," Melanie said, her brow creasing as she started walking away.

Sighing, Izzy entered her room and immediately peeled off her drenched costume, sending a spray of water droplets across the floor. She quickly gathered her belongings and made her way to the bathroom.

As Melanie had predicted, the shower offered soothing heat. Izzy stood under the water, letting her muscles relax. Steam filled the room, wrapping her in a comforting fog. Her thoughts drifted to the upcoming Halloween party at the Shark Tank Pub, reminding her that she didn't have much time to get ready.

Exhausted, her mouth curved downward. She wanted nothing more than to sink into her bed and escape into sleep. The past week had been nothing short of a nightmare, and the prospect of immersing herself in a crowd of intoxicated partygoers was the last thing she needed.

However, Kyler's irritated face flashed in her mind, his anticipated disappointment outweighing her longing for solitude. The idea of adding yet another person to the list of those she had let down lately seemed unbearable to her.

Her mood swiftly plummeted as she begrudgingly shut off the shower. Stepping out onto the cool tiled floor, a shiver ran through her. She quickly dried off and, moments later, emerged from the bathroom dressed in a different costume.

"Who are you supposed to be? Morticia Addams?" Melanie called out from her perch on the couch, one eyebrow arched as she took in Izzy's appearance.

Holding the dirty laundry aside, Izzy glanced down at the black gown that draped her frame. It clung to her figure, flattering her form with its floor-length design. She looked up, meeting Melanie's gaze with a slight frown. "No, I'm supposed to be a vampire."

Melanie's eyebrows lifted, and her heavily painted red lips pursed thoughtfully. "Ah, the gothic vampire look, I see it now."

"I guess so. I didn't give it much thought," Izzy admitted, shrugging as she pushed open the door to her room. She flung the damp towel onto the back of her desk chair, where it slumped in a sodden heap.

Melanie followed, her gum popping in a rhythmic beat. "Clearly," she said, eyeing Izzy's outfit.

Izzy spun, tongue out in retaliation, then grabbed her brush and worked it through her wet hair. Deciding to keep it loose, she slipped a hair tie around her wrist for later.

"Seriously? "You're not even going to style your hair or put on some makeup? It's a Halloween party, Iz!" Melanie's eyes widened as she surveyed Izzy's minimal effort. "At least tell me you got some fangs to complete the look."

Izzy carefully stowed her phone, keys, and money inside a compact black purse. She turned to Melanie, who had made herself comfortable on her bed. Melanie's costume was a tantalizing short black dress, leaving little to the imagination. Her makeup was flawlessly applied, and her long auburn hair had been transformed into meticulous curls. Perched atop her head, a classic witch's hat added a whimsical touch to her polished look.

Izzy's gaze landed upon a pair of plastic fangs resting on her desk. She playfully waved them at Melanie before slipping them into her purse. "I'll put these on once we arrive," she grinned. Walking to the door, she paused, giving Melanie a moment to join her. "You know, aren't witches supposed to be all haggard and ugly?" Izzy asked, smirking at her friend.

"Not this witch," Melanie declared, the loud smack of her gum punctuating the air just before she let out a high-pitched screech. A crash echoed in the room. Izzy spun around to find Melanie sprawled on the floor, her purse's contents scattered around her. Dropping to her knees beside her friend, Izzy reached out to help her sit up.

"Are you okay, Mel?" She picked up the crumpled witch's hat, carefully smoothing out the wrinkles before placing it gently back in Melanie's hands.

"I'm fine." Melanie's voice became sharper than usual as she scooped up her belongings. "Damn Arlo and his stupid weights! Nearly twisted my ankle," she muttered under her breath.

Arlo's abandoned workout equipment lay near Melanie's feet. Izzy rolled her eyes and began to help her collect the scattered items from the floor.

"Geez, Mel. It's like you've packed everything but the kitchen sink," Izzy joked. She picked up a small, lumpy bag from among Melanie's possessions. Holding it up to the light, a frown creased her brow. "What is this?" she asked, bringing the bag closer to her face to examine the strange stitching keeping it closed.

Melanie reached forward and took the bag from Izzy. "I'm not sure . . . this was in my purse?"

Izzy nodded, rising and making her way to the kitchen. She came back with a pair of scissors in her hand and gestured for Melanie to pass her the bag. With deliberate care, she snipped at the jagged stitches, gradually loosening the tight seal. Finally, the bag gave way, spilling its contents into Izzy's hands.

In the centre of her open palm rested three glass vials, each holding a strange substance. An opal was nestled among them, its hues catching the light with a subtle shimmer. Red hair weaved through the odd assortment, adding to the peculiarity of the find.

Izzy's fingers closed around a vial filled with red liquid. She pulled it to her face for a closer look. "Jeepers!" she exclaimed, her grip slacking, sending the vial clattering to the floor.

"Is that . . . blood? And dirt?" Melanie examined another vial, tilting it to catch the light. Inside, a clear liquid shimmered. "What do you think is in this one?"

"Spit, Mel. Probably spit," Izzy quipped. With a knowing glance at Melanie, her voice softened with concern, "And that hair looks like yours. Maybe you really were hexed!"

Melanie gathered the items and pushed herself to her feet, a faint tremble betraying her nerves. She smoothed out her dress and spun toward Izzy, her eyes alight with sudden terror. "The psychic was right!"

A smirk played at the corners of Izzy's mouth. "So, whose boyfriend did you mess around with, Mel? It seems you've ruffled someone's feathers."

Melanie squirmed uneasily, her eyes darting away from Izzy's gaze. "Not funny," she muttered. "That crap isn't real anyway," she added, striding to the door.

"It's real to someone," Izzy murmured.

Once outside, the girls merged with a stream of students crossing the campus toward the college pub. The rain had stopped, leaving an earthy scent that wove into the chilly night air. Nearing the entrance, Melanie's spirits visibly lifted; she clutched Izzy's arm, pointing out the array of costumes around them with renewed enthusiasm.

A couple, their costumes transforming them into a comical cheeseburger and fries, playfully hopped into line behind them. Their infectious giggles filled the air, spreading laughter among the surrounding students. Izzy sighed, moving closer to Melanie, suddenly regretting her decision to attend the party.

As they approached the entrance, the rhythmic throb of music seeped out from behind the large, double doors. Melanie nudged Izzy and reminded her to put on her plastic fangs. She slipped them into her mouth just as they reached the front of the line.

A tall man guarded the entrance, his sole task being to collect entrance fees. He barely acknowledged Melanie, casting an uninterested glance her way as he accepted her payment. Izzy carefully extracted a twenty-dollar bill and handed it to him. Her fingers brushed against his elongated ones. A ripple of discomfort surged through her, causing her to quickly withdraw her hand.

"Cute costume," he remarked, his smile crinkling the corners of his eyes as he smoothly secured Izzy's money into the cash box.

Izzy's words stuck in her throat. She was mesmerized by the dangerous allure of the doorman's twin fangs, which curved sharply downward from his upper jaw. They gleamed under the dim lighting with a cold, predatory glint that promised nothing short of danger.

Izzy's heart thudded against her ribcage, mimicking the frantic flutter of a bird confined in a cage. She could only stare wide-eyed until Melanie's sharp tug snapped her from the trance, pulling her into the pub.

Her eyes twitched as the lights swirled and spun, leaving dizzying trails in their wake. The rhythmic thrumming that was a faint heartbeat outside now swelled into a relentless tidal wave of bass inside, rippling out from unseen speakers to vibrate through the floorboards.

Melanie's grip tightened on Izzy as they navigated through the writhing throng of twisting bodies, making their way toward the distant glow of the bar.

"Did you see his teeth?" Izzy shouted over to Melanie, struggling to be heard over the pulsating beats.

"Whose teeth?"

"The doorman. His teeth, they were actual fangs!"

Melanie spun around, the brim of her witch's hat narrowly missing Izzy's face. "I didn't see a thing, Iz," she said, her frown deepening. "He looked like an oddball—probably filed them to look like fangs. People do that, you know." As they reached the bar, her attention shifted, and she started waving to catch one of the bartenders' eyes.

A shiver prickled Izzy's skin, but she quickly brushed it off, refusing to let it take hold. Standing there, waiting for Melanie to order their drinks, her gaze wandered around the room. Carved pumpkins and untouched gourds were scattered in corners, their candlelit innards casting trembling shadows.

Garlands of orange and black streamers danced whimsically overhead, crisscrossing the room like mischievous spirits. Along the walls, grotesque monsters dangled, their eerie eyes glowing otherworldly whenever an unsuspecting dancer strayed too close.

"Here," Melanie said, presenting Izzy with a cloudy blue drink. "Kyler's band should be coming on soon. Didn't he want you to sit up front?"

Izzy nodded and accepted the glass from Melanie, her fingers curling around it. "Don't worry, there's no alcohol in that. I remembered," Melanie reassured her.

Izzy let out a sigh of relief, the weight of Melanie's words dispelling her tension. The bitter memory of her father's passing had forever changed her relationship with alcohol, extinguishing any desire for its taste or effects.

As Izzy and Melanie navigated through the crowd, they edged closer to the front, where the stage stood bathed in a halo of spotlights. At the foot of the stairs leading up to it, a man with dark hair and soft brown eyes glanced up from his guitar.

"Hello, Izzy," he greeted, his voice carrying a melodic softness. Melanie brushed past him, climbing the stairs and disappearing onto the stage.

"Hi, Lovepreet," Izzy said, cradling her drink. "How's your Halloween going so far?"

Lovepreet's shoulders slumped. "My housemates and I bought candy to give out, but only a few kids came to our door."

Izzy's heart sank at Lovepreet's crestfallen expression. Since his house was nestled in a busy residential area, the absence of visitors could only mean one thing. "You've been here since seven o'clock, right? Maybe some of the older kids arrived after you left . . ."

"Ah, Izzy, do not worry. We are a house full of unfamiliar international students. The parents are likely just being cautious."

Izzy's grip on her glass tightened. "It's not okay! Every house you visit on Halloween is filled with strangers. Parents should accompany their children to the doors. I bet they went to other houses on your street, didn't they?"

Frustration welled up in Izzy, a tide of restlessness urging her to act. Yet she was acutely aware of her limitations—as a young woman, her voice would be drowned out. She suspected that the subtle threads of discrimination woven into the fabric of behaviour around her went largely unrecognized.

"Truly, Izzy. It's all right. Next year will be better," Lovepreet continued, rising to his feet and slinging the guitar strap over his shoulder.

She watched as he ascended the stage, her thoughts darkening. Anger ignited in her belly, prompting her to purse her lips tightly. The international students at her college were not only friendly but also incredibly polite. Many, like Lovepreet and Vishvesh, simply wanted to build a new life in Canada.

They already had numerous hurdles to overcome. Their challenges were plentiful and daunting—a labyrinth of paperwork to navigate, homesickness, and more. Having to advocate for acceptance from the community shouldn't be an additional burden.

Izzy's thoughts were abruptly disrupted as Kyler leaped off the stage. He landed in front of her, almost making her spill her drink.

"Hey, babe," he said, taking the cup from her hand and setting it down. He wrapped her in a sudden embrace, their kiss a long, drawn-out affair that seemed to pause the noise around them. She broke away first, her cheeks flushing a telltale pink.

"You're late," he stated.

Izzy glanced toward the stage where the instruments were still being set up. "But you're still getting ready," she said, biting her lip.

"Yeah, but I wanted you here early to watch us set up," he snapped, the corner of his mouth pulling downward.

"You wanted me here early just to watch you set up . . ."

Ignoring her, Kyler asked, "What do you think of the costumes Lovepreet is making us wear?" He shot a disdainful glance toward his bandmate, who, at that moment, was preoccupied with adjusting the stage microphone.

Stepping back, Izzy took in Kyler's outfit, realizing it differed little from his usual daily attire. He was clad in black jeans paired with a slightly elongated leather jacket—its hem uneven, dipping lower in the back than the front.

"It doesn't look too bad," she remarked delicately, not pointing out that he might be overreacting.

"Doesn't look too bad?" he echoed, raising an eyebrow. "Just look at the hats he wants us to wear." With a dramatic flourish, he presented a top hat to which a long, pale blond wig was attached, thrusting it toward her. "I am not putting on this garbage. It will ruin my hair."

Izzy glanced at Lovepreet, who now sported the hat with a wide grin plastered across his face. Turning back to Kyler, she wove her fingers through his. "Come on, Ky. It's Halloween," she coaxed. She leaned in, kissed his lips, then drew back slightly. "Besides," she teased, "I think it's kind of sexy."

Kyler placed the hat atop his head, arranging it so the long blond hair spilled over his shoulders. He shot her a suggestive look, one eyebrow cocked, and pulled her into another kiss. "So this does it for you, huh?" he asked, drawing her closer. As his hands began to roam, slipping down to her rear, Izzy's reaction was instantaneous—her body stiffened, recoiling from his unwanted advances.

Kyler was oblivious to her reaction. "For you, I'll wear the hat." Nodding in Lovepreet's direction, he added, "I better go before Apu gets his turban in a twist."

Izzy's stomach churned as she watched Kyler leap onto the stage, striding to his spot beside Lovepreet. The fluttering butterflies that used to dance in her stomach at the sight of him had mutated into a sharp prickle of distaste.

She tensed, hugging herself tightly as Kyler's words echoed in her mind—a racist remark that repeated itself, amplifying the turmoil within her. She turned away from the stage, her feet carrying her forward. Partygoers, lost in their revelry, jostled against her as she made her way through the crowd.

Drawn back to the bar, Izzy's hands brushed against the delicate cobwebs clinging to its front. She set her purse down on the worn counter and started rummaging for her money.

"What do ya want to drink?" a raspy voice snapped, jolting Izzy from her search. She looked up, her mouth dropping open. The bartender stood before her. Impatience creased his deep red face as he drummed his fingers on the counter, the edges of his mouth turning down. Coiled black hair wound around two curved horns jutting from his head.

Izzy laughed, pulling out her money. The faint aroma of paper and ink filled the air, mingling with the bar's ambient scents. "Great demon costume," she said, extending a crinkled twenty-dollar bill toward him.

"I ain't wearin' no costume, witch," he barked, flinging his dirty dishcloth onto the counter beside her.

"I'm supposed to be a vampire," Izzy retorted, her gaze lifting to meet his unnerving orange eyes. "Sure looks like a costume to me," she muttered as he gruffly snatched the bill from her hand.

Her eyes tracked his movements, captivated by a peculiar transformation that unfolded before her. The bartender's skin seemed to ripple, a subtle change sweeping across it, transitioning gradually to a light almond hue. As she watched, his horns began to recede into his head until nothing remained that marked him as anything other than ordinary.

Izzy recoiled and stumbled backward as he extended a bottle of water to her. "Y-y-your horns . . . where did they go?"

His eyebrows shot up. "Oh, you're human?" His eyes flickered with panic as he quickly scanned his surroundings. Refocusing on her, he dropped her change into her purse and then, with a bit more force than necessary, placed both the bag and the water bottle into her arms. "You've had too much to drink. Go home."

"I haven't had anything to drink," she protested, her voice quivering. A panicked look flickered in her eyes as she slowly backed away from the bartender. He opened his mouth to respond, but she spun around and bolted. Her pulse thundered in her ears as she weaved through the room in a blind rush, colliding with unsuspecting partygoers.

A firm grip closed around her wrist, halting her frantic escape. With a startled cry, she whirled around, her fist raised defensively, only to find herself face-to-face with Melanie.

"Are you okay, Izzy?"

"I . . . I'm just not feeling well. I think I'll head back to my room and lie down."

"Your face looks really pale," Melanie said, loosening her grip on Izzy's arm. "Do you want me to come with you?" Her gaze flickered to the stage, carrying a wistful longing.

"No, Mel. It's okay. Stay and have fun," Izzy replied, zipping up her purse and slinging it over her shoulder.

A faint, relieved smile broke out on Melanie's face. "I'll check in on you when I get back," she promised.

Izzy turned and weaved through the crowd, focusing on the exit. As she stepped outside, a refreshing coolness swept over her heated face, offering soothing relief.

The early evening was still bustling with people flocking toward the college pub as she made her way home. Despite the mundane scene, a tingle of unease gripped her, accelerating her heartbeat. Her mind entertained the unsettling possibility that these people could be more than just ordinary humans.

"I can't be going crazy," she muttered to herself. "He didn't think I was human." As confusion and fear intermingled within her, Izzy unlocked the apartment door and stepped into the vacant kitchen. She walked through the common room, and her eyes drifted toward Emily's door. Her mind suddenly filled with thoughts of the peculiar little man she had encountered twice now.

Fear coursed through her again, propelling her into a panicked sprint toward her room. She slammed the door shut behind her, the sound reverberating in the stillness. Finally, safe within her room, she flung herself onto her bed, her imagination conjuring images of monsters lurking underneath.

Her mind raced, replaying the series of peculiar occurrences she had witnessed: the irate bartender, Emily's strange cat, and the vivid hallucinations that plagued her. She paused at the thought of the hex bag in Melanie's purse. Was it possible that someone was deliberately toying with Melanie? Much like Emily, Melanie wasn't particularly well-liked within their program.

However, the encounters with the doppelgänger in the bathroom and the vampire guarding the pub door seemed to go unnoticed by others. Izzy was hit by an overwhelming sense of isolation, the stark realization that she was the sole witness to these phenomena—seeing things like an unstable person.

A different kind of fear washed over her, a suffocating grip she could not escape. A wrenching sob burst from deep within her chest. For the second time that week, she buried her face into the comforting embrace of her pillow. The soft cotton absorbed the sound of her shaking sobs as they ripped through her.

As her tears gradually receded, Izzy clung to her pillow, seeking solace in the darkness of her room. Little did she know that the events of this Halloween night were merely the beginning of the twisted journey she was about to embark upon.

CHAPTER THIRTEEN

THE BITTER TASTE OF LOSS

The dream materialized from the depths of nothingness, a hushed whisper weaving its way through the inky blackness. The surrounding emptiness around Izzy melted away, replaced by an ever-changing swirl of colours. She was amid an ocean of deep blues and purples, an ethereal glow casting a soft light around her.

A pull at her hand, soft as a breeze, beckoned her forward. She passed through a mural of colours, each hue blending seamlessly into the next as she went. Gradually, from within the swirling abyss, buildings and trees began to take shape.

Izzy swayed on the curb, her bare toes curling into the concrete as she tried to regain her balance. A hiccup burst from her lips, the abrupt motion sending her tumbling back onto the grass. Sitting up, she giggled and smoothed out her dress.

Having given up on trying to stand, she tucked her legs beneath her. She casually dropped the sandals she had been holding onto the ground. The distant laughter of her friends spilled out from the townhouse behind her, blending with the sultry strains of music. Closing her eyes, Izzy savoured the kiss of the cool breeze on her flushed cheeks.

The world began to tilt, sending her into a nauseating spin. Her eyes opened, a hand flying over her mouth as she fought the overwhelming urge to vomit. Clearly, indulging in that last shot of vodka hadn't been the wisest choice on her part.

Her gaze locked onto the cars driving down the street. Squinting, she tried to focus on their blurred outlines. The roar of each passing vehicle sent a jolt through her, her stomach churning with every whoosh.

Finally, the deep purr of an engine she knew all too well vibrated in the distance. The car's profile cut a sharp line against the evening sky, its dark form gleaming under the streetlights. The driver's door opened with a flourish, and the twangy strains of a banjo tune spilled out.

Footsteps echoed around the front of the car, and a moment later, strong hands gently scooped Izzy up from the ground. A startled squeak escaped her, quickly dissolving into giggles as she sank into her father's warm embrace.

"Hiya, Daddio." The words were thick on her tongue as she tried to look up at him.

The passenger door issued a soft click, and Izzy found herself being eased onto the warm leather seat of the car. Blinking up at her father's face, she caught the flicker of amusement warring with sternness in his expression.

"Izzy-boo, I told you to wait inside," he scolded, leaning in to secure her seatbelt.

"Sorry, Dad," Izzy mumbled, sinking back as the seatbelt latch clicked. He glanced down at her, scratching his brown hair absently, his bright blue eyes clouding with a perplexed expression.

He sighed, giving her shoulder a reassuring pat. "Let's get you home, kiddo." Izzy winced as he shut the door, the noise hurting her head.

As her father settled behind the wheel, Izzy leaned over, her fingers fumbling with the stereo buttons. After a moment, she found the volume dial and quickly turned it down, cutting off the screeching sound of the fiddles that filled the car.

"Hey, I was listening to that!" her father complained, easing the vehicle away from the curb. Casting a brief glance toward Izzy, he rolled down her window just a crack, allowing the cold November breeze to waft gently inside.

Izzy tilted her head toward the open window, relishing the cool rush of air that surrounded her. Her eyes lingered on the scenery slipping by, the tranquil neighbourhood with its serene trees and quiet townhouses slowly falling away. Before long, the calm tableau was replaced by the dizzying rush of traffic as they merged onto the 401 on-ramp.

The crinkle of wax paper pierced the silence. As her father unfolded a greasy take-out bag, the tantalizing aroma of a cheeseburger filled the air. Izzy groaned, the scent amplifying the turmoil in her stomach.

"Seriously, Dad, you stopped for food?" she murmured, inching closer to the window for fresh air.

"I thought you might be hungry," he replied, offering her one of the burgers.

Izzy pushed the burger away, a moan escaping her lips as a fresh wave of nausea hit. Her father's eyes darted quickly toward her. "Do you need me to pull over? Your mom will kill me if you puke in the car."

"Mom's going to kill you for eating in her car."

Her dad's chuckle rumbled through the confined space of the vehicle as he deftly maneuvered the burger out of its wrapping. "Hey, what do you call a burger that is afraid of the dark?" he asked between bites.

Izzy's stomach lurched again, and she winced. "I don't know," she managed to say, her mouth filling with saliva as she struggled to hold back her vomit.

"Chicken burger!" The corners of his mouth twitched into a self-satisfied smile. "Aw, come on, Izzy-boo, that was a good one. Not even a smile?" he prodded, stealing another glance at her.

The car swerved abruptly, tires grumbling against the highway's warning strips and sending a shudder through the frame. Her dad's hands were quick and sure as he corrected their course. Fresh waves of nausea rose within Izzy, and a sour taste filled her mouth as she started to gag.

Her father's expression twisted in alarm as he leaned over, his fingers fumbling in search of the empty cheeseburger bag. "Hold on, kiddo," he urged, unfastening his seatbelt to reach the bag at her feet. The car jerked as the tires lost their grip on the asphalt.

Izzy's eyes flew to her father, his face a mask of sheer terror as he fought for control. The piercing screech of tires filled the air, blending with the odour of burning rubber as her father vigorously pumped the brakes, struggling to slow down the vehicle.

The sickening crunch of metal and shattering of glass reverberated through the air as the car collided with something solid. Izzy lurched forward in her seat, her body propelled against the restraint of her seatbelt. An airbag burst forth, striking her with brutal force and blanketing the cabin in a powdery haze.

The car careened out of control, flipping onto its side and skidding across the highway before slamming into the guardrail. Pain seared through Izzy as she struggled to lift her head from the deflated airbag. Suspended at a sickening angle by her seatbelt, she hung there, disorientated.

"Dad?" Izzy's voice was met by silence. She frantically swatted at the lingering cloud of powder veiling the air. Her eyes swept over the vacant driver's seat, her mind reeling from the absence where her father should have been. Numbness crept over her as she grappled with the inconceivable thought that her father had vanished.

"Dad!" Izzy's voice trembled as she called out again. She fumbled with her seatbelt, struggling to get it off as it cut into her skin. Tears welled up in her eyes as she screamed out for her father, her heart aching for a response. Engine smoke billowed into the car, making it nearly impossible to see. A fit of coughs seized her, her lungs feeling like they were on fire.

Suddenly, the door above her screeched open, letting in a rush of air that swiftly dispersed the dark smoke. A woman peered down into the car. Her pale face flooded with relief as she realized Izzy was alive. Speaking rapidly in an unfamiliar language, she unbuckled Izzy from her seat. With her assistance, Izzy managed to clamber out onto the side of the vehicle.

She turned, captivated by the smoke billowing from the sports car. It was a tangle of twisted metal with crushed glass scattered around it. Her gaze followed the trail of wreckage to a truck halted in the middle of the road a short distance away.

A smaller shape caught her attention, lying off to the side between the two vehicles. Frowning, she shrugged off the woman's attempts to guide her away. The woman's voice rose in pitch as she tried to turn Izzy around. Ignoring her, Izzy stubbornly made her way across the highway, shards of glass piercing her bare feet. Whether due to the lingering effects of alcohol or shock, Izzy remained numb to the pain.

As she drew closer to the shape, a vice-like tightness gripped her chest. A sob caught in her throat when she recognized the familiar black dress shoes of her father. His body was motionless and sprawled face down on the harsh asphalt. Blood gathered by his head, staining the road crimson. In the distance, the wailing sirens grew louder as emergency responders raced closer.

A tender hand touched the small of her back. Izzy's knees buckled beneath her, and a torrent of sobs wracked her body as she crumbled into the woman, seeking solace in her soft, reassuring embrace. She buried her face into the woman's glossy black hair, hiding from the heart-wrenching sight of her father's lifeless form.

The vibrant hues and details of the dream began to blur and fade, overtaken by an encroaching darkness. It seeped into the fringes of Izzy's slumbering consciousness, engulfing her dream world until a black abyss was all that remained. Within this vast emptiness, Izzy felt an intense pang of loss, a hollow echo in the space where her father's comforting presence once was.

The void's silence was pierced by a faint buzzing, at first barely discernible. It swelled, permeating the darkness with a pulsating, almost hypnotic rhythm. Izzy's attention honed in on the sound, which seemed to originate from the very core of her being. As the persistent hum wrapped around her, she gave in to its embrace, allowing it to steer her from the sorrow of her dream into a different realm of consciousness.

CHAPTER FOURTEEN

INTO THE UNKNOWN

Izzy's eyes snapped open, alarm coursing through her as the buzzing noise from her dream escalated. It seemed to reverberate through her entire being, its intense vibration sending goosebumps prickling along her skin. Struggling to sit up, she found herself pinned by an unseen source. Paralyzed, she could only stare at the ceiling while a tingling sensation spread slowly through her limbs.

Panic swelled in her chest as an electric current hummed throughout her body. Her thoughts raced, seeking logic, grasping for reason amid the inexplicable. Fear took over as a rational explanation eluded her grasp.

An ear-piercing noise resounded throughout the room, reminiscent of a kettle reaching its boiling point. It assaulted Izzy's ears, each wave a throbbing pulse in her head. As the clamour continued, a bizarre sensation emerged—a series of unsettling pops rippled through her as if countless bubbles were bursting within her body. Then, a curious weightlessness took hold, as if gravity had suddenly relaxed its unyielding embrace.

Izzy shot upright with a sharp gasp, finding herself suspended in midair. Her legs thrashed, seeking solid ground, yet their movements only sent her into a more erratic spin. Rotating helplessly, her gaze finally settled on her bed, and her hands flew to her mouth in shock. There, lying in a peaceful sleep, was her own body. Her tangled hair framed her face, serene and undisturbed by the chaos unfolding above it.

After several futile attempts, Izzy managed to right herself into a standing position. However, her feet remained inches above the ground. She hovered beside her sleeping form, her gaze anchored to the peaceful rise and fall of her chest.

Izzy rationalized that she couldn't possibly be dead. Concluding that this must be another layer of the dream, her eyes wandered and caught her reflection in the floor-length mirror across the room.

She gasped at the mesmerizing view—a shimmering cord snaked along the floor from her slumbering form, ascending up her back, and disappeared into the base of her neck.

Intrigued, Izzy swiftly turned her head, and to her astonishment, the cord mirrored her movements as if it were an extension of herself. Her hand trembled as it rose toward her neck. The moment her fingers brushed against the ethereal strand, a cool whisper of air slipped through her touch as though her skin had disturbed a curtain of mist.

A peculiar thought flitted through her mind as she recalled a concept she had come across in one of the spiritual books—astral projection. Could this be what she was experiencing now? When she had purchased the book, she had skimmed over the chapters on out-of-body experiences, dismissing them as mere fantasy.

Yet, now, a seed of excitement took root in her stomach as her mind entertained the possibility. Shaking her head, she dismissed the idea as impossible. Her experience wasn't how the book described astral projecting. This had to be a dream.

Taking one last reassuring glance at her sleeping form, Izzy approached the door of her room with anticipation. Her outstretched hand moved toward the handle, only to pass through it. A strange, prickling feeling crawled up her arm, causing her to quickly retract her hand. She shook it, trying to dispel the uncomfortable tingling.

Holding her hand close to her face, she examined it but found no visible changes. Trembling, she brought it near the door again, the tips of her fingers blurring as if dipping into water.

She took a hesitant step forward and felt her body merging with the door—a strange, suction-like sensation tugged at her entire being. Opening her eyes, she stood in the common room, having emerged seamlessly through the barrier.

Glancing over her shoulder, she noticed the shimmering cord trailing behind her on the floor. It flickered with each step she took away from her body, its glow gradually fading to transparency. A faint tug at the base of her neck reassured her of the cord's unseen presence.

In the common room, shadows pooled in the corners, cast by the dim lighting that gave the space an eerie ambiance. Izzy's gaze settled on the stove clock, its illuminated numbers cutting through the gloom to show that it was only ten o'clock.

Driven by curiosity and the thrill of a dreamlike adventure, she moved forward, stepping through the apartment door. She grimaced once more, the peculiar feeling of being simultaneously pulled and tugged greeting her as her ethereal form crossed the threshold.

Once outside, she paused for a moment. Despite the absence of warm clothing—her attire consisting of a tank top and flannel pyjama pants—Izzy couldn't sense the chill in the air. *Well, that's one upside of the dream world,* she thought, a faint smile on her lips.

Appreciating the stillness of the night, she wove her way across the college campus. As Izzy approached the college pub, the quiet night transformed, bustling with the vibrancy of nightlife.

A colourful array of college students, donning clever costumes inspired by eras long past, mingled along the path. Among them, a young woman captured Izzy's attention. She excluded the glamour of the 1930s, with her fiery red hair set in a short bob, crowned by a sparkling headpiece that caught the moonlight's gleam.

"Hello?" Izzy called out, waving her hand in greeting. The woman's gaze, however, stayed locked on the conversation with her friend, seemingly oblivious to Izzy's presence. Tentatively, Izzy reached out and touched the girl's bare arm. In response, the girl shrugged her shoulder as if brushing off an imaginary bug. Unfazed, she continued walking past Izzy, her laughter mingling with the night air.

Izzy's frown deepened, then morphed into a startled cry when an intense tickling sensation coursed through her spectral form. She felt her body momentarily compress and elongate as a man passed right through her. He stopped short and shivered. Rubbing at his neck, he looked around in confusion before shaking it off and continuing to the pub to join his waiting friends.

Izzy marvelled at the strangeness of this dream. Her hand moved to her stomach as if to soothe an invisible wound. She stepped off the path, making way for a stream of students laughing and chatting as they headed toward the Halloween party. She followed along behind them.

The door was tended by the same man as before. Izzy approached with caution, each step measured and light, as though she feared even the slightest disturbance might ripple in the air around him. She slipped past him into the pub and wove toward a vantage point with an unobstructed view of the stage. The set lay barren, signalling a break in Kyler's band performance.

Lovepreet caught her attention as she spotted him standing at the side of the stage. His face was beaming joyfully as he enthusiastically pointed out the Halloween decorations. He seemed oblivious to the growing flock of girls gathering around him. A smile tugged at the corners of Izzy's lips as she watched him, relieved that the night was looking up for him.

Her smile waned as the memory of Kyler's derogatory remark about Lovepreet resurfaced, washing over her in a tide of shame. How had she ever been charmed by someone capable of such ugliness? His good looks were undeniable—the wavy blond hair and captivating green eyes—but the attraction had to be more than superficial. There had been an inexplicable pull, a connection she couldn't quite rationalize, that had initially drawn her to him.

Izzy struggled to understand her oversight of Kyler's flaws. Throughout their brief relationship, his attention never seemed to extend beyond using her as a trophy to impress his friends. And then there was the constant, unwanted touching. Her spine tingled with a wave of cold realization as she finally understood how wrong their relationship was. Relief washed over her as she resolved to end things with Kyler come morning.

She leaned against the wall, forgetting her ethereal nature, only to find herself sinking into the concrete. The wall seemed to close in, pressing against her chest. With a sharp intake of breath, she jerked forward, peeling away from it with a sucking noise. Edging away from the wall, she moved toward the exit and stepped outside again. The earlier tingling sensation, once unsettling, now diminished to a mere afterthought as she looked around, uncertain of her next move.

A familiar flash of auburn hair caught Izzy's attention, causing her to spin around just in time to see the silhouette of a woman—Melanie—vanish into the dark woods beside the college. A sinking feeling gripped Izzy's stomach as Melanie's form disappeared into the shadows. Why would Melanie risk the woods at night?

Izzy's concern for her friend spurred her off the path, drawing her to the edge of the woods. She wasn't sure what help she could provide if Melanie encountered trouble, but Izzy knew she couldn't simply stand and watch her friend wander off alone.

She slipped into the forest, carefully navigating between the towering trees as she trailed behind Melanie. The woods came alive with the rustling of startled animals disturbed by Melanie's passage. An owl's hoot echoed distantly, mingling with the soft patter of a nocturnal creature darting underbrush.

Melanie's head turned sharply at the sound, her eyes scanning the dark depths of the forest. Izzy watched as a gloved hand slipped from the shadows, wrapping around Melanie's waist. Her scream ripped through the night, abruptly muffled as another gloved hand clamped over her mouth.

As Melanie struggled against her captor, Izzy's instincts kicked in. She launched forward, her hands thrusting deep into the attacker's chest as if the solid flesh had turned to air. The shocking sensation of her hands passing through his body startled him into releasing his grip on her friend.

Melanie tumbled to the forest floor, the pointy brim of her witch's hat veering off into the undergrowth. "Run!" Izzy's cry fell silent in the night, her voice seemingly swallowed by the darkness. She watched, feeling helpless, as Melanie clambered to her feet.

"Are you okay?" Melanie's voice wavered uncertainly as she approached the shrouded figure lurking in the shadows.

"What are you doing? Run!" Izzy reached out to tug at Melanie's wrist, but her hand slipped through as if swiping at nothing. Melanie recoiled, hastily rubbing at the goosebumps that erupted along her skin.

"I'm fine. Just felt a weird chill." Izzy's eyebrows shot up as Kyler stepped out of the shadows, a cocky grin stretching across his face.

Izzy's mind churned with confusion as she watched Melanie's deliberate, sultry approach toward him. It all came sharply into focus when Melanie's face softened into an unmistakable lovesick gaze as she folded into Kyler's waiting embrace.

Izzy's heart plummeted as the harsh reality struck her—her boyfriend was cheating on her with her best friend. Anger flared within Izzy, her hands balling into fists as she watched them embrace. They were entwined, lost in a passionate kiss that seemed to last an eternity. Kyler's hands boldly explored Melanie's body, his fingers provocatively tracing the bare skin of her thighs, toying with the hem of her tight black dress.

He drew even closer, his lips grazing her neck, inciting a giggle from Melanie. "Kyler," she protested lightly, pushing him back. "When are you going to end things with Izzy?" The words hung between them, her teeth catching her bottom lip as she waited for a response.

Surprise flickered in Kyler's eyes as he looked down at her. "Break it off with Izzy? Why would I do that?"

A shadow of hurt passed across Melanie's face. "I just thought that . . . you know, we've been hooking up for a while now. It would be nice to be together openly . . . as a couple."

"A couple?" His lips twisted into a smirk as he regarded her. "Come on, Mel, you know this is just a casual fling. I made that clear from the beginning." Ignoring her crestfallen expression, he pulled her in for another kiss.

Rooted in place, Izzy's disbelief deepened. A wave of anger rolled through her, her gaze piercing Melanie with a silent accusation. Kyler's betrayal was a sting, yet predictable. But Melanie . . . Melanie was a different story.

This was someone with whom she had shared her darkest grief, who knew every layer of her—her aversion to alcohol, her yearning to connect with her father's spirit. The depth of their friendship made this act of betrayal all the more devastating.

Emotions whirled within Izzy, a dark torrent of rage, grief, and despair. Her friendship with Melanie, once a pillar in her life, now joined the rubble of her shattered certainties. Tears brimmed, spilling down her cheeks only to be absorbed back into her ethereal form. Her chest felt constricted, each breath a struggle.

A dark shape sliced through the night sky, hiding the couple from Izzy's view. Wiping her face hastily, she dismissed it as a trick of her eyes—until another shape whizzed by, a wing grazing her. She jerked back, her hand flying to where the touch lingered and spun around to find the source. Craning her neck, she searched the night sky, a gasp escaping her lips.

From the darkness, small forms emerged, blotting out the stars as they converged upon her with alarming speed. Izzy had no time to brace herself before a swarm of bat-like creatures enveloped her, their talons clawing at her skin.

A scream tore from her throat, echoing into the night as she was hoisted into the air. She flailed about, her hands connecting with one of the fur-covered creatures. It wriggled from her grasp to snatch at her foot, its red eyes gleaming malevolently.

Engrossed in one another, Melanie and Kyler were oblivious to Izzy's desperate screams for help. She struggled in the grip of the demonic creatures, rising higher above the earth. Below, the couple dwindled to mere specks, lost against the vast canvas of the planet.

Panic flooded through Izzy as she ascended beyond the earth's atmosphere. Soon, she found herself gazing down upon the stunning blue planet she called home. It diminished in size, soon becoming a dot in the vastness of space. Then, abruptly, a shimmering blue line, pulsating with otherworldly energy, materialized ahead. The bats, sensing its power, veered toward the radiant anomaly, dragging Izzy into the unknown.

Overwhelmed by fear, she unleashed one last piercing scream—a cry that cut through the silence before she was swallowed by the portal's depths. And then, as sudden as it had appeared, the gateway vanished, erasing any sign that a supernatural occurrence had ever occurred.

CHAPTER FIFTEEN

THE REALM OF NIGHTMARES

A chilling wind swept relentlessly across the desolate landscape. With it came a haunting wail that reverberated through the darkness, piercing the silence. Gusts whipped up dirt particles, forming swirling clouds that scatted across the land and descended in clumps, coating the terrain in layers of dust.

A blinding blue light erupted in the sky, transforming into a jagged, luminous line that sliced through the darkness like a lightning bolt. From the heat of the pulsating light, a glowing figure fell. Then, as abruptly as it had appeared, the blue light vanished, plunging everything back into darkness.

Izzy landed in an unceremonious heap, her body hitting the ground with a thud that sent clouds of dust billowing in the air. She struggled to her feet, her body protesting the movement.

Fatigue clung to her, yet adrenaline coursed through her veins, driving her to swipe at the air, warding off the unseen attackers. A minute passed before it dawned on her that the demonic bats had vanished.

Izzy's gaze swept across her surroundings, the subtle glow from her body casting a faint light around her. Instinctively, her hand rose to the back of her neck, finding the cord still tethered there—a brief relief before despair set in as she realized she was trapped in this strange realm.

Her stomach twisted, and she tugged at a strand of blond hair. The gnawing feeling grew, and an overwhelming dread wrapped around her like a suffocating cloak.

An icy blast slammed into Izzy unexpectedly, triggering an involuntary shiver through her body—the first chill she'd felt since her ethereal journey started. Wishing for warmer clothes, she wrapped her arms around herself. Taking a deep breath to steel her resolve, Izzy pressed forward, her steps crunching on the dirt as she went.

Before long, the ominous silhouette of a tree grove loomed out of the shadows. Approaching, Izzy noted the eerie stillness; the trees, much like the rest of the landscape, seemed empty of life. Rotted trunks leaned on the brink of collapse, and barren branches stretched like skeletal fingers, grazing the dust-blanketed ground.

Another gust of wind tore through the grove, catching Izzy off guard. She stumbled and then collided with a tree. A sharp cry burst from her. Her hands scraped against the rough bark, clinging on for support. Above the howl of the wind, a loud creak resonated. Casting an uneasy glance around, Izzy strained to see what had made the noise. Yet she saw nothing but the tree she clung to.

Huddled against the trunk, Izzy pressed her back to its rough surface. A branch snapped overhead with a crackle. She recoiled, losing her balance as the tree trunk shifted.

Unease mounting, Izzy pulled away and looked up. There, in the darkness, a pair of red-hued eyes glared back at her. As they inched closer, the twisted visage of the tree emerged.

It snarled, its mouth opening to reveal splintered teeth. The ground beneath Izzy quivered; a massive root burst forth, flinging her toward another tree. She scrambled to her feet, narrowly dodging a decayed branch that swept at her in a vicious arc, intent on sending her crashing down again.

The grove around Izzy came alive with a sinister energy. The air itself seemed to crackle as more glowing eyes pierced the darkness. Trapped in a harrowing ballet of survival, she wove and dodged among the gnarled branches, avoiding their hungry grasp. Her pulse thundered in her ears, drowning out the growling of the animated trees.

The ground beneath her started to glow green, bathing the tree grove in an otherworldly luminescence. Fatigue washed over her, and her energy plummeted alarmingly. Then, a deep, rhythmic breathing filled the air, drawing her gaze upward. She watched, her mouth dropping open, as the nearest tree bent over in a grotesque bow, inhaling as if savouring her presence. Cold dread pooled in her stomach, and she stood, paralyzed by the terrifying spectacle.

The grove thrummed with a chorus of heavy breaths as the trees seemed to lean in, greedily drawing in the essence of her presence. A chilling thought crept into Izzy's mind—were they intentionally terrifying her to feast on her fear?

Exhaustion hit her like another wave, yet she pushed on, darting between the trees. A root snagged her foot mid-stride, and she stumbled out of the grove's embrace. As she rolled to safety, the pulsating green glow abruptly blinked out, casting the forest back into shadows. A symphony of snarls and haunting howls filled the air, heightening the terror of the sudden darkness.

Izzy collapsed onto the coarse dirt, its grit pressing into her back. She closed her eyes and took a deep breath, fighting to steady her racing pulse. Time stretched as she lay there, but eventually, determination overcame weariness. Brushing off her clothes, she pushed herself up. Despite the lure of rest, the need to distance herself from the grove spurred her on.

As she pressed forward, the wind's mournful lament finally waned, leaving silence in its wake. Then, from the stillness, a new sound surfaced—a cry for help. Izzy felt a sudden surge of exhilaration; she wasn't alone. The unmistakable human cries kindled a spark of hope within her.

Blindly running through the darkness, her haste led to misfortune when she slammed into a large boulder. Startled and falling backward from the impact, she lay there momentarily dazed. Then, cautiously, she reached out, her fingers tracing the rock's smooth surface.

Izzy carefully edged around it, her movements deliberate and calculated so as not to draw attention. From her vantage point, she caught sight of a young woman aglow with the same soft luminescence that surrounded Izzy. Tendrils of wavy, brown hair framed the woman's downturned face. Curled into a ball, she rocked gently, her sobs a haunting melody in the otherwise silent world.

"Wake up," the woman moaned, a tremble of desperation in her voice as she buried her face in her knees. "Wake up, wake up!" Her voice rose, her words now a frantic cry that filled the empty expanse with its urgency.

Izzy, about to step out from her hiding place, froze as the other woman lifted her head, her eyes wide with a dawning fear as though she sensed the presence of another.

Three grotesque creatures slithered from the shadows, a nightmarish fusion of human and insect, with twisted, grasshopper-like bodies. They skittered forward on long limbs, their elongated mouths gaping wide to reveal rows of serrated teeth. A spine-chilling shriek pierced the darkness.

Izzy winced, her hands flying to her ears. Frozen in place, she watched as they encircled the woman, their shrill cries forming a chilling song. Thick, black tongues slithered from their mouths, reaching for their prey. Izzy pressed her hands against her mouth, tears welling in her eyes as she fought back a scream. Beneath the woman, the earth began to glow with a sickly green pulse.

And then, the woman's form started to fade. Her screams died away into silence. Thwarted, the creatures unleashed a cacophony of shrieks and turned on each other. Their vicious battle caused the ground to throb with light again as they fought to steal each other's energy.

Izzy pressed her body tightly against the rock, silently praying for the creatures to pass by. Time stretched in agonizing slowness, each second an eternity as she waited. Finally, to her relief, she watched the demonic creatures turn away, disappearing into the darkness.

She slumped against the stone, knees drawn to her chest, and squeezed her eyes shut. Her thoughts spun in a whirlwind of fear and uncertainty. This had to be a dream, a nightmarish creation conjured from the depths of her imagination.

Regret gnawed at her as she berated herself for delving into those spiritualism books, which had likely sculpted this hellish landscape. Lost in her thoughts, Izzy almost missed the murmurs approaching from the other side of the boulder. Her eyes flew open, her muscles tensing as the voice grew louder.

Peeking from behind the rock, Izzy felt relieved as she spotted another human figure. A boy, no older than sixteen, wandered aimlessly toward her, murmuring incoherently.

Noticing the shimmering cord trailing from his neck, cutting through the dark like a graceful serpent, Izzy felt reassured that he was indeed human. She rose from her hiding place and cautiously approached him.

"Hello," she whispered. The boy brushed past her without responding. Izzy paused, glancing back at the boulder, then hurried to catch up with him.

"Hello," she said louder, grasping the sleeve of his flannel pyjama top. The boy remained oblivious, his shirt slipping through Izzy's fingers. Frustration mounting, she quickened her pace, determined not to lose him.

She stepped directly into his path and planted her feet firmly. With a forceful grip, she shook his shoulders. He stopped, his tousled red hair framing a vacant expression. His lips moved rapidly, a stream of incomprehensible mumbling filling the air around them.

Izzy shook him again, harder. Suddenly, a howl pierced the silence. She closed her eyes briefly, trying to reassure herself that it was only a dream. But her fingers clung to the boy's shirt as another howl, closer now, cut through the dark. Despite her resolve, fear prickled across her skin, her body tensing involuntarily.

Dogs, of all things, she thought, her mind cursing her vivid imagination. The image of Ms. Penny's little rescue dog nipping at her as a child flashed through her mind. It had left a lasting mark, fueling an irrational fear of dogs that clung to her ever since.

She shook the boy, mustering all her strength in an effort to snap him out of his daze. But he remained still, his vacant eyes staring out into the shadows that loomed ahead. Tears breached Izzy's eyes, tracing paths down her cheeks as frustration washed over her in crashing waves.

Her desperation surged as she shook the boy with all her strength, hoping to snap him out of his trance. As the distant howling grew louder, panic gripped Izzy's heart. She looked upon the boy's face, so serene and youthfully oblivious, and her voice broke as she pleaded with him.

"Please, wake up!" Her shaking hands clasped onto his. The thought of leaving him behind was unbearable. Her mind reeled with images of the savage dogs tearing into his body.

Another howl tore through the air, closer this time. "I'm sorry!" Izzy cried out, releasing his hands. She bolted past him, driven by the raw instinct to survive.

Her breath came out in jagged sobs as she darted forward, the ground blurring beneath her pounding feet. Behind her, the howls crept closer, a relentless reminder of the threat at her heels.

Izzy risked a glance over her shoulder. A pack of dogs emerged; their mangy forms were just visible in the faint glow from her body. Fiery red eyes bore into her like embers in the dark.

The distance between them shrank. Izzy shrieked and sprinted forward, trying to outpace the snapping jaws behind her. Their hot breath grazed her ankles. The wind howled, lashing her with dust, and she nearly stumbled.

Then, as she teetered on the edge of a fall, something sharp dug into her shoulder, jerking her upward. She rose in the air, the snarling figures shrinking into the void below.

Izzy's eyes lifted, and with them rose a chilling realization—she had been ensnared by yet another nightmarish being. This new tormentor resembled a demon with twisted horns, bat-like wings, and a grotesquely humanoid torso. Yet it was the face—or the lack thereof—that was the most horrifying. The ravaged skin had been brutally torn away, exposing muscles, cartilage and jagged bone beneath.

From the empty eye sockets, a malevolent red light shone, casting an ominous glow. The creature tilted its head, the remnants of its face contorting into a vile smile. Izzy's breath hitched in her throat, her mind racing for a way to escape from this living nightmare.

In one swift motion, the creature tossed her higher into the air with its clawed feet. Izzy found herself ensnared again, pressed against its sinewy chest. With a swift reversal, they hurtled toward the ground, the wind's icy fingers clawing at them.

Her eyes clamped shut, and every muscle in her body tensed for the inevitable end. Yet, in a bewildering twist of reality, the expected collision never came. Instead, the solid ground dissolved into an illusion, and they plunged through the earth's surface into an abyss, darker and more sinister—a realm that promised an even deeper terror.

As they descended further, a creeping weariness overtook Izzy. Her strength ebbed away with the passing of each moment, leaving her feeling drained. She whispered a silent prayer for help as the darkness around her threatened to consume her consciousness.

CHAPTER SIXTEEN

A MYSTERIOUS CONNECTION

A blinding flash of light tore through the dark, searing through Izzy's tightly shut eyelids with a brilliance that rivalled daylight. She struggled to pry her eyes open. As the demon shifted its grip to secure her under his other arm, it let out a menacing growl.

Peering through half-closed lashes, Izzy saw a figure falling toward them—its beauty rendered Izzy breathless. Majestic wings, pristine as snow, spread wide from its back, accentuating the figure's imposing stature.

The demon snarled. Within seconds, a crude-looking sword materialized in his hand. The demon thrust it before the winged creature's face. "This isn't your realm, angel. You don't belong here."

"Neither does she," the angel retorted, her expression darkening as she pointed at Izzy. She drew her own sword from behind her back, its blade concealed by wisps of energy that resembled flickering flames. "Release her to me, demon."

"I'll release her into the depths of hell!" he responded. His grip on Izzy slackened, and she fell from his grasp, plummeting downward. Above her, the angel's eyes blazed with an unnatural glow. The demon lunged toward her with his sword aimed to strike.

With a graceful maneuver, she sidestepped his attack and redirected his sword hand with a deft strike, forcing it aside. Then, she retaliated, her sword arcing down to slide through his neck. The air crackled with energy as the demon dissolved into a shower of purple sparks.

Wasting no time, the angel dove through the fading cascade of sparkles, her hand reaching for Izzy's outstretched one. In one seamless motion, she pulled Izzy close, cradling her against her side. Izzy leaned her head against the cool metal of the angel's chest plate. As she closed her eyes, a tranquil peace washed over her, and she felt the gentle ascent as the angel carried them upward.

As they rose higher, a flow of revitalizing energy coursed through Izzy. Finally, they slowed to a gentle stop, the surrounding scenery coming into focus. Izzy found herself amid the splendour of a breathtaking garden. Soft grass carpeted the ground, stretching out into the horizon. Nearby, a tranquil pond shimmered with crystal-clear water, reflecting the garden's brilliant hues. Lily pads floated on the surface, while below, koi fish shimmered as they swam, their scales catching the sunlight.

A meandering pathway crafted from intricate mosaic pebbles directed Izzy's gaze through the garden. It wound toward a gazebo perched atop a raised flagstone platform. The lush vines entwined around the structure were ablaze with fiery orange flowers whose sweet fragrance perfumed the air.

A gentle squeeze on her arm brought Izzy back to the moment. "Thank you," she whispered, looking up at the angel. "Where are we?"

The angel's serene smile carried a calming energy that wrapped around Izzy. "I felt your deep longing for love and protection. So I have brought you to the one person your soul yearns for the most."

Hope swelled inside Izzy's chest; her father's image projected vividly in her mind. The realization struck her with overwhelming force—she was about to be reunited with her father. "You brought me to my dad?" she asked, her voice cracking. The angel remained silent, her pleasant smile speaking volumes as she inclined her head, urging Izzy to look behind her.

Izzy spun around, her gaze sweeping across the garden until it settled on a towering hedge at the far end. A figure with curly blond hair emerged and sauntered toward the gazebo. He halted abruptly, his eyes locking onto Izzy. Without a moment's hesitation, he broke into a sprint, charging toward her.

Irritation flared within Izzy as she whirled back to face the angel. "You brought me to Kyler? Are you kidding me?" She arched an eyebrow, only to find the space beside her empty—the angel had disappeared.

"You're back!" The voice that rang out was familiar, but it didn't belong to Kyler. Izzy turned toward the approaching man, studying his form. Though undeniably not Kyler, an uncanny resemblance left her with an overwhelming sense of déjà vu. It was as if their souls had met before. Lost in his green eyes, she felt an irresistible pull drawing her closer. Her heart quickened, instinctively recognizing a sense of safety and trust in his presence.

Her gaze trailed up to the man's face, and there it was—a small, distinct scar along his jawline, partially hidden by stubble. She knew that scar, and the familiarity of it sent a shiver down her spine.

The man looked over Izzy's shoulder, his gaze fixated on something beyond her view. The light in his eyes dimmed for a moment. "No. I suppose you're not truly back, are you? Just here for a visit, then. I guess that means you don't remember much, do you?"

"My memories are just fine . . . Although I don't remember this place," she admitted. "And what do you mean by 'not truly back'?"

Silence encircled them as the man's gaze lingered on Izzy. A blush flushed her cheeks with a delicate rose hue, and a warm sensation spread through her body under his intense scrutiny. "Why are you looking at me like that?"

The man's eyes darted to the side, a sheepish grin creeping onto his lips. "I'm sorry. It's just that . . . it's been such a long time since I've had the chance to speak with you."

When their eyes met again, Izzy was caught off-guard by the dance of golden flecks playing within the depths of his green eyes.

Interrupting the moment's intensity, he said, "You have an astral cord." He paused, seeking permission with a gesture. "May I?" Izzy nodded, and he leaned forward, carefully brushing her hair aside to expose the transparent cord attached to the base of her neck. "This connects your soul to your physical body. You're still alive."

As Izzy's fingertips glided along the cord, its luminous presence intensified. "So, you're saying this isn't a dream, then? This is actually real?" Memories of the nightmare she had just fled crept in, and she shuddered.

"Why don't we go sit down," the man suggested, extending a hand toward the gazebo. "By the way, I'm Dax."

Walking along the pathway, Izzy noticed the meticulously placed pebbles forming mosaics beneath their feet. Each depicted a sinuous black snake coiled around a gleaming silver circle. Izzy's lips parted in astonishment as she noticed that every snake had an emerald embedded in its eye.

"It's the symbol of Orbistia," Dax called out from the gazebo.

Izzy paused to take in the intricate details, then hurried to catch up with Dax, who stood waiting for her.

"You're not dreaming," he said, settling across from her. "Your physical form is back on Earth, fast asleep." Leaning back, he grinned broadly at her. Seeing her blush, he quickly adverted his eyes. "Sorry. I just can't believe that you are actually here."

As his voice faded, a vine crept closer to Izzy, its tendrils gently nestling an orange flower by her ear. Startled, she swivelled to face the vine, which seemed to tremble with mirth, letting the flower fall softly into her lap. Wide-eyed, she turned to Dax and asked, "Where exactly are we? Is this . . . is this heaven?"

"Well, some might refer to it by that name, among others," he replied, gesturing at the lush garden around them. "This is the realm of Orbistia. It's where all souls journey to after death . . . at least most souls. This is our home."

A gentle breeze danced through the gazebo, carrying the subtle hint of the seaside. "Why do I smell the ocean?"

"Oh, we are near the Astral Ocean," Dax said, his eyes lighting up. "Do you want to see it?"

A grin spread across her face, drawn in by his enthusiasm. "I've just met you, and you're already inviting me to wander off with you?" she teased, rising to her feet.

"I keep forgetting that you don't remember me." His smile faltered. "I'm sorry if I was too forward. We can just stay here if you want."

"I'm just teasing!" Izzy said, hopping down from the gazebo. She waited for him to join her before asking, "How do we know each other anyway?"

"I'm not quite sure how to put this without making you uncomfortable . . . I don't want things to feel weird between us," Dax said, his shoulders hitched up slightly.

As Dax spoke, their steps led them past a pear tree heavy with fruit. Izzy reached out, her fingers brushing against a ripe pear, but she recoiled, dropping it as the tree erupted in screams. "I'm exposed!" it wailed, shaking as it clumsily shielded its stripped limb with its other branches. The tree trembled so violently that several more pears plummeted to the ground.

Quickly, Izzy stooped to gather the fallen fruit and offered it back to the weeping tree. It snatched the pear back, letting out a series of disgruntled noises, and then picked up its roots, stomping away.

Izzy turned back to face Dax. "I'm sure that whatever you're about to tell me can't be as bizarre as that," she said, waving her hand toward the agitated tree.

Dax gave a warm chuckle. "No, I guess not," he agreed, a smile flickering across his face. "You handled that exceptionally well, by the way." Reaching out, he tenderly grasped her shoulder, pulling her to a stop. The corner of his mouth twitched uncertainly, and he reached up to tug at his hair.

"You're making me nervous," Izzy replied, reaching out to pull his hand away. The moment their skin touched, an exhilarating energy passed between them, sending waves of power rippling through Izzy. Reluctantly, she let go of his hand. "What was that?" she whispered, breathless from their electrifying touch.

Dax closed his eyes for a brief moment. When he opened them again, his gaze settled on her with a newfound intensity, his green irises shimmering as though lit from within. An affectionate, almost sappy smile spread across his face. "That," he said, his voice rich with excitement, "was a demonstration of what I've been trying to tell you. Izzy. . . we're soulmates."

Izzy looked at him, dumbfounded. Soulmates? The idea seemed plucked from a fairy tale—charming, yet implausible. Was he serious, or could this be a figment of her dream, woven by her vivid imagination?

While she pondered, Dax gave her a moment of silence, his gaze never waning. Izzy carefully studied his face, her eyes tracing the distinct features that set him apart from Kyler. The scar, the curly hair, even the slight height difference—these details stood out, challenging the notion that this was just her imagination. Could a dream ever be this detailed, this consistent?

A sudden realization struck her. What she had felt toward Kyler might have been an echo of her connection with Dax—a soul's yearning for its counterpart, mistakenly finding solace in Kyler's familiar features. She paused, eyes closed, clinging to the hope that this second possibility had.

"Soulmates," she murmured, testing the word on her tongue. Her mind returned to the angel's words, and she quickly shared the revelation with Dax. "So that's why the angel led me to you!" But the look of horror on Dax's face halted her. "What is it?" she asked, a knot tightening in her belly.

"You were brought here by an angel? How did you cross paths with *an angel?*"

"It's okay," Izzy replied, trying to reassure him. "I ended up in some nightmarish place, but the angel came to my rescue," she explained, skipping the more harrowing details.

A scowl crossed Dax's face. "One of your guides should have been waiting for you when you astral projected!" His mouth set into a hard line as he reached up, his fingers pulling at his hair again. "It's their job!"

Izzy winced and eased his hands down. "I understand why that bothers my aunt now," she murmured.

As Dax gazed at their conjoined hands, a smile began to play at the corners of his mouth. "You can't feel pain in your spirit form," he said, giving her hands a soft squeeze. He gently pulled her forward, resuming their walk through the garden with their hands swinging lightly between them.

Gradually, the texture beneath their feet transformed—the grass giving way to sporadic patches of sand. They passed a cluster of purple lilac trees, the heady floral scent slowly yielding to the crisp, salty tang of the ocean air. Izzy gasped as the shimmering water came into view, stretching out endlessly before them. Its horizon blended seamlessly with the sky. With each step, her feet sank into the sun-warmed sand, drawing them closer to the shore where the waves lapped gently in frothy ripples.

The sandy shoreline of the beach extended for miles, curving to shape a scenic harbour where several ferry boats were moored. Their forms rose and fell with the distant swells. "That's the Orbistian Terminal," Dax explained, pointing toward the ships. "It's a major gateway for carnies coming into the realm."

"Carnies?" Izzy's eyes narrowed as she focused on the busy port. She could just make out the faint, ethereal glow of souls disembarking from the boats and filling the docks.

"It's what we call souls who have reincarnated. You're considered a carnie until your memory block is removed after your 'death.'"

Izzy's gaze lingered over the ocean's vast expanse, entranced by the fluid dance of the greens and blues. "This place is beautiful. Why would anyone willingly leave this realm to reincarnate?"

"Our lives are endless here, Izzy. Reincarnation gives us purpose. It's an adventure, an opportunity for growth and development," Dax explained. "There are other reasons, too, but I really shouldn't say more." He paused, a hint of mystery flickering in his eyes. "You're not supposed to know about any of this—they placed your memory block on for a reason."

"If I'm not supposed to know about this, why would the angel bring me here?"

"Funny enough, the angels don't care much about our rules. They believe in doing the right thing, and I suppose, in your case, that meant bringing you here to me."

She tilted her head to look up at him, a gleam in her eyes. "Our rules?" He chuckled and playfully nudged against her shoulder.

"Quit fishing for information! You're going to get me in trouble with your head guide. She's a terror, that one," he said, pulling a dramatic face that set Izzy into a fit of laughter.

Her laughter came to an abrupt halt when a small, plump woman appeared from behind a distant sand dune. Her short, curly brown hair bounced with each determined step she took toward them. The sunlight glinted off the silver brooch pinned to her blue blazer—a raven perched proudly on a compass. Izzy's stomach tightened. Ravens had become an inescapable presence in her life.

Dax sighed. "Here comes Miss Priss," he muttered, throwing a disdainful glance toward the advancing woman. His gaze met Izzy's, his eyes dimming with a sadness that etched deeper lines into his face. A sense of growing unease tightened in Izzy's chest as she braced herself for whatever new threat awaited her.

CHAPTER SEVENTEEN

UNVEILING THE RAVEN

"Of course, I would find her here with you!" The woman marched across the sandy shore, kicking up clouds of fine grains as she moved toward them. She planted herself firmly in front of them, her arms folded across her plump body, eyes blazing with disapproval.

"Good to see you too, Priscilla," Dax said, his voice laced with cheerfulness that didn't quite reach his eyes.

"And to bring her into this realm of all places. What were you thinking, Dax?" Priscilla's voice rose to a shrill note, and she glared at him, her nostrils flaring.

Dax's fingers tightened around Izzy's, yet his expression remained unreadable. "She was brought here by an angel," he said, his eyes narrowing at Priscilla. "She was in the Kingdom of Nachtmahr."

Colour drained from Priscilla's face, and her hand flew to her chest as if to quell a sudden fluttering. "The Realm of Nightmares?"

Dax bent toward her, his tone edged with accusation. "Isn't it part of your job as a spirit guide to chaperone carnies when they astral project?"

Ignoring him, Priscilla swiftly turned to Izzy. Her abrupt movement caused her orange and blue striped tie to become untucked from her blazer. "Hello dear," she said, adopting a warm and motherly tone. With a lift of her chin, she announced, "I am Priscilla, your head spirit guide."

"It appears you have had quite the adventure," she continued. "I apologize for any scare you may have had." Priscilla cast Izzy a reassuring look as she started patting down her pockets. "I can only imagine how overwhelming this must be for you."

With a furrowed brow, Priscilla reached deeper into her pocket. "Damn that Roger, if only he hadn't walked away from his screen," she muttered.

Dax's lips curled into a smirk, his eyebrows shooting up, "Trouble with your new guide?"

Priscilla bristled, her gaze lifting to glare at Dax. "Certainly not," she said. "There was a power outage at the Department of Spiritual Guidance and Support, and our screens shut down. An abnormality, really, nothing to be blamed on any of the guides."

She looked at Izzy, her eyes softening. "Such chaos it caused—carnie pick-ups being missed, astral projectors left unaccounted for . . . I'm dreadfully sorry, dear. I assure you that most out-of-body experiences are more pleasant than what you have experienced."

Izzy leaned forward, examining Priscilla's brooch. "It was you, wasn't it?" she asked, pointing at the raven. "You've been following me around all week!"

Priscilla let out a heavy sigh as if reluctant to answer her. "Yes, we were trying to warn you, dear," she admitted. "Your roommates . . . the incident with your sister. Unfortunately, most people ignore their spirit guides. Lately, you've been more attuned to the spirit world . . . We were hoping you would pick up on the signs."

Incredulity flashed in Izzy's eyes, her mouth falling open in a silent gasp of disbelief. "Warn me? The whole car incident was supposed to be a warning? You nearly scared me half to death!"

Priscilla shifted her eyes away from Izzy. "Yes, well, I do apologize for that incident. Roger . . . well, he's new to the role. He got a little carried away."

"I'll say," Izzy grumbled, shooting Priscilla a scathing look.

Priscilla resumed rummaging around in her jacket, her movements growing more frantic. "Anyway, we really must be getting you back to your body. Now, where is that amnesium ball . . ."

Dax stepped forward, positioning himself between Priscilla and Izzy. "You're not going to erase Izzy's memories."

Priscilla's eyes snapped up to meet Dax's. "It is protocol, Dax. She's not supposed to be here," she insisted, gesturing to their surroundings.

"It should be her choice," Dax replied, his jaw clenching.

Priscilla straightened, inflating her chest out. "One purpose of reincarnating is to rediscover a sense of mystery in life, Dax. You know this." She adjusted her tie, tucking it back neatly into her blazer. "Besides, it is against the rules for her to be here," she added, giving Dax a pointed look as if implying that he should be well aware of the regulations.

Izzy's eyes lingered on Dax, and a warmth spread through her as she noticed the protective look on his face. It struck her then—despite the terrifying start to this experience, she wasn't ready for it to end. An unsettling wave of anxiety washed over her at the thought of having to let go of Dax after just meeting him.

"Actually," she said, leaning closer to Dax, "I thought I might stay here a bit longer and do some exploring. You could always erase my memory afterward," she suggested sweetly, smiling at Priscilla. "That is if you'd be willing to show me around," she added, turning to Dax.

His eyes lightening up, he replied, "Absolutely!"

"Absolutely not!" Priscilla exclaimed, her voice taking on a stern tone. "Now, really dear, I must insist. We need to get you back before the council finds out," she added, her gaze darting around as if she expected the council to be eavesdropping on their conversation.

"Why? Afraid they'll reprimand you for your screw-up." Dax's face grew thoughtful, and he continued, "You know, I don't recall there actually being a rule prohibiting a carnie from visiting Orbistia, only that they shouldn't retain any memory of it." A smug smile curled the edges of his mouth as he gazed down at Priscilla.

Priscilla's composure faltered, her hands flying up in exasperation. "Of course there is a rule!"

"Prove it," Dax countered, his smile widening. "I'll get Maddy out here. She's a keeper of knowledge at the Akashic Hall of Records. She'll have the information."

"I know what your sister does," Priscilla said darkly. She sighed at their expectant faces. "Fine. Summon your sister. I am sure she will agree with me."

Dax's face lit up with excitement. He held out his palm, facing upward, and said, "*Flamma Nuntius*" loudly. Izzy watched in awe as a tiny flame sprung to life in the centre of his hand.

Holding the flame closer to his face, he said, "Maddy, I need your assistance. Meet me on the beach just beyond the lilacs." As each word left his lips, it appeared in bold, black writing within the centre of the flame. The words adjusted to fit the flame's flickering form. Satisfied with his message, Dax closed his fist around the fire, extinguishing the flame in a wisp of smoke.

After several minutes, the rustling of branches signalled someone's approach. Izzy turned her attention toward the lilac trees bordering the beach's edge. A tall, slender woman emerged from the foliage. She was clad in a white blouse with a yellow and grey tie beneath a yellow blazer. A large, embroidered silver eye decorated the breast pocket. Her eyes narrowed into a subtle scowl at the sight of Izzy.

Dax grinned and beckoned his sister closer. As Maddy neared, Izzy sensed a coolness from her, confirmed by the rigidness of Maddy's acknowledging nod. Dax seemed oblivious to the tension, but even as Maddy's features briefly relaxed into a smile when hugging her brother, her eyes flickered toward Izzy, and the smile vanished, replaced by her earlier reserve.

Dax turned to Izzy with gleaming eyes. "This is Maddy, my sister."

Maddy glanced at her brother, her brow knitting together. "Why are you introducing us? She already knows who I am."

"Izzy's astral projecting right now. Priscilla insists that Izzy needs to return to her body, but I'm not convinced that there's any law stating that she has to go back right this second."

"There is," Priscilla snapped, her arms folding across her chest.

"Could you look it up, Maddy? See if it's really a thing?" Dax asked, ignoring Priscilla.

Maddy's sharp, brown eyes narrowed as she glanced at Izzy, her lips forming a tight line. "Dax, you have an appointment at the Department of Reincarnation," she reminded him. "You're supposed to select your incarnated body today, remember?"

Dax waved his hand dismissively. "I can reschedule. This is more important."

Maddy cast Izzy a cool glance as she addressed her brother. "It could be months before you get another appointment. Are you seriously going to postpone it . . . for her?"

"Please, Maddy," Dax said, his shoulders dropping.

With a weary sigh, Maddy reached into her yellow blazer and took out a paper roll. With a flick of her wrist, it rapidly unfolded into a long scroll that touched down to the sand. Priscilla quickly joined her, leaning in to consult it together.

Dax moved closer to Izzy, his whisper warm against her ear. "You sure you want this?" She nodded silently, reaching out for his hand. Using his free hand, he reached into his jeans and retrieved a coin engraved with the letter *M*. Closing his fist around it, he muttered, "*Pasporta Dorasalite.*"

Izzy's heart thrummed with anticipation as a green portal unfolded behind Maddy and Priscilla. She bit her lower lip, her eyes fixed on the vortex's mesmerizing dance.

Dax gently tugged on Izzy's arm. He led her forward with a murmured pretext of admiring the ocean as they slipped by the two women.

"Trust me," Dax whispered.

As they drew nearer, the portal pulsated, growing brighter. Squeezing Izzy's hand, they stepped through together—the magic whisking them away from the beach and the looming presence of Izzy's spirit guide.

CHAPTER EIGHTEEN

THE ASTRAL HIGHWAY

The portal opened, revealing a dark plain stretching before them. Unlike the nightmare realm, where everything had been consumed by pitch black, this place held a different kind of darkness. Overhead, the skies unfurled like an inky canvas, pierced by stars twinkling like distant diamonds. The ground underfoot mirrored the heavens. It was composed of smooth, reflective sand reminiscent of a crystalline floor. With every step they took, ripples of light danced across the surface.

"Where are we," Izzy asked, her eyes darting around as the portal closed behind them.

"The Astral Plains," Dax replied, his smile widening as he looked at her.

She glanced at him, catching his expression, and burst into laughter. "You really need to stop doing that!" she exclaimed, warmth flooding her cheeks.

"I can't help it. I didn't expect to see you for at least another eighty years. I'm just . . . really happy right now."

A thrill raced through her as he spoke, and her pulse quickened. None of her past relationships had ever stirred such a sensation within her. With Dax, she felt profoundly important, as if she held a cherished place in his life.

"We should get going," he said, leading the way across the twinkling landscape. "We need to get to the Astral Highway—it's the safest place for travelling around here."

"Is this place . . . dangerous?"

Dax squeezed her hand reassuringly. "It can be. The demons also have access to this realm, but angels closely monitor it, as well as members of the Guard, so we should be relatively safe."

Noticing the fear in Izzy's eyes, he stopped beside a towering tree, its branches heavy with oversized white flowers. "We can protect ourselves, Iz. Here, watch this." He closed his eyes and fell silent. Then, in a firm tone, he called out, "*Advo Telum.*"

A boomerang, aglow with a brilliant light, materialized in his hand. Its intricate designs pulsed with a blue shimmer, captivating her gaze. He held the weapon out to her, inviting a closer inspection. "It's so beautiful," she murmured, her hand pausing before reaching to caress its smooth surface.

"It's my spirit weapon." He threw the boomerang into the air, catching it easily as it returned to his hand. "It has the power to break down energy forms into their purest state," he continued. "It takes souls and demons years to recharge after that."

"I saw that happen," Izzy said, leaning against the tree trunk. "The angel took out the demon who had me. He exploded into a shower of purple sparks."

Dax's brow creased as he looked at her. "I can't believe you ended up in the Realm of Nightmares. How did that even happen?"

Izzy quickly recounted her ordeal, ensuring not to omit any details. When she reached the part about the bats, Dax nodded, comprehension dawning on his face. "Demons are drawn to negative emotions," he said. "They must have been nearby and picked up on your reaction to Melanie and Kyler." With a roll of his eyes, he added, "That guy's such a douchebag. I never liked him."

A flicker of surprise passed over her face. "You never liked Kyler? How do you even know him?"

Dax's eyes shifted away from hers, his neck reddening with a telltale blush. "Well, I don't personally know him," he confessed. "But I've seen how he treats you, and he just seems like a jerk."

"You've been watching me?"

He lifted his hands in a gesture of defence. "I know how it sounds, but watching over loved ones is something we do here." His shoulders slumped as he continued, "Time works differently in this realm. Sometimes, it moves really fast, and other times it slows down. Nineteen years have passed for you, but for us, it's been thirty-two."

He toyed with his boomerang, eyes not meeting hers as he spoke. "There's a proper process to visit the physical realms—paperwork, permission forms, all that bureaucratic stuff." A sheepish grin appeared on his face. "It can be time-consuming, but there are always loopholes if you know the right person." His smile shifted, taking on a mischievous edge. "Priscilla busted me a few times for using those shortcuts. I don't think she's particularly fond of me."

A smile played on Izzy's lips. "Yeah, Priscilla definitely seems like a stickler for rules." After a brief pause, she added, "It's a bit odd but understandable. If I were in your shoes, I'd likely do the same thing."

A slight upturn of Dax's mouth conveyed his relief at her understanding.

"So," she said, changing the subject. "Will you show me how to do that?" She motioned toward the glowing weapon in his hand. "How do you get it to appear?"

Nodding, Dax let his boomerang dissolve into the air. "Okay, close your eyes and visualize your own spirit weapon."

"Except I don't know what my spirit weapon looks like."

Dax laughed. "Oh, right. That would help. Yours is a sword—a really cool, Viking-like sword."

Izzy's eyebrows arched skeptically. "Aren't those swords heavy? Why would I choose something like that?"

"Spirit weapons are weightless," he reassured her.

With her eyes closed, Izzy imagined the sword securely in her hand. Minutes passed in focused silence before she opened her eyes and looked at Dax, her voice a soft whisper. "Now what?"

"Now, say the words *Advo Telum*," Dax instructed. "And say it with confidence."

Despite his encouraging words, Izzy struggled—each attempt to materialize her weapon ended with only a wisp of faint blue light wavering in her hand. On her third unsuccessful effort, Dax's reassurance was immediate. "You actually are quite good at calling it forward. It's probably not working because you can't visualize it properly."

A wave of defeat washed over Izzy, and her outstretched hands dropped to her sides. "I guess you'll have to handle any demons we come across on your own," she said, her shoulders sagging.

Dax's eyes softened as he met Izzy's gaze. "Come on," he said. "We're almost at the highway. I'm sure we'll be fine."

Leaving the tree's shelter, they resumed walking. Underfoot, the terrain subtly shifted from flat ground to mounds of glittering sand. With each step, these hills grew, evolving into rising and falling sand dunes. The rolling curves and majestic peaks wove a breathtaking pattern that stretched into the horizon.

While they walked, Izzy continued sharing her ordeal in the Realm of Nightmares. When she reached the part about the mumbling teen, her gaze dropped to the ground, and she halted mid-sentence—gripped by the shame of having abandoned him.

"Sounds like he astral projected but remained in a deep sleep. Without fear or negative energy, the demons would have had no interest in him," Dax explained.

"I still shouldn't have left him. I—"

Their conversation was abruptly overtaken by the roar of an engine, pulling their gaze to a nearby dune. Dax waved cheerfully toward a Jeep cresting the sandy rise, its occupants squealing with delight and clutching their seats tightly. The vehicle soon slipped from view, its engine growl diminishing with the widening gap.

"Tourists," Dax explained.

"Tourists?" Izzy's eyebrows shot up in surprise. "You mean other astral projectors like me?"

Dax shook his head. "No, not astral projectors. I mean actual tourists from neighbouring universes visiting ours," he clarified. "There's a designated realm that guides take projectors to, and that's where you should have gone."

"You're talking about aliens!"

Dax chuckled. "Think of it more like visitors from a foreign country."

"Visitors from another universe . . ." A bright smile took over Izzy's face. "This is unreal."

Dax absently scratched his cheek and squinted at the faint glow cresting the next hill. "I know this is a lot to take in," he said. A shadow of uncertainty crossed his features as he turned to her. "Maybe . . . we shouldn't go any further. There are more than mere tourists where we're headed . . . I'd hate to cause any upheaval in your current life."

"Priscilla will wipe my memory anyway, so what difference does it make?" She glanced over her shoulder at him. "I'm not a child, Dax. I can handle it."

Scrambling up the sand dune, Izzy came to a halt. Her eyes widened at the sprawling view that unfolded before her. A soft "Wow" escaped her lips. Dax caught up, joining her to gaze upon the dazzling highway snaking through the landscape like a luminous serpent.

Gesturing toward it, he said, "That leads to Sparklafex."

As they neared the freeway, Izzy's attention was drawn to a group of souls sitting in a meditative pose at its edge. One figure caught her eye. "Is that a fairy?" Izzy asked, bouncing on her toes. She pointed at a woman whose pale beauty was accentuated by the delicate, sparkling wings resting behind her.

"Yes," replied Dax, his tone casual as if fairy encounters were commonplace. "She's a carnie from Tír na nÓg." He gestured toward the other souls—some draped in peculiar robes, others in more mundane clothes. "The highway's positive energy is a magnet, attracting souls here. In this deep of a meditative state, these carnies cannot be harmed."

Izzy nodded, her eyes still fixed on the fairy. "But a fairy, Dax. A freaking fairy!"

"I told you, it's not just tourists around here. Earth isn't the only habitable planet in our universe—there are a number of other ones, and each has its own form of carnies. Some are humans, some not so much."

Excitement flooded Izzy as she stared at the fairy. A planet of fairies—what else existed here? The beauty before her was in sharp contrast to the nightmarish ordeal she had endured earlier, making her feel like Alice tumbling into Wonderland.

Reluctantly, she shifted her gaze to the radiant stretch of road before her. It extended into the distance, alive with a throng of souls, each navigating its own unique mode of transportation. Her mouth fell open in a slight gape as a man adorned in the clothing of a bygone era swept by on a unicycle.

A stunning woman with flowing black hair followed, seated regally on a white horse. She rode side-saddle, her dress billowing over her feet while the horse trotted past. Hot on her heels, three hobgoblins on oversized rubber balls bounced along, clutching the handles tightly. They jostled each other playfully, their laughter reaching Izzy's ears.

"How do we get on?"

"It's similar to summoning your spirit weapon," Dax explained, his hand waving toward a man riding by on a pogo stick. "You just need to visualize the mode of transportation in your mind, and it will manifest."

"Well, this I can do," Izzy said, closing her eyes.

Dax clasped her hand, his eyes alight with encouragement. "Do you have it in your mind?" Izzy nodded, her lower lip caught between her teeth. "Step forward now," Dax urged. Together, they stepped out onto the highway.

Izzy settled into a plush leather seat and, opening her eyes, let out a delighted squeal—she was behind the wheel of a classic 1967 Chevy Impala. Dax lounged beside her, a smirk on his lips as he caught her expression. "Really?" he said, arching an eyebrow.

Izzy's smile widened into a full-fledged grin as she shrugged. "I'm a massive *Supernatural* fan."

"I can tell." Dax chuckled. "Just don't get it in your head that we're going demon hunting anytime soon."

Izzy's laughter rang out as she settled comfortably into the seat, feeling the highway take over the steering. "Don't worry, demon hunting isn't on my bucket list."

As they moved along, Dax pointed out several off-ramps to Izzy, each leading to the entrance of a different galaxy's habitable zone. "Most people here," he said, "are either visiting loved ones or embarking on explorations. They have the necessary paperwork to gain entry."

Leaning over her, he pointed to a line of vehicles queued at an off-ramp. "That exit leads to Katswyn," he said, a wistful expression crossing his face. "You and I once incarnated there together," he added. They continued, leaving the exit behind as Dax sank back into his seat, still ensnared by the past.

Breaking the lingering silence, Izzy said, "So, tell me more about Sparklafex."

Dax's gaze sharpened, pulling away from his distant thoughts. "It's the last stop on the Astral Highway," he explained. "The only city within the Astral Plains. Tourists stay here when they visit, but it's also where all the immigrants come to live."

"Immigrants?"

"Yes. Refugees too," Dax said, his face growing sombre. "Many souls travel into our universe to escape their own for various reasons. They are denied entry into the realm of Orbistia," he continued, his eyes hardening, "so they come to Sparklafex. Refugees founded the city."

Izzy sighed. "Orbistia . . . Yet another place obsessed with differences," she murmured, her brows furrowing in disappointment. Beside her, Dax nodded, his silence speaking volumes.

The highway's population thinned as souls veered off onto various exits. Soon, the barren land gave way to an array of trees and shrubs punctuated by occasional structures that hinted at a settlement ahead. Nearing their destination, the luminous path of the highway transitioned into a lively street, its edges flanked by buildings. On the sidewalks, an electric mix of souls caught Izzy's eye, some so unusual they could easily pass for aliens.

Dax turned to her, his tanned face aglow with excitement. "Welcome to Sparklafex."

CHAPTER NINETEEN

The Unassuming Shopkeeper

As they ventured deeper into the city, Izzy pressed herself against the driver's window—completely mesmerized by the vibrant storefront and peculiar characters strolling along the sidewalks. Dax leaned over, pointing out various sights as they passed by.

"There's where you can sign up for hunting demons," he said, gesturing toward a storefront. Its entrance was an elaborate cut-out of a menacing creature—a sign overtop read *Astral Adventorium*. Izzy watched as several tall souls with shrivelled faces disappeared into the establishment through the gaping mouth of the cut-out.

Next, Dax directed Izzy's attention to another landmark. "And there's the Smoky Quartz," he exclaimed. His finger aimed at a building crafted entirely from the mineral it was named after. It sparkled like a gem under the starry sky. As they drove past, the club's door burst open, and a wave of hypnotic music spilled into the air, enveloping them in its rhythm.

Their journey concluded as the road ended, and the Impala dissipated into the ether, depositing them on a narrow, cobbled lane. It was just wide enough for a single cart to pass.

Directly across, nestled among thick pine trees, stood a charming shop. The trees loomed overhead, their branches forming a protective canopy over the building. An intermittent flicker of a neon sign danced above the door, displaying the words *Mogworm's Multiverse Escapade*.

"What are we doing here?" Izzy asked.

"Well, remember when I mentioned using loopholes if you know the right person?"

Izzy squinted through the shop's dusty windows, her vision thwarted by the veil of grime. "So, this is your guy then?" she asked, turning to Dax.

He responded with a nod, his hand hovering over the brass doorknob of the faded blue door. "Marlo Mogworm. He's . . . well, a bit unusual. Priscilla is probably going to come searching for us here soon. We should go to Earth—She won't expect that."

A contemplative look settled over Izzy's face as she considered their options. "So, we could go anywhere on Earth? And your guy can get us there?"

Dax nodded. "Yes, and it would be undetected. Once we got there, we could travel around pretty easily."

"I've always wanted to visit Australia," she said, her voice filled with a hint of longing.

Dax laughed. "Sure, we can also visit New Zealand while we're there. So is that a yes?"

Izzy nodded and moved to stand next to Dax. He twisted the knob, and with a groan, it swung open to unveil the shop's interior, which was cloaked in shadows and a layer of dust. A wooden desk stood in one corner, its surface a chaotic mix of paperwork and coffee cups. Along the walls, several large-screen televisions hung, each paired with dangling headphones. Below these screens, small tables held thick binders.

Izzy's gaze swept over the room—ordinary, to her dismay, devoid of the magic she had anticipated. Edging closer to Dax, she murmured, "What kind of service does your friend even offer?"

"Timeline travel," a deep voice resonated behind Izzy, making her startle and stumble backward into Dax.

A man of average height was standing near the window, his attention fixed on the world outside. He turned slowly, a black Toronto Raptors baseball cap shadowing his eyes. Izzy's mouth fell open as she took in his peculiar attire—ratty blue jeans and an oversized hoodie that seemed to swallow his frame. Was this the contact that Dax had mentioned?

"Izzy Adams," the man said as he moved toward them, a smile on his face and his hand extended in greeting. "It's a pleasure to finally meet

141

you," he continued, lifting his head. Warmth sparkled in his soft brown eyes, visible beneath the brim of his hat. "Dax has spoken of you often—I feel like I already know you," he said with a chuckle.

Despite her initial reservations, Izzy returned his smile and shook his outstretched hand. "You must be Marlo."

Marlo ambled toward his desk. "I must be," he replied with a touch of humour. He sank into his office chair and propped his feet up on the desk, sending a flurry of papers drifting down to the worn carpet below.

Dax, his voice filled with admiration, explained, "Marlo has the unique ability to transport souls to different timelines."

"Only timelines that have already passed or the ones that never came to be," Marlo interjected, leaning forward to scrutinize the collection of coffee cups on his desk. He picked up one, took a sip, then wrinkled his nose, setting the cup back down.

Dax headed to one of the binders along the wall, swiftly flipping it open and gesturing for Izzy to come for a closer look.

Izzy stepped nearer, her attention drawn to the passage Dax pointed out:

Planet: Earth
Timeline: If Trump had served two consecutive terms.

A sheer look of bewilderment crossed Izzy's face. "Who would want to experience that?"

Marlo chuckled. "Surprisingly, there are many who find it intriguing. If you're curious, I can show you a brief preview," he offered, nodding toward the television screen.

Izzy snapped the book shut and stepped back from the screen. "No, that's all right. I think I'll pass."

Dax walked to the desk and took a seat across from Marlo. He leaned forward, adopting a serious expression. "We need a Meli coin."

"I expected as much." Marlo rubbed his long, thin nose. "But what will you give me in return?"

"We're planning on going to Earth. Do you have anything you need collected?"

The room fell silent as Marlo's gaze drifted off, lost in contemplation. "Earth, you say . . ."

Izzy returned to the binders, leafing through the pages while waiting for Marlo to speak again. She cast a curious glance his way, struggling to understand how he could be one of the immigrants Dax had referenced. The man seemed utterly ordinary—more suited to attending a basketball game than manipulating time. He was the last person she would have suspected of possessing such power.

As Marlo discussed a proposed exchange with Dax, Izzy's attention sharpened at the mention of *Bloodstone* and *Massachusetts*. Her expression morphed from curiosity to horror when, through the shop's window, she spotted a familiar figure hurrying down the cobbled streets.

"We need to go now!" she said, her eyes urgently meeting Dax's.

"He still has to create the Meli coin, Iz."

"It shall only take a moment," Marlo added, glancing at the grey sports watch on his wrist. "It's only two o'clock in the morning in Ontario. You will have plenty of time to explore Earth."

"It's not that," Izzy said, her eyes flickering toward the door. "Priscilla is across the street, checking out the other stores. We need to leave now!" She faced Marlo, her eyes wide and pleading. "Please send us to one of your timelines. Just until she's gone."

Marlo sat up straight, his feet hitting the floor with a thud as he swung his legs off the table. "And what will you offer me in return, Izzy Adams?"

"Izzy, please, don't make a deal—"

"Anything!" Izzy reached up, fingers tugging at her blond hair as the doorknob jiggled. "Just send us anywhere. Please!"

"Very well," Marlo mused, rubbing his chin thoughtfully. "A future favour. Yes?"

Izzy nodded, ignoring Dax as he groaned and slumped back in his chair. She thrust her hand into Marlo's, shaking it. A warm surge of energy tingled up her arm as their hands met, and suddenly, the world's edges smeared into a cascade of shifting shades, each blending into the next. The shop faded from view, leaving Izzy and Dax suspended in a weightless limbo between the folds of time and space.

CHAPTER TWENTY

A Journey into Chaos

Izzy's soul fragmented into an infinite number of particles. Amid the disarray, she maintained a sense of Dax's presence nearby—their connection remaining unbroken. Together, they hurtled through the tunnel of colours that stretched endlessly, as if the fabric of reality was melting away.

Izzy was yanked backward, her soul melding together once more. The brilliant kaleidoscope of colours faded, giving way to an expanse of soft blue. She was freefalling through the open sky, the exhilarating wind whipping past her. Below, a speck of brown rapidly grew more prominent as the ground loomed closer.

In mere moments, the distant peaks of a forest came into view, followed by a small clearing nestled within it. Two figures lay sprawled in the grass, their stillness like a frozen snapshot. Panic surged through Izzy as the horrifying realization hit—she was hurtling toward the bodies. Her arms flailed wildly, a frantic attempt to counter the unstoppable descent.

A sharp pop echoed through the air as Dax materialized beside Izzy. With effortless grace, he flipped onto his back, casually resting his hands behind his head.

"Don't worry, Iz," he shouted over the rush of wind. "You won't get hurt, but you might want to flip around. If you fall into your body backward, you'll be looking out through the back of your head!"

His face broke into a mischievous grin, and he winked at her. Then, with a burst of energy, he sped up his descent, disappearing into one of the lifeless bodies below. Izzy's eyes widened, and she made a frantic effort to turn herself midair, her body contorting.

As she managed to shift onto her side, time appeared to slow. She felt a gentle guidance directing her toward the figure on the ground. A peculiar sensation wrapped around her as her soul melded with the body, claiming it as her own.

Izzy blinked, her eyes slowly adjusting to the blue sky above. She sat up quickly and surveyed her surroundings. Instinctively, her hands flew to her face, tracing familiar contours and confirming the reassuring presence of her nose. She breathed a sigh of relief—she was indeed, in her body, properly orientated.

Laughter erupted from beside her. Izzy turned to see Dax sitting up, tears of mirth streaming down his face as his gaze met hers. "I'm sorry," he choked out between bouts of laughter. "I couldn't resist. The look on your face was priceless."

"I thought I was going to be stuck seeing through the back of my head, Dax!"

Dax collapsed with laughter as Izzy's eyes caught sight of a cluster of mushrooms. With a smile, she grabbed them and flung them at his chest. "You're an arse!" Their shared laughter reverberated through the clearing, intertwining with the gentle rustle of grass beneath them. Gradually, they regained their composure, rising to their feet.

As she flicked away specks of dirt from the thin sweater and jeans she now wore, her eyes swept around the area. Towering trees surrounded them, their upper reaches forming a natural canopy that provided respite from the heat. Sunlight, broken by the leafy branches, filtered through the foliage to cast enchanting patterns of light upon the forest floor.

"Marlo must have sent us into an alternate timeline," Dax said, dusting off his pants. "It felt like we were moving forward rather than backward."

Izzy ventured ahead, her fingertips delicately tracing the rough bark of a tree. "Do you think we're actually on Earth?" she asked, studying the sticky sap that clung to her hands. "It looks like Earth . . ."

"Possibly. Tír na nÓg is far more vibrant, and Katswyn is an apocalyptic planet. I haven't incarnated on all the planets, so I can't say for certain."

Turning toward her again, he reached down and clasped her sticky hand. "We'll find out soon enough," he said, guiding her through the dense underbrush. "I caught sight of a road in this direction when we fell."

They pressed on, footsteps sinking into the moss that carpeted the ground. "I wish you hadn't made a deal with Marlo," he added, pushing aside overhanging branches.

"I didn't really think about it," Izzy admitted. "I panicked. I just didn't want Priscilla to catch us."

Dax squeezed her hand reassuringly. "I know. It's just that Marlo is a bit of a shifty character. I like him, but I don't really know him . . . I'm not sure if it's good that you owe someone like him a favour."

"Someone like him?"

"He's a god, Izzy. Now you owe a god a favour."

Izzy came to a sudden stop. She turned to Dax, disbelief etching itself across her face. "Marlo is a god? Are you kidding me?"

Dax nodded, swatting at a mosquito that had landed on his neck.

"He doesn't look like a god," she said.

Dax chuckled. "Well, what do you imagine a god should look like, Iz?"

"I don't know . . . Marlo just looks so ordinary."

"He's humble. That's what I like about him," Dax said, pausing to use a twig to clear a sprawling spiderweb from their path. "There are other gods who probably look more like what you're imagining, but they don't usually leave Orbistia.

Izzy recoiled, her face contorting in disgust as she watched him discard the stick. She hurried to follow, avoiding the lingering web strands that fluttered in the soft breeze.

Her mind spun with countless questions. The afterlife bore no resemblance to anything she had expected—multiple gods, immigrants from different universes, and time-travelling escapades. Her mother would have a fit if she knew.

Dax's voice cut through her whirlwind of thoughts, bringing her attention back to the conversation. She realized she'd missed a significant portion. "Marlo's one of the good ones; otherwise, he would have been banned from Sparklafex. He's just a bit unusual. His sense of humour is . . . twisted," he explained. "I'm a little nervous to see where he has sent us."

"How do you even know Marlo?"

"I run errands for him, find missing items . . . stuff like that. In return, he makes me Meli coins. Only gods can create them."

"Why do you need so many Meli coins?"

"To get around with."

"Wouldn't it just be easier to go through the proper channels you mentioned before?"

Dax glanced back at her, his face taking on a sheepish expression. "Well, I used to go through the proper channels, but then the Department of Astral Observation and Broadcasting Support cut me off. Priscilla lodged a complaint—said it was unhealthy for me to visit you so often."

As they emerged from the forest's edge, an offensive stench invaded Izzy's nostrils. She instinctively wrinkled her nose, recoiling from the putrid odour that wafted through the air.

"Oh my gods," Dax gasped, doubling over to retch into the nearby ditch. "What is that smell?" he choked out, hastily covering his nose with the hem of his shirt.

"Rotting flesh," Izzy said, climbing onto the highway.

Dax, pale and shaken, joined Izzy on the road. Together, they pressed on, their footsteps resonating on the hot asphalt as they drew closer to the intersection. A desolate gas station and an abandoned coffee shop marked the edges of a town.

Izzy's voice pierced the unnatural quiet as she pointed to a sign displaying the name Madoc. "Marlo sent us to Earth," she said, nostalgia flooding her. She turned to Dax, a soft smile playing on her lips. "My grandparents used to live in this town."

"I don't think anyone lives here anymore," he said. He buried his nose in his arm as another gust of decay blew in their direction.

They walked past an impressive, two-storey house with a veranda encircling the entire building. A white bedsheet, tightly fastened to the railing, billowed in the breeze. Izzy's gaze lingered on the sheet, and an unsettling shiver shot up her spine.

As they ventured deeper into the town's core, more houses adorned with white sheets came into view—draped over bushes and wound tightly around mailboxes. Izzy caught a glimpse of movement behind a curtain, a fleeting sign of an unseen observer. Beyond that brief hint of presence, a stillness covered the town, the streets devoid of life.

The further they advanced toward the village square, the more the pungent stench of decay intensified. Without warning, Dax halted, yanking Izzy into the alcove of one of the storefronts. "Look," he whispered, nodding toward a red-bricked gazebo.

The structure's octagonal silhouette, once a beacon of charm, now presided over a tableau of death. The surrounding gardens, once meticulously cared for, had succumbed to neglect—flowers laying lifeless among encroaching weeds. Yet, it was the square that held the true horror. Mounds of motionless bodies were scattered across the ground, shrouded in white sheets. These coverings proved futile in hiding the repulsive blood stains and decay oozing through the fabric.

Underneath the gazebo, a dozen tables were arranged haphazardly. Each bore a figure barely recognizable as human. Despite Dax's protests, Izzy found herself drawn closer. She edged near one table, her pulse pounding in her ears, and then staggered back, gasping at the sight of the woman lying there.

Beads of sweat streamed down the woman's contorted face, merging with her bulging eyes. She clawed frantically at her throat in a desperate gasp for breath, her nails tearing into the flesh and leaving behind raw, bloody wounds.

Frantically, Izzy's gaze darted around, her mind racing for a way to help her. She spotted a table nearby cluttered with supplies and hurried over. After a quick rummage through the medical equipment, she seized a bundle of bandages. Without a moment's hesitation, Izzy moved to secure the woman's flailing hands to the sides of the table.

"What do you think you are doing!" A high, authoritative voice cut through the air, halting Izzy's actions instantly.

Startled, she let go of the white tension bandage, her attention snapping to the tall figure advancing toward her. Dark hair cascaded around a face defined by intense, moss-green eyes that burned with unmistakable anger.

"Where is your face mask?" the woman demanded, stopping at a distance.

"We don't have any," Dax said, coming to stand beside Izzy.

The woman's finger jutted out, pointing toward the nearby table Izzy had just rummaged through. "Get one now!" she ordered, her voice stern. "And sanitize your hands first."

Following her instructions, Izzy and Dax headed to the overturned box filled with masks and hand sanitizer. After equipping themselves with the necessary items, they returned to the woman, only to discover that she had finished binding the dying lady's arms to her side.

"You're not from around here, are you?" the townswoman exclaimed, her voice heavy with suspicion. She turned and called, "Louella!" to another lady emerging from a store with a water bottle. "Do you recognize them?" she asked, nodding toward Izzy and Dax.

Louella approached, her mask dangling loosely from her chin while she took small sips from her bottle.

"No," she said.

"We're from Belleville," Izzy explained. "We got turned around while hiking in the woods."

Louella raised an eyebrow skeptically. "Hiking in the woods?"

"Yes, we came to visit my grandparents' grave," Izzy replied, the lie weighing heavy on her tongue. "What is happening here?" she asked, gesturing toward the lifeless bodies around them.

The two local women exchanged puzzled looks. The first woman narrowed her eyes, suspicion creeping into her expression as though she suspected Izzy was making a sick joke.

"What do you think is going on?" she snapped, her voice weary and edged with anger. "People are dying from the plague worldwide, and you hiked fifty-six kilometres to visit your grandparents' grave?" She scoffed in disbelief, turned on her heel, and strode away.

Izzy turned to Louella, a frown tugging at her lips. "The Black Plague?"

"The Crimson Plague," Louella corrected. "You know, because they all bleed out in the end." Her voice dropped to a whisper. "Dr. McKenzie-King is just exhausted. There aren't many of us left to help her."

As Louella moved to aid the doctor, Dax faced Izzy, anger sparking in his eyes. "Damn that Marlo," he muttered.

"He dropped us right in the middle of a pandemic," Izzy whispered back, her voice trembling with fear as the gravity of their situation took hold. They were trapped, unable to escape until Marlo chose to retrieve them . . . if he ever did. As the cries of the suffering echoed around them, they could do nothing but wait, their future clouded in uncertainty.

CHAPTER TWENTY-ONE

THE WORLD THAT NEVER WAS

A short while later, Izzy and Dax were engrossed in a whispered conversation, considering their next course of action. Louella had ventured off to fetch more water, momentarily leaving them alone. Meanwhile, Dr. McKenzie-King seemed oblivious to their presence, focusing on the afflicted patients at the far end of the gazebo.

The distant growl of a vehicle sounded through the empty street, drawing their attention. A battered, brown pickup truck rumbled to a stop before them, its tires stirring up dust. With a creak, the passenger door swung open, revealing a tall, robust woman. Her long, blond braid swayed against her shoulder as she leaped out of the vehicle, laughter still playing on her lips.

Surprise flickered in her gaze as it settled on Izzy and Dax, her face quickly becoming a broad smile. The smile, however, was short-lived—it swiftly turned to panic when she realized she was without her mask. She glanced toward Dr. McKenzie-King and, with hurried movement, pulled her crumpled mask from the pocket of her overalls, fitting it securely in place. Meanwhile, the driver's door slammed shut with a finality that drew their eyes. The noise was jarring in the quiet street. An older man came into view as he rounded the front of the truck, his expression stoic, giving nothing away.

"Well, howdy there," the woman greeted, drawing near to Izzy and Dax. "You folks ain't from around these parts, are ya?"

Izzy's response was practised, smoother this time. "My grandparents were born and raised here," she shared. "We came to pay our respects at their gravesite but ended up getting lost in the woods."

"Who were your grandparents?" the woman asked, stooping to fasten her shoelace. "Name's Jody Cassidy, by the way."

"Edward and Gertrude Adams," Izzy replied. "I'm Izzy, and this is Dax," she added, gesturing toward her soulmate.

Jody rose, a spark of recognition igniting in her eyes. "Oh, hey, I remember them! They used to buy eggs from our farm!" Her expression softened as she continued, "I heard about their son . . . your dad, I suppose. I'm sorry for your loss."

Izzy tensed, a pang of grief clenching her chest. Even here, the haunting shadow of her father's death seemed inescapable. "Thanks," she murmured. Her gaze drifted to the man who had arrived with Jody. He was hunched over a covered body, his arms embracing the lifeless form as he struggled to lift it onto the back of the truck.

Jody noticed Izzy's gaze and quickly moved to help him. "Ya gonna take a break, Caleb?" Jody asked as she bent down to lift the feet of the body.

"No," came Caleb's gruff reply, weary but resolute.

The guttural sounds of retching drew Izzy's attention to Dr. McKenzie-King. The doctor was struggling to roll a patient onto his side, spittle and blood spraying onto her hospital gown. Izzy dashed forward to help. The man's body convulsed abruptly, his spine arching violently before he slumped back, his eyes devoid of life.

Dr. McKenzie-King checked the man's pulse, her expression sombre. "We've lost another one," she called out.

Caleb, his head bowed, gave a silent nod as he and Jody lifted another corpse onto the truck.

The doctor's gaze landed on Izzy as if only just noticing her. She zeroed in on Izzy's bare hands and barked, "Gloves!" Then, without further comment, she turned and collapsed into a nearby camping chair, her slouched form mirroring the defeat that shadowed her eyes.

Jody approached Izzy, a floral print bedsheet clasped in her hands. Her voice shook as she spoke. "That was Mr. Peterson," she murmured. "He was my high school math teacher."

Caleb joined them at the table, and together, they wrapped Mr. Peterson's body. Dax came forward with visible reluctance, his unease clear as he helped carry the deceased man over to the truck bed.

Louella reappeared from the store, her arms holding a case of bottled water. "Over here," she beckoned, nodding toward a group of empty chairs spaced away from the gazebo.

Jody, visibly relieved, quickly made her way to Louella, taking a water bottle with a nod of thanks and sinking into a chair. Meanwhile, Caleb accepted his water without a word and withdrew to the solitude of his truck. Louella glanced at Izzy, shrugging as if Caleb's behaviour was to be expected.

Shifting her chair back away from the others, Louella broke the silence. "So," she began, "what's it like in Belleville? Do you still have power? Ours went out three days ago."

Izzy twisted the cap off her water, taking a long sip before answering. "Yeah, ours is out too."

Louella nodded as if she had anticipated such a response. "I heard they called in the military for assistance, but that was weeks ago . . . did Belleville receive any support? We never received any."

Beside her, Dax gave a slight shake of his head, his eyes evading hers.

"Strange," Louella mused thoughtfully. "Considering how close Belleville is to the airbase, I would have expected . . . Oh well, never mind." She took a sip of her water and reclined in her chair.

"We could've really used their help," Jody said, setting her nearly empty water bottle down at her feet. "We lost a lot of our elderly in the first few weeks," she added, her eyes tearing up.

"Most people are staying indoors, leaving only for essential supplies," Louella remarked, smoothly shifting the conversation to a different topic.

"What's the deal with all the white bed sheets draped around the houses?" Dax asked.

A shadow crossed Louella's face. "That's how they signal if someone has passed away inside. Jody and Caleb are responsible for collecting and transporting the bodies for burial."

"Oh," Dax said, the word escaping his lips softly. The group fell silent—the only noise from the pained moans within the gazebo.

"Well, what are ya going to do now?" Jody finally asked, her fingers playing with the silver buttons on her overalls.

"I guess go back to Belleville," Izzy said.

Jody's eyes sparkled with excitement. "Tell you what, how about you let Caleb and I give you a ride? We were gonna go after we dropped off this last load. The town is running low on supplies."

"Oh . . . well, that would be great. Thanks."

Jody rose abruptly, her camping chair wobbling. "Well, I suppose we better get going. Caleb doesn't like to sit too long."

"Thank you," Dax said, nodding at Louella. He glanced at Dr. Mckenzie-King, still slumped in her chair, snoring softly. "I would say goodbye, but . . ."

"Don't," Louella replied, the corners of her eyes crinkling with laughter. "Trust me, you'd regret it the moment you tried."

They bid Louella farewell and made their way back to the truck. Dax leaned closer to Izzy. "So, Belleville?" he said, his eyebrows arched questioningly.

Izzy shrugged. "We can see if my Aunt Audrey is still around in this timeline. If not . . . We'll find somewhere to hide until Marlo pulls us out."

Reaching the truck, Jody yanked open the rusty back door and gestured for them to climb in. "All right with you if we bring them along to Belleville?" she asked Caleb, settling into the front seat beside him. Caleb gave a noncommittal grunt and turned the ignition key, the vehicle groaning in protest before it rumbled to life.

As the truck pulled away from the curb, Jody twisted in her seat and began speaking animatedly. After a moment, she removed her mask, stuffing it between the seats. "Hope you don't mind," she said, rolling down the window to allow a refreshing breeze to sweep in. "I figure I'm probably immune by now if I haven't caught it already. Besides, it's hard to talk in one of those darn things."

"Um . . ." Izzy began, but Jody didn't wait for her to finish.

"My dad owns the slaughterhouse off 62, so I'm used to all the death. Doesn't faze me one bit, 'cept, of course, when it's someone you know," she said, her voice quivering. Jody paused to collect her thoughts. "My dad had planned to pass down the farm to my older brother, but they're no longer with us. So, I guess I'll be inheriting it after all. It's just me and my gran now." She offered Izzy a warm smile. "Anyway, that's enough about me. What about you guys? I heard you grew up in Toronto, Izzy. What was that like?"

The conversation continued as they drove further from Madoc—townhouses giving way to stretches of tree and underbrush. Before long, a shimmering lake unfolded before them. Its surface was a mesmerizing tapestry of blues and greens. Quaint cottages and boathouses dotted the shore, enhancing the charm. Yet, despite the summer heat, the beach lay deserted. The dock was quiet, untouched by the excitement of swimming children. The road then curved right, guiding them away from the lake's allure and up a steep hill.

Towering trees flanked their path, their canopies sporadically broken by homes tucked with the greenery. Izzy, keen to divert the conversation from herself, leaned forward. "And what about you, Caleb? Do you have any family in this area?"

"Dead," Caleb replied curtly, his gaze fixed on the road ahead.

"I'm sorry to hear that," she murmured.

Caleb grunted, and the air inside the vehicle thickened with awkwardness. After a pause, Jody turned to Izzy and Dax with manufactured brightness. "So Dax, how did you and Izzy meet? College?"

Before he could respond, a bang echoed through the truck, sending it careening to the side. Caleb's hands clenched the steering wheel, his arms rigid as he wrestled for control. With deft movements, he brought the truck to a standstill, a cloud of gravel ballooning around them as they came to rest at the roadside.

As the dust settled around the truck, Izzy's fingers slowly relaxed their hold on Dax's arm. She glanced at him, a knot of unease in her stomach. Exhaustion swept over her, leaving a residue of shock as the adrenaline ebbed away.

"It's okay, Iz," Dax murmured, pulling her close. Izzy shifted, resting her head against the comfort of his chest, her eyelids squeezed shut as she focused on steadying her breath.

Outside, Jody and Caleb had exited the truck. Then, cutting through the calm, Caleb's voice erupted. Izzy, her curiosity piqued, extracted herself from Dax and stepped out of the vehicle. Dax was quick to follow.

They joined Caleb and Jody on the passenger side. "All four tires are shredded," Jody explained, looking up at them. Rising to her feet, she walked back toward the road, her blond braid swaying in rhythm with her steps.

"Hey, Caleb," she called out, bending down to retrieve a glimmering object from the road. "What do you think this is?" She held up a spiked metal strip, the sunlight glancing off its sharp points.

Caleb's expression hardened. "A spike strip," he muttered, the colour draining from his face. "Jody, get back over here." His voice was sharp with urgency.

"What?" Jody's response floated back, laced with bewilderment as she moved toward them.

"Get back over—" Before Caleb could finish, a chilling whistle cut through the air, ending in a sickening thud. Jody's cry shattered the stillness. She took a faltering step backward, shock splintered across her features, and then collapsed—the handle of an axe protruding from her head.

Time seemed to stop. A suffocating silence wrapped around them as Izzy's pulse thundered in her ears. Jody's still form lay in the road, the liveliness and warmth she had once radiated brutally extinguished. A quiet sob broke from Izzy, muffled by her hand as sorrow gripped her, bending her body with its weight.

Abruptly, a strong pull at her arm drew her down, Dax's arms enfolding her as they crouched together. The sound of footsteps disturbed the quiet, approaching from the other side of the road. Fear swirled through Izzy's thoughts, a torrent of questions about what might come next.

CHAPTER TWENTY-TWO

THE PRICE OF MAGIC

"Yeee, boy!" a voice bellowed from the edge of the woods, followed by a chorus of hooting and catcalling.

"Ya got 'er clean in the head, Willy," a deep, male voice rang out.

"Yup. Wasn't hard to miss. The woman was a giant," responded another, his voice brimming with pride.

As the men clambered over the ditch and neared Jody's body, their voices grew louder. Izzy shrunk further into Dax's arms. Her shoulders and chest tightened with each passing moment, constricting her breath as her heart pounded wildly against her ribcage.

The air was filled with a sickening, squelching sound as the axe was pulled from Jody's head, followed by a burst of crude laughter that turned Izzy's stomach.

"Ya gonna wash that axe off first, Willy?" a man with a high-pitched, nasally voice asked.

"Heck no," Willy drawled slowly, "gives it character."

The deep-voiced man chuckled. "Did ya see 'er drop like a sack of potatoes?"

"Yeah, man, she went down hard," Willy replied, his voice tinged with satisfaction.

As the men revelled in their kill, Caleb sent a sharp glance to Izzy and Dax. From his position by the front tire, he pressed his fingers to his lips, signalling silence. Then he motioned for them to start crawling toward the safety of the woods' edge.

Willy's voice sliced through the tension, halting them mid-motion. "Come on out, old man. We just want your supplies."

After a tense pause, the high, nasally voice broke the quiet. "We won't hurt ya . . ."

The snickering that followed did little to ease Izzy's fear. Caleb shot another look at Izzy and Dax, his nod resolute as if making a decision.

"You've been warned, old man. Come on out now, and we'll let ya go on your way," Willy called out, a note of impatience colouring his tone.

"Don't," Izzy whispered to Caleb as he slowly rose. He cast a fleeting glance at them and tipped his head subtly toward the woods, silently imploring them to escape. He emerged from the truck's front, advancing cautiously toward the men with his hands raised in surrender.

"We can't just leave him," Izzy said, inching forward for a glimpse from behind the front of the truck.

"He's giving us a chance," Dax murmured, his breath a warm caress against her ear. "I don't think they know we're here. We need to move now!" His hand found hers, fingers intertwining in a silent plea.

But Izzy gently disengaged from his grip, repositioning herself for a better view. Her gaze locked onto Caleb as he neared the group of men. Willy was standing with an untied boot on Jody's outspread braid, idly twirling the bloody axe handle. His gaze sharpened on Caleb, who stopped short, leaving a cautious distance between them.

"There aren't any supplies in the truck, boys," Caleb stated calmly, his hands still held high above his head.

"What are ya talkin' 'bout, old man. It's full of supplies," Willy said, jabbing a finger at the truck bed.

"Dead bodies," Caleb replied, his voice devoid of emotion.

As Willy raked a hand through his dishevelled brown hair, suspicion etched into his features. "You're lying," he said sharply, then he turned and nodded toward one of his friends. "Go check it out, Jeff."

Izzy huddled close to Dax, her palms growing sweaty. The sound of Jeff's heavy boots approached, growing louder until he reached the rear of the vehicle and flung the tailgate open.

The air, thick with a charged silence, was broken by the harsh sound of someone retching. A pungent, acrid stench followed.

"He ain't lying, Willy," Jeff gasped between gagging fits.

"Now what?" the nasally-voiced man complained, his arms folded in a display of irritation as he shot a resentful look at Willy. "You promised we'd be bringing home supplies tonight. Lorna's gonna kill me if I show up empty-handed!"

"Shut up, Eric," Willy snapped, his face contorting into an ugly scowl. "We'll just have to head to town then, start checkin' out some houses." His eyes settled on Caleb, and a malicious grin crawled across his face, exposing a crooked set of teeth. "We'll start with his place first."

While he spoke, Izzy's attention was drawn to a peculiar sight—a pink mist danced within Caleb's fingers. It swirled around, glittering in the afternoon light.

Her nudge was urgent against Dax's side. "Do you see that?"

"He's a wizard," Dax murmured, his eyebrows shooting up in wonder.

Izzy's mouth fell open. "Seriously? A wizard?"

"Yeah."

Izzy watched as Caleb snapped his wrist in Willy's direction and yelled, "*Serpentstoneola!*" in a commanding voice.

As the pink erupted from Caleb's fingers, Willy's hands shot up in surprise. The mist swirled around Willy, seeping into his skin. His mouth dropped open, his face donning a comical expression. A grey pallor swiftly overtook his skin, and in moments, he was immobilized, his form solidified into stone.

Izzy watched as Caleb staggered backward, exhaustion carving deep lines into his face as he struggled to steady himself. "What's wrong with him?" she whispered to Dax.

"He used up most of his energy with that spell. Magic comes with a cost," Dax said. "We should go, Iz," he urged, gently tugging at her arm.

"We can't leave him, Dax."

"Izzy, they have weapons, and we don't. He went out there so we'd have a chance to get away. Don't waste his sacrifice."

As Izzy glanced back, she saw Eric close in on Caleb, a knife flashing in his grip. Eric pounced, but Caleb, though visibly weakened, managed to cry out, *"Whirligigium!"*

The spell took immediate effect—Eric was hoisted into the air, his form twisting as he tried to fight the invisible force. He flipped onto his back, his knees jerked to his chest, and he began to spin. His screams pierced the air as Jeff scrambled to pull him down.

Caleb slumped against Willy's stone statue, beads of sweat trickling down into his grizzled beard. He glanced toward the truck and locked eyes with Izzy. He mouthed a single word to her—"Run."

She hesitated and then shook her head no. Caleb fixed her with a stern gaze, his lips moving in a silent incantation. A strong gust of wind struck, hurling Izzy and Dax backward into the ditch.

They landed in a muddy patch surrounded by cattails and weeds. "Don't make Caleb waste any more energy on us," Dax whispered, helping her up. On their hands and knees, they moved forward toward the forest.

They scrambled up the steep embankment, stumbling into a thicket of pines. Sharp branches scraped against their skin as they ran. After what seemed like an eternity, they emerged into a small clearing. Exhausted, Izzy collapsed onto a fallen log, clutching her side and struggling to catch her breath.

"This isn't right, Dax," she said, mustering the strength to stand again. "We need to go back to help."

"Izzy, we could get killed. If that happens, we'll pop back into Marlo's store, and Priscilla might still be there," Dax replied, stepping forward to block her path.

"It's been hours, Dax. She's probably gone by now," Izzy said, attempting to sidestep him.

"Time works differently here, Iz. It's likely only been minutes since we left," Dax explained, gently removing a twig from her blond hair. As his hands brushed her face, a distant bang rang out. Startled by the sudden noise, Izzy clung to his arm.

"We need to go back for him," she insisted, her blue eyes welling up with tears.

"Iz, this is just a simulation of an alternative timeline in our universe. The real Caleb is back on your Earth," Dax said, taking her hands into his. "I know it feels real, but it's just Marlo's magic. The people here are duplicates . . . they don't have souls." He gently pulled her into his arms, stroking her hair to comfort her. Izzy sank into his embrace, her eyes closing as hot tears spilled down her cheeks and soaked into his cotton shirt.

"I still feel awful leaving him behind."

"I know."

A cracking noise resounded behind them, followed by the heavy thud of approaching footsteps. Dax released Izzy, quickly picked up a fallen branch, and wielded it like a baseball bat. At the same time, Izzy seized a large rock from the ground.

The snapping of twigs underfoot startled a flock of birds into flight, their wings fluttering noisily above. Seconds later, a man lurched into the clearing, his movements heavy and uncoordinated. Tripping over the gnarled roots of a tree, he crashed into Dax, and they both tumbled to the forest floor in a chaotic heap.

Izzy rushed over, her rock poised overhead, ready to be thrown. She halted, gradually lowering her stone, and then dropped it on the ground. "Caleb!" Recognition dawned as she gazed at the older man sprawled at her feet. He returned her look through half-closed eyes, his complexion pale and smeared with blood. With a groan, his head lolled to the side, his hand falling away from his waist to unveil the blood-soaked fabric of his shirt.

Izzy struggled to process what she was seeing. Blood seeped from the wound, staining the pristine forest floor crimson. Her eyes flickered to Dax, who was trying to stand. His face had lost its usual colour, now a ghastly pale at seeing Caleb's injury. The idea that Caleb was merely a soulless duplicate seemed ludicrous now—his agony, the very essence of his life seeping into the ground, felt all too real.

163

Overcome with a paralyzing sense of helplessness, Izzy felt her mind racing to act. Yet, she remained immobilized by the horrific sight. She yearned to do something—anything—to stem the flow of blood, to save him, but her limbs were leaden, her brain numbed by shock. The world around her seemed to blur, and her pulse thundered in her ears, each beat echoing the life ebbing away before her.

CHAPTER TWENTY-THREE

A Gruesome Discovery

Jerking back to reality, Izzy moved toward Caleb. She quickly peeled off her sweater and pressed it against his wound. Dax was right beside her, and together, they helped Caleb into a sitting position.

"I'm fine," he insisted through clenched teeth, gently pushing them away to look at the injury. Lifting his blood-soaked shirt, he revealed a deep wound with a jagged piece of metal protruding from it.

"We heard a gunshot," Izzy said, her eyes widening as she looked at the metal. "Is that a bullet fragment or something?"

Caleb's chuckle was feeble, and it quickly turned into a wince as his wound seeped more blood. "It wasn't a gunshot," he said with a rough edge to his voice. "I used an incineration spell. The fire got out of control and blew up the truck," he admitted, regret tainting his words.

Dax's eyes shifted toward the woods. "So, they're all dead then?"

"Yes, nothing left to see but scorched dirt," Caleb confirmed, a sombre expression crossing his features. "Jody is gone now, too," he murmured, his voice heavy with grief.

"I'm really sorry," Izzy said. A wave of grief washed over her as she thought of the warm-hearted farmgirl. Visions of their brief time together swarmed her thoughts.

Caleb just nodded his jaw firm, retreating into a heavy silence. Another wince crossed his face as he looked down at his injury, his eyes sharpening with discomfort. Ignoring the protests from Izzy and Dax, he seized the metal shard and jerked it out, flinging it away. The trickle of blood that followed was more pronounced now, staining the fabric of his jeans.

"You shouldn't have done that," Dax said, applying pressure to the wound.

Caleb swatted away Dax's hand. "I'll be fine."

A delicate, pink mist seeped from Caleb's fingertips, hovering around the wound before gently settling into the marred flesh. Izzy's eyes widened in amazement as the laceration began to close before her, the torn skin weaving itself back into wholeness until only a minor cut was left.

"Was that the last of your energy?" Dax asked, concern lacing his voice. He swiftly wrapped Izzy's sweater around Caleb's waist, safeguarding the wound. Offering a steadying arm, he assisted the other man to his feet. Caleb wobbled unsteadily, leaning heavily on Dax for support.

"Yup, best I could do," Caleb responded, his eyelids drooping with exhaustion. "Won't be much use to you now." A deep yawn escaped him. "Might as well leave me here. I need to close my eyes for a bit."

"Don't be ridiculous," Izzy said, stepping closer to Caleb and slipping his free arm over her shoulder. "You can't stay here. It's not safe."

With Izzy on one side and Dax on the other, they began the journey back through the woods toward the highway. The sun's rays pierced the thick canopy above, bathing them in heat. As sweat drenched their backs, they shouldered the full weight of Caleb, who had fallen into a deep sleep.

"So, witches and wizards actually exist?" Izzy asked, a hint of breathlessness in her voice as they climbed a rocky incline.

"Witches, warlocks, vampires . . . they're all real."

Surprised, Izzy nearly lost her footing on the loose soil. "I thought I was losing my mind," she confessed.

"What do you mean?"

As they continued their ascent, Izzy described her encounters with Emily and the disturbing visions that had been haunting her. "So Emily's a witch then," she concluded, brushing away sweat from her forehead.

Relief spread across Dax's features as they crested the hill. "Almost there," he said, batting away the black flies that buzzed persistently around his head. He glanced at Izzy, continuing, "And yes, Emily is a witch, and so is your friend Rhylynn."

Izzy halted in her steps. "Rhylynn? A witch? I don't think so, Dax. I would have noticed," she said firmly, shaking her head.

Dax arched an eyebrow, pausing to lean on a nearby tree for support. "Oh, would you have?" he said, his tone skeptical. "She's the one who put the hex bag in Melanie's purse," he added, carefully easing Caleb to the ground as the man let out a loud snore. "I saw her do it."

Izzy gaped at Dax, absorbing his words. "Rhylynn, a witch," she repeated, her face knitting in contemplation. "I suppose . . . I mean, she always smells like herbs. I just thought it was because she likes to cook. And then there was that eye I saw on her grandma's door . . ."

Dax stretched out, popping his back before leaning over to get a firm grip on Caleb's arms. "Think you can carry his feet?" he asked Izzy, nodding toward Caleb's dusty brown work boots. "It might be easier to carry him this way."

Izzy nodded, bending down to lift Caleb's legs. "So, supernatural beings . . . are they like special souls or something?"

"No. Any soul can incarnate in a supernatural body. It will just cost you more tokens," Dax said, guiding them past a broad tree.

"Tokens?"

"Yeah. If you want to incarnate, you need to earn tokens."

Izzy adjusted her hold on Caleb's legs, her fingers tightening around the fabric of his jeans. "I was under the impression that one of the upsides to dying was not having to work anymore."

Dax chuckled, offering her an amused grin. "Well, you don't *have* to work. Most souls do, though. Reincarnation is appealing. It's like a vacation, really."

"I guess it does make sense," she mused, glancing at him. "So, what kind of job do you have?"

Dax hesitated, the slight redness on his neck betraying his discomfort. "Oh, well, I just pick up different roles here and there. I thought about becoming a spirit guide, but it takes up a lot of your time . . ." He looked away from her shyly. "Hey, isn't that a driveway up ahead?"

Izzy followed his gesture to where a gravel driveway snaked through the trees. As they approached, a large, two-storey brick house came into view. The once-manicured lawn was now a tangle of weeds, and the house stood silent.

They positioned Caleb down near a red Toyota parked in the driveway and then turned their attention to the building. "You stay with Caleb," Dax said, moving toward the front door.

Izzy rolled her eyes and quickly caught up, brushing past Dax to press the doorbell firmly. A loud, resonant chime echoed inside the house. After a brief pause, she pushed it again, complementing the ringing sound with loud knocks, her knuckles rapping sharply against the wood.

"Maybe they're too afraid to come to the door," Dax said, leaning on the stair railing as he surveyed their quiet surroundings.

Izzy's gaze shifted to the narrow window beside the door. A shadow crossed her expression, her smile disappearing. Pressing her lips into a thin grimace, she said, "No. It's not that."

Her fingers wrapped around the door handle, the metal warm to the touch, as she turned it slowly. With a quiet creak, the door opened, unleashing the vile stench of sulphur and decay.

Dax's complexion lost its colour, taking on a greenish hue as he grimaced, his hand flying to his mouth. "I'm going to be sick," he muttered, a hint of panic in his voice before he spun around, dashing down the steps.

Izzy raised an eyebrow at Dax's retreating form before pivoting and stepping into the entranceway. There, amid the white tiles and exquisitely carved wooden bench, was a woman splayed out in a pool of decay. Her body was bloated, her skin a nightmarish palette of plum and crimson, stretched tight by the gasses within. Her head was turned in Izzy's direction, the tongue swollen and lolling out—her eyes bulging unnaturally out of their sockets.

Steadying her stomach, Izzy approached the body, ignoring the swarm of flesh flies that feasted upon the remains. She was no stranger to witnessing bodies in differing stages of decomposition. Yet, she had to admit, she'd never encountered one quite this ghastly.

A wave of compassion washed over Izzy as she pictured the woman in her final moments—the desperate gasps for breath as she scrambled to reach the door. She had met with an excruciating end, wracked by pain and all alone.

Izzy shivered and diverted her gaze from the corpse, focusing instead on the purse nearby, its contents scattered across the floor. Keys glittered back at her, partially submerged in a puddle of decomposing fluid near the woman's arm.

She inched forward and crouched down to retrieve them. As her fingers curled around the cool metal, a beetle scurried out from beneath the woman's skin, trailing a slimy streak of ooze in its wake. Its movement caused the skin to slip off, collapsing onto the floor with a nauseating, wet thud.

Startled, Izzy stumbled backward, knocking into a vase by the wall. It crashed to the ground, its shards flying across the room. Clutching the keys tightly, Izzy turned on her heel and fled the house, leaping over the entrance steps in her rush to leave the gruesome scene behind her.

Dax reappeared from around the side of the building, his pallor a stark contrast to his usual demeanour. "Everything okay, Iz?"

"Yup, I'm fine. I found the car keys. Do you want to drive?" she asked, lobbing them in his direction. He caught them, but his expression soured as he registered the body residue on them. Suppressing a gag, he dropped the keys and bolted toward the bushes for a second time. Laughing, Izzy retrieved the keys and wiped them off against the grass.

"That wasn't funny," Dax grumbled, returning minutes later.

"Not even a little bit?"

"Not in the slightest," he said, moving to help her as they made Caleb comfortable in the backseat.

"I'm sorry."

Dax's expression softened as he looked at her. "Let's just put all this behind us," he said softly. "We'll find a quiet place around here to ride this nightmare out, okay?" He shut the back door and then slid into the passenger seat. "Let's head back to town first. Drop Caleb off with the doctor."

Izzy nodded as she made her way to the driver's side. The engine hummed to life, and the air conditioner kicked in. They drove in silence, the scenic lake they passed earlier now enveloped in the soft, golden light of the setting sun, the surface of the water shimmering in hues of deepening orange.

Within minutes, they arrived back in town. Izzy maneuvered the car to a stop beside the gazebo. Before the engine could even cool, an exasperated voice confronted them. "Why are you back?" Dr. McKenzie-King marched toward the vehicle, her eyes sharp with irritation. "For God's sake, put your masks on," she scolded, halting at a safe distance.

Izzy quickly retrieved hers from her pocket and secured it over her face. Dax, looking slightly mortified, made his way to the supply table and came back wearing a new one. Following close behind him was Louella, her face creased with concern. "Where is Caleb and Jody?" she asked.

Dax spoke softly as he moved to stand beside Izzy. "We were ambushed on the road," he said. "Jody . . . she didn't make it. We got away, but Caleb was hurt," he explained, nodding toward the backseat of the Toyota where Caleb lay motionless. "I'm really sorry," he added as Louella burst into tears.

Dr. McKenzie-King, taking command, strode over to the car and yanked the door open. "Help me get him out," she ordered. With Dax's help, they lifted Caleb carefully from the backseat and carried him to a nearby table.

"He was injured on his side," Dax said, pointing to Caleb's blood-soaked shirt. "He pulled out the metal piece before we could stop him."

"Stupid man," the doctor muttered, snipping Caleb's shirt open with a pair of scissors. "Louella, save your tears for later," she said, gesturing for her assistant to join her.

"What can we do?" Izzy asked.

"Nothing," the doctor said, her hands already cleaning Caleb's wound.

Louella's voice, heavy with sadness, broke in, "I live at the end of the street—the house with the red roof. Go there for the night."

"Thank you," Dax said.

Leaving the downtown area behind, Izzy glanced around. The streets emanated a sense of desolation, underscored by white towels tied around trees and mailboxes. "I can't believe this could've been the current timeline on Earth," she said, removing her mask and shoving it into her pocket.

As they neared a cozy, one-storey home, a sweet, childish voice filled the air. A little girl, no older than four, sat on the front lawn. She sang softly, her small hands busy with toys in the tall grass. When Izzy and Dax approached, the girl looked up and waved, her smile bright and unguarded. Izzy returned the wave.

The exchange was cut short when a woman, visibly pregnant, came over quickly. She picked up the child, eyeing Izzy and Dax with caution as they passed.

"Why would anyone choose to reincarnate into a world like this?" Izzy asked as she quickened her pace, eager to escape the mother's hostile stare.

"You can experience so much more when you have a physical body, Iz. Everything tastes better and smells better. Plus, there's a lot you can learn, even in a place like this," Dax replied, slipping his mask off.

Izzy shot him a skeptical look. "If you think it's so great, then why haven't you incarnated since I left? Why does your sister have to push you into it?"

Dax gently pulled her to a stop beneath a lilac bush stretching over the sidewalk. "The truth? I've been waiting for you," Dax admitted, his fingers brushing her cheek with deliberate tenderness. "I only want to reincarnate if you're by my side."

Izzy was taken aback by his confession. Warmth spread throughout her body, flooding her face with colour. She found herself staring into his eyes, unable to look away. A ripple of anticipation fluttered in her chest. Her fingers reached up to caress his face—grazing the rough stubble on his cheek and exploring the smooth scar along his jawbone.

"Izzy," Dax whispered, his hands cradling her face.

Closing the space between them, Izzy rose to her tiptoes, her lips meeting his in a kiss charged with soft electricity. Her breath caught, and when their lips parted, a smile blossomed on her face.

As Dax leaned over, his lips nearing hers again, a strange sensation swept over Izzy. The world around them began to lose its definition, edges blurring and colours melting away. A wave of nausea seized her. She tightened her hand around Dax's arm, seeking his steadiness. Then, just as suddenly, the sensation ebbed, leaving her breathless and confused. When she dared to open her eyes again, the streets of Madoc had vanished. They were somewhere else entirely.

CHAPTER TWENTY-FOUR

MOCHAS AND MEMORIES

Once more clad in her pyjamas, Izzy stood in Marlo's dusty little shop. She nervously scanned the room, her gaze cutting through the dust motes suspended in the air. Eventually, her eyes settled on Marlo. He appeared utterly unfazed, lounging in his swivel chair with his sneakers resting nonchalantly on the cluttered desk.

He fixed her with an intrigued look and sipped on a slushy, slurping up the last drops. He then crushed the cup in his hands. With the finesse of a skilled basketball player, he tossed the cup toward the large hoop across from his desk. It sailed through the air, the net swooshing as the cup passed. The lid of the garbage can swung open. To Izzy's astonishment, a fat, slimy tongue shot out, wrapped around the trash and retracted quickly. The lid slammed shut, but not before emitting a disgusting burp.

"Manners, Trevor," Marlo said, facing Izzy and Dax.

"Is Priscilla really gone?" Izzy asked.

"Indeed, she most certainly is," Marlo said, wiping his hands on his jeans. "My apologies for not bringing you back sooner," he continued, his legs coming off the desk as he sat up straighter in his chair. "A client walked in moments after your guide left. It appears that Meli coins are in high demand today."

Dax's eyes narrowed. "You left us there longer because you made another client a Meli coin?"

"Certainty not," Marlo said with a cheerful smile. "I refused to help him. Guides have Meli coins allotted to them for their duties. If he wanted one off the books, his intentions are likely less than honourable."

173

Dax looked at Marlo with interest. "Which guide was it?"

"To reveal such information would breach the sacred trust of confidentiality. It would not bode well for business," Marlo responded, his eyes gleaming from beneath the brim of his baseball cap.

"You're right. I shouldn't have asked," Dax said, his ears burning red.

"It's quite all right," Marlo said. "Now, tell me, did you enjoy your trip?"

"Did we enjoy our trip? You sent us to an apocalyptic timeline! What were you thinking?" Izzy narrowed her eyes at him as she folded her arms.

"Were you not hoping for an adventure?" Marlo asked, a half-smile playing on his lips. "Is that not why you came here for a Meli coin?"

"Not the kind of adventure we had in mind, Marlo," Dax said.

"My sincerest apologies." Marlo removed his cap to scratch at his tousled, silver-streaked hair.

Izzy approached the desk, her arms falling to her side. "That was definitely a dead timeline, right? It's not really going to happen, is it?" An anxious tingle spread across her neck as she waited for him to respond.

"No, Miss Adams. Rest assured, that particular timeline is no longer set in motion."

"How can you be so sure?"

Marlo stood, unfolding with a deliberate stretch. "In the timeline you just experienced," he began, his voice tinged with sadness, "the man who would have played a crucial role in developing the vaccine for the virus was murdered in a senseless hate crime years before the outbreak."

Marlo approached a nearby television screen and pushed it to one side, revealing a hidden safe. "In your current timeline," he continued, "this man is still alive, having never crossed paths with the officer who killed him. So, you see, Izzy, I am quite certain that timeline will never come to be.

He turned back toward them, holding a velvet bag. "Hate always has repercussions," he said, returning to his desk. "Carnies often focus on superficial distinctions like skin colour. But in the spirit world, those differences vanish. Here, every soul shines with equal brilliance, reflecting the intrinsic beauty within us all."

Marlo opened the bag, spilling its contents onto the desk. Several coins engraved with an *M* tumbled out. They produced a soft clinking as they collided. "Now, I believe this was what you came here for," Marlo said. He selected two coins and placed them into Dax's outstretched palm.

"Thank you," Dax said, his eyes lighting up.

"You're most welcome." Marlo cleared his throat and glanced at his wristwatch. "Now, I must be off, or I'll be late for the next Skyscuttle match." He strode toward the door, a spring in his step. "It's the Plasma Punks versus the Dainty Demons," he added, his voice tinged with excitement. He held the door open, a patient look on his face, as he waited for Izzy and Dax to step outside.

"You should take in some of the game before you head off on your next exciting adventure, Miss Adams," Marlo said, winking at Izzy. "I suspect you might find it highly entertaining."

He paused, eyeing Izzy's pyjamas. "Although," he added thoughtfully, "you may want to change your attire. You'll stand out like a sore thumb in your nightclothes." With a smile, he turned and ambled down the cobbled street, quickly becoming another face in the crowd.

"He's got a point," Dax said, turning to Izzy. "Regular clothing would help you blend in better."

"I don't have any tokens to buy new clothes."

"You don't need tokens. Just close your eyes and picture yourself in different clothing. Maybe think about your favourite outfit."

Following his instructions, Izzy squeezed her eyes closed, conjuring the vivid image of herself clad in her college sweatshirt and jeans. When she opened her eyes, her gaze fell upon the familiar faded blue of her sweater.

"That was a lot easier than trying to summon my spirit weapon," she said, a smile spreading across her face. She slipped her hands into her pockets and looked up at Dax. "So, what now?"

"I need to contact Maddy," Dax said, leading the way down the cobbled street lined with storefronts. A whimsically painted shop named Loki's Laughs and Nifty Novelties caught her eye. Through the glass, she saw several souls inside, laughing and indulging in candies. To her astonishment, a strange enchantment seemed to take hold of them, their bodies fading out until only their heads remained, bobbing like untethered balloons.

"Why do we need to contact your sister?" Izzy asked, reluctantly tearing her gaze away from the store.

"I made a deal with Marlo. I need to locate and retrieve a Bloodstone talisman in exchange for the Meli coins. It's somewhere in Salem, Massachusetts." He paused, stepping aside to make way for a group of animated trees—decorated with twinkling Christmas ornaments—to walk by. "Since Maddy works at the Akashic Hall of Records, she can find out who currently has it."

"Uh huh," Izzy murmured, gawking at the brightly lit trees as they meandered away, their bulbs bouncing in rhythm with their strides. She almost bumped into Dax when he came to an abrupt halt in front of a quaint building with grey stone walls. The entrance boasted a hefty wooden door intricately carved with mythical beings. The door was nestled between two windows, the wavy glass warping the inviting glow of the flickering lights inside.

Dax gestured toward a wooden plaque with elegant gold lettering above the door that read *Ancient Grounds.* "This is the only place Maddy will come to in Sparklafex."

"She's not going to be happy with us," he warned, pushing against the door. As it swung open, the tantalizing scent of freshly ground coffee drifted out, accompanied by the faint sound of piano music.

Izzy stepped into the café behind Dax. Her eyes were immediately drawn to the lofty ceilings crisscrossed with timber beams and the dark oak flooring beneath their feet. "Wow," she breathed out, coming to a halt. Across the room, through the glass wall, a pristine tropical beach was bathed in the warm gold of a stunning sunset.

The scenery changes with Thea's mood," Dax explained.

"Thea?"

Dax sank into a velvet armchair situated near the glass wall. "She's the owner of the café."

As Izzy took her place across from Dax, two menus appeared on the table as if by magic. "Crocodile Loaf," she read aloud, a quizzical arch forming in her brow as she looked at Dax.

He chuckled. "It's an ancient Egyptian dessert. It's only shaped like a crocodile. Thea can create any food or beverage ever made. It's one of her gifts."

"Another god?"

"Yup. Only gods can create on a grand scale. The rest of us average Joes are limited to things like controlling our appearance."

Izzy shook her head, lowering her menu to the table. "This is all . . . well, it's a bit overwhelming," she admitted, settling back into her seat.

"It won't be when your carnie life ends. Once they remove your memory block, none of this will seem strange," he said, gesturing to the room around them. Izzy's gaze wandered, taking in the peculiar assortment of souls lounging in armchairs around the room. She watched as a neon-pink blob inched toward a chair near the fireplace, a slick trail of slime marking its path.

"If you say so," she said.

Dax extended his hand and murmured, "*Flamma Nuntius.*" A small, flickering flame danced to life in his palm, and he began dictating a message to his sister. Once again, Izzy was mesmerized as the words elegantly swirled into existence within the orange glow. The message complete, Dax clenched his hand, extinguishing the flame.

"She should be here soon." Dax glanced toward the room's far corner, where a shining, circular metal platform was guarded by a figure shrouded in black. The man's face lay concealed under the deep shadow of his hood, secured at his neck with a pendant that bore an image of an eagle in flight above a thunderbolt.

"Who's that?"

"A member of the Guard," Dax replied. "They're the military of the spirit world." He pointed toward the metal platform where the man stood. "He's guarding the Transcendent Transmuter."

"The Transcendent Transmuter?"

"It's a way for souls to travel in the spirit world. This one allows travel between Orbistia and Sparklafex, but you must be an Orbistian to use it."

As he spoke, the air hovering above the Transcendent Transmuter stirred, rippling and quivering as though disturbed by an unseen force. Izzy watched, spellbound, as a spectral shape began to form, its contours flickering between solidity and mist. The figure sharpened gradually into the form of a woman. When Dax's sister finally took shape, her expression irritated. Her gaze swept the room in rapid assessment before fixing resolutely on their table.

"What were you thinking, Dax?" Maddy's voice cut through the room as she approached their table, her brown eyes alight with anger. "I can't believe you left me with that woman!" she complained, halting in front of them with her arms folded tightly.

"Sorry, Maddy," Dax said with a rueful grin. He rose and embraced his sister, then gestured to his seat. Despite her scowl, she took the offered chair, tucking her legs to the side of the table.

"*She* shouldn't be here," Maddy said, waving her hand dismissively toward Izzy. "You're going to get yourself into a lot of trouble."

"It's fine, Maddy," Dax replied, moving to stand behind Izzy, his hand resting on her shoulder. "Carnies astral project all the time."

"They don't make their way into Orbistia, Dax," Maddy said, her eyes darting toward Izzy.

"It's not my fault," Izzy said, fixing Maddy with a glare. She couldn't help but feel a growing dislike toward Dax's sister.

Before Maddy could reply, a woman with long, wavy brown hair approached. She laid a pale hand on Maddy's shoulder. Izzy observed as Maddy's posture softened, and a gentle smile crept across her face as she tilted her head up to greet the newcomer.

"Hey, Thea," Dax said, greeting her cheerfully.

"Good afternoon, Dax. And Izzy, what a nice surprise. It has been many years, has it not?" Thea responded warmly, gently setting down a steaming mocha for Maddy.

"Thank you, Thea," Maddy murmured, cradling the hot beverage.

"Izzy's astral projecting right now," Dax said.

Understanding flicked in Thea's eyes. "Oh. Well, I imagine this must all be strange to you." A steaming cup of coffee appeared in her hand, and she placed it in front of Izzy. "Everything looks better after a cup of coffee, don't you think?" she said, her laughter filling the room.

"I don't have anything to pay you with."

"Thea accepts happy memories as payment," Dax explained. "You just need to share one with her."

Izzy regarded Thea with hesitation. Did that mean parting with her memory forever, leaving an empty space in her mind?

Thea smiled down at Izzy, her face taking on a gentle expression as if reading her thoughts. "I do not keep them," she reassured Izzy. "I simply make a copy and use it to fuel my energy."

"All right then. I suppose that's okay."

Thea moved closer, placing her warm hand atop Izzy's. A wave of comfort embraced Izzy, and her eyes fluttered shut, a memory unfolding in her mind. She was transported back to her toddler years on the beach with her family. The sun's warmth kissed her skin, punctuated by the refreshing caress of lake water that lapped at her skin. The air was infused with the moist aroma of earth and a subtle hint of fish.

Kate swam toward Izzy, her body skimming the surface, letting the gentle waves bring her to shore. She knelt beside Izzy, cradling her chubby hands within her own. "On the count of three, we'll sit down together, okay? One. Two. Three!"

Together, they plopped down, Izzy's delighted squeal mingling with the splash as the cool water hugged her waist. Giggles escaped her lips as Kate scooped up the lake's mud, holding it aloft for Izzy to see as it oozed and slipped between her fingers.

The memory receded, leaving Izzy awash with nostalgia. There had been a time when her sister had made her feel safe and cherished. But those days were distant memories. She glanced at Thea, tears threatening to spill from her eyes, and quickly looked away before anyone could notice.

"Thank you," Thea murmured, her smile warm with understanding as she moved away.

Maddy's gaze locked onto Dax. "Why did you summon me?"

"I made a deal with Marlo for some more Meli coins."

"You did what?" Maddy's voice rose alarmingly, and she accidentally sloshed mocha from her cup. "Dax, I asked you to stay away from him!"

"He's not that bad."

"I don't trust him!"

"You don't trust anyone, Maddy!" Dax said, running his hand through his hair. "I want to have fun with Izzy before she returns to her body. You know, go to the top of Mount Everest, deep sea diving, that sort of thing."

Izzy felt the weight of Maddy's glare and recoiled into her chair. A pang of guilt gnawed on her—Dax was risking himself to help her. He had delayed his incarnation appointment, possibly losing his spot in line. Now, according to Maddy, he was breaking some rules for her. It suddenly dawned on her that Maddy's resentment might have some merit.

"I just need you to track down the last known whereabouts of the Bloodstone talisman last seen in Salem, Massachusetts. It was originally owned by a witch named Sarah Good," Dax said, his eyes widening as he pleaded with her. "Please, Maddy. I already made the deal, so I have to do it."

Maddy's hostile demeanour softened as she looked at her brother. "Fine," she relented with a sigh. She lifted her mocha, indulging in a deep sip, then rose to her feet. "I suppose you need this now," she added, straightening out her yellow blazer.

"Yes, please. Before Priscilla finds us," Dax replied, hugging her. "You're the best, Maddy!"

Maddy returned his hug and then turned to Thea and thanked her for the mocha. Ignoring Izzy, she made her way back to the Transcendent Transmuter.

She paused before the guard, who carefully scanned her with an unusual black device. It beeped, growing green in approval. The guard gave a curt nod, signalling her to step onto the metal platform. She cast one final glance at Dax, and then she started to fade from view until only her eyes were left floating in the air—they blinked once and then vanished from sight, leaving an empty void in their place.

CHAPTER TWENTY-FIVE

SPIDERS IN SILK SLIPPERS

After Izzy gulped down the final sips of her coffee, she and Dax set out into the throng of souls crowding the main street. They made their way toward the Astral Arena, deciding to take in the Skyscuttle match while waiting for Maddy to return. Dax led her through the city, passing by even more storefronts, each donning a unique name, like *Soulaxation* and *Spectral Treasures*.

Finally, they arrived at an immense arena that seemed to sprawl endlessly into the distance. A group of enthusiastic men, clad in vibrant red blazers with red and black ties, stood near the main entrance, eagerly distributing team merchandise. As they walked by, Izzy's eyes were drawn to the theatrical masks embroidered onto the breast pocket of their jackets. One of the men leaned toward her, offering a colourful team flag. It featured the image of a humanoid figure covered in green slime, sporting electric blue hair and nose rings.

As Izzy hesitated, Dax reassured her that no payment was necessary. "The games are organized by the Orbistian Bureau of Magical Entertainment and Athletics," he explained, guiding her into the building. "Most things are free in Orbistia. Skyscuttle matches are held in Sparklafex because our gods only permit Orbistians into their realm, and many teams are made up of immigrants."

"If the gods are so opposed to immigrants, then why do Thea and Marlo live in Sparklafex?"

"They aren't Orbistian. They're immigrants, too."

Before Izzy could respond, she and Dax were swept up by the crowd. The air buzzed with animated chatter as everyone eagerly made their way inside. Dax gripped her hand firmly, ensuring they wouldn't lose each other amid the swarm of souls. They followed the stream of people into the illuminated arena, quickly finding two seats near the railing that promised a perfect view of the unfolding action.

As they settled into their seats, the lights flickered out, plunging them into darkness as excited screams rippled through the area. "We made it just in time," Dax said, squeezing Izzy's hand.

Above the arena, fluorescent gobs of hot pink slime began forming on the ceiling, gradually building up before dropping onto the floor with a sickening splat. Izzy watched, fascinated, as other neon colours merged into drops of goo, creating a rainfall of colour in the darkness. Before long, the floor was coated in a thick kaleidoscope of slime.

From the concealed speakers, a voice erupted, "Brace yourselves for the arrival of the . . . Plasma Punks!"

Loud music tore through the arena, startling Izzy, so she jerked back in her seat. In the middle of the stadium, a figure with shocking green hair appeared, riding on a magic carpet adorned with metal studs and dangling chains. With a fierce expression, she belted lyrics in sync with the deafening music. One by one, five other riders emerged to join her.

As the music swelled in intensity, Izzy clamped her hands over her ears. Through the din, she caught a glimpse of Dax, who was singing along, his face lit up in a wide grin. Just as the music seemed about to swallow her whole, it stopped, leaving the Plasma Punks visibly disappointed.

A shiver raced down Izzy's spine as a chittering sound echoed through the arena. From above, a swarm of diminutive spiders began their descent, their grotesque forms at odds with the delicate satin slippers adorning each of their eight legs. Izzy couldn't suppress a high-pitched squeal, recoiling and pressing herself against the plastic chair.

What began as a sense of terror quickly dissolved into absurdity. As the demonic spiders touched down, they seemed bewildered, their hairy faces twisting in confusion. They slide across the slimy surface, bumping into each other. Their legs flailed about comically as they struggled to shake off the gooey plasma. The audience erupted in laughter, drowning out the anguished cries of the spiders.

"Not to be outdone, let's hear it for the Dainty Demons!" the announcer's voice boomed once more.

A new group of carpet riders emerged from thin air, garbed in gentle pastels. Their hair was woven in elaborate braids. Sailing through the arena on carpets embellished with bows and lace, they cast disdainful glances at the disarray beneath them.

Several Dainty Demons stood atop their carpets, shaking their fists indignantly at the Plasma Punks, who revelled in the crowd's laughter. The scene teetered on the edge of confrontation when a deep voice cut through the noise. In the centre of the arena, a hologram flickered into view, showcasing a bright green man with curly tusks that twisted into an absurd semblance of an elaborate mustache.

"Welcome, friends, to the opening game of the Skyscuttle season!" the man paused for dramatic effect. His grin broadened as the arena erupted in thunderous applause and cheers. "Joining us tonight, we have the Plasma Punks," he announced, gesturing toward the far corner—the team's eccentric-looking members bounced on their carpets, hooting and pounding on their chests. "And facing them, the Dainty Demons," the host continued, nodding toward the other team. The Dainty Demons responded with sulky glares directed at their rivals.

Izzy leaned back in her seat, her pulse quickening with anticipation. The Plasma Punks took to the air, zipping around the arena on their carpets.

"Representing the Plasma Punks, we have Merrick 68975, Zed 254, Frankie 54620, twins Sarah and Terra 235647, and of course, their beloved guardian, Yuko 14577."

The Plasma Punks delivered a performance that held the audience spellbound. They soared through the air, performing somersaults and daring acrobatics. The animated carpets they rode on pretended to buck them off.

Once the applause waned and the Plasma Punks retreated to their corner, the game host redirected the crowd's attention to the Dainty Demons. They gazed eagerly at the audience, ready to showcase their skills and claim their moment in the spotlight.

"Representing the Dainty Demons are Mildred 112235, Bob 159, Mercedes 54986, Coco 1124547, Raven 978452, and their guardian, Sandy-Ann 456482!"

Izzy watched as Bob 159 briefly lost command of his ride, spiralling through the holographic projection of the host. His hands clutched at the fringes of his carpet as he sought to regain control. The host, undisturbed, let out a robust chuckle, joining in the crowd's amusement as Bob 159 tumbled into another team member.

"What's with all the numbers?" Izzy asked, moving closer to Dax.

"The numbers represent the year we were born," Dax explained. "It's like our last name."

Izzy's brow knitted in confusion. "So . . . Bob 159 . . ." she began.

"Is really, really old," Dax interjected with a smirk. "Although you wouldn't know it. The guy doesn't seem to have much experience, and he's a bit of a dolt."

Their exchange was interrupted by the announcer's voice. "And now, what does the Bureau of Magical Entertainment and Athletics have in store for us tonight?" As he spoke, the ground quaked beneath them. The demonic spiders, previously stuck in slime, morphed into a formidable landscape of volcanic rock.

Towering boulders and skeletal trees sprang up, transforming the arena into a nightmare. At the epicentre stood a colossal volcano, spewing molten lava while dense ash and smoke billowed in the sky. The stadium stretched out, growing to encompass the new playing field.

Above the smoke, dragon-like shapes glided through the air, their shimmering scales intermittently visible through the dense ash. Izzy turned to Dax, her eyebrows raised in alarm.

I know it looks dangerous," he began, "but it's not. Souls can't die, remember?" He regarded her with a cryptic expression, hinting at a secret. "You're going to love Skyscuttle, Iz. Trust me."

Their focus shifted back to the arena as the announcer spoke again. "Ah, a volcanic wasteland, love it! A brilliant recovery from last year's closing games, which I am sure you all remember, included giant fluffy kittens and cotton candy clouds—how absolutely terrifying." The game host performed an exaggerated eye roll, provoking a few laughs from the stands.

He patted down his glittering gold suit and continued, "Well, let's just be glad that Game Developer Karen 64564 has incarnated back to Earth. Hopefully, we have kitten-free games for at least a hundred years, folks!" The crowd roared with laughter, and Izzy couldn't help but join in, caught up in the excitement.

"Okay, now on with the show! Each team will take their flag and hide it on their assigned side of the volcano!" The announcer's voice echoed through the arena as the two groups split up, heading in opposite directions. However, Bob 159 lingered behind; his eyes fixated on the Plasma Punks' guardian as she strategized with her team on the optimal location for their flag.

"Ahh, hold on a second, first a privacy spell to discourage peeking!" Bob 159's face fell in disappointment, and he changed direction, hurrying to catch up with the rest of the Dainty Demons. The game host chuckled. With a snap of his green fingers, he muttered, "*Secretum!*" Izzy's eyes widened in wonder as a pink shower of glitter enveloped each team, obscuring them from view.

A gentle hum began at Izzy's feet, drawing her attention downward. Within moments, a small screen emerged, rising to her eye level. It flickered on, offering a live glimpse of the Plasma Punks huddled in mid-discussion atop their carpets.

Izzy edged forward, entranced by the scene on the tiny screen. Yuko, the team's guardian, craned her spiky black head, surveying the game field. She clutched her team flag firmly in her hand and glided over to the rugged base of the volcano, dodging ash and sizzling fragments of rock. Hovering next to a burning log, Yuko wedged the flag into a well-concealed pile of stones. She then flew a short distance away, taking cover behind a collapsed hut.

"Risky move," Dax said.

"How so?"

"Their flag is practically on top of the division line for their territory. Too close if you ask me." His grin grew wider as a horn reverberated through the arena. The game was starting.

"All righty then, some quick rules before we start!" the game host bellowed. "Riders, if you fall off your carpet, you're out! The victory goes to the last team member still flying or the team that seizes their opponent's flag! No magic is to be used by any player unless they find a mystery ball! And remember, friends, this is a FULL contact sport, so get out there and have fun! Let the games begin!"

The Plasma Punks took to the skies, flying low beneath the ash clouds. Despite her clear vantage point from her seat, Izzy was drawn again to the television screen, seeking a closer look at the unfolding action. The camera zoomed in on Yuko, concealed behind the remains of the crumbling hut.

Izzy's pulse sped up as the first Dainty Demon crossed over the mountain, breaching the boundary into the Plasma Punk domain. At that moment, Yuko erupted from her hiding spot, a radiant blue orb pulsating in her grasp. Balancing on her carpet, she stood and took aim at the unsuspecting rider above.

As the orb made contact, it burst into a cloud of blue dust, trapping the Dainty Demon in a writhing net of dark serpents. The rider let out a startled cry as she plummeted to the ground. Izzy held her breath, riveted, as the earth cleaved open, swallowing the player up.

"Yuko 14577 takes out Mildred 112235 with a Medusa's hug! How did she get her hands on a mystery ball so soon?" As the announcer spoke, Yuko withdrew to the safety of her shelter. Izzy noted another pair of Dainty Demons navigating past the volcano, cautiously avoiding the residual blue mist.

"Clever girl," Izzy murmured, her smile broadening as she kept her eyes on the screen. "Now they're avoiding the area where the flag is hidden; they must think it's a trap."

A murmur fluttered through the audience, and Izzy turned to see what had captured their attention. Her sharp intake of breath punctuated the air as she spotted a player slicing through the skies, his bald head disappearing into the dark clouds as he flew higher. "What's he doing?"

"Trying to view the whole arena," Dax replied. "Stupid move. The game makers always have some aerial beast to patrol the skies—finding the flag from above would be too easy."

Izzy's breath caught again as a sinuous red tail flicked out from the clouds, vanishing as quickly as it appeared. Then, in one heart-stopping moment, a dragon burst forward, snatching the player in its jaws. The player's carpet drifted downward, disappearing into the volcano's depths.

"And the Plasma Punks lose Frankie 54620. Well, we all saw that coming! Don't worry, folks, he'll be pooped out whole later, good as new! What a game, what a game!"

Izzy watched as Bob 159 pumped his fist and performed a daring flip mid-air. His performance cost him more than just a few laughs. Unbeknownst to him, a pink-skinned Plasma Punk hurtled toward him. The collision sent Bob 159 into a tailspin, crashing into the side of the mountain.

"Bob 159 has been taken out by Terra 235647! It never pays to show off, folks. I guess age doesn't always reflect wisdom."

Laughter echoed across the venue, only to be replaced by a collective intake of breath as the crowd's focus snapped to the spectacle unfolding at the far end of the arena.

"It looks like Zed 254 has stumbled upon a mystery ball!"

The screen transitioned to a new scene. A wiry man with a mohawk soared through the air in pursuit of a beautiful woman wearing a frilly white dress. Her green eyes flashed with urgency as she coaxed her carpet into greater speed. The man took aim, hurtling the blue orb in her direction, grazing the edge of her rug.

Abruptly, it stiffened under the woman, catapulting her into the air. She collided with one of her teammates, and together, they spiralled downward. A chorus of cheers erupted from the audience, their applause thunderous. The game host's exhilarated voice echoed throughout the venue, "Brilliant shot, Zed 254! Mercedes 54986 and Coco 1124547 have been taken out. The Dainty Demons are now down to just two players!"

"This game is awesome," Izzy gushed, turning to look at Dax. But his attention was elsewhere, locked onto a stout woman navigating through the seats below them. From her elevated position, Izzy could spot the glimmer of the raven brooch the woman wore. Izzy's shoulders dropped.

"Are you freaking kidding me," she said, glaring down at the woman. "There are thousands of souls here, and she's still searching for me."

"She's persistent, that's for sure," Dax replied, gently tugging Izzy to her feet. "Come on, we need to go," he said, leading her toward the aisle.

Izzy allowed herself a final, longing glance at the game before trailing Dax through the dark drapes that concealed the exit. As the cheering from the arena faded behind them, a weight settled on Izzy's chest, knowing that Priscilla was always just a few steps behind them.

CHAPTER TWENTY-SIX

THE VAMPIRE'S EMBRACE

Dax guided Izzy along the narrow pathway tucked behind the shops they'd passed earlier on their way to the arena. With Priscilla's pursuit hanging over them like a dark cloud, they avoided the bustling main streets, rewinding their way back toward Ancient Grounds. After a harrowing sprint that lasted several minutes, they emerged into a quiet courtyard.

Izzy slid onto a stone bench beside Dax. "I don't think Priscilla saw us; we should be okay," he said, extending his legs in front of him.

"I wish we could have seen the rest of the game," Izzy murmured, a shadow of regret on her face. Visions of magical carpets and blue orbs danced in her thoughts.

She sighed and turned her attention to the small theatrical performance unfolding in the courtyard. An actor, wearing clothing reminiscent of the mid-eighteenth century, was barking orders at a trio of cowering figures. Their faces were hidden behind grotesque masks.

"What do we do now?" Izzy's voice drifted away as she watched the fake demons move awkwardly around the square.

"We wait for Maddy to summon us," Dax said, swatting away the hand of an overly eager demon as it reached out for him.

Izzy gave the actor a bemused look. He shrugged and wandered toward a group of onlookers gathering to watch the show.

"What's this all about?" Izzy nodded toward the demons, coaxing laughter from the crowd as they playfully grabbed at them.

"It's a reenactment of the Siege of Sparklafex." Dax chuckled. As they watched, a stilt-walking actor in faded brown trousers and a pinstriped jacket joined the demons. He flung a handful of blue powder above them. In response, the demons fell into a line dance, moving in harmony to a silent rhythm. The leader shook his cane at them and stormed into some nearby bushes.

"It was during the War for Orbistia," Dax continued, his eyes on the performance. "Satan led the attack on Orbistia, while the dark god Mammon of Midas sought to seize control of Sparklafex."

He pointed toward the stilt-walker who was attempting to join the line dance. His wooden legs became entangled, causing him to tumble into a nearby flowerbed. "That character is meant to portray Loki, an Orbistian god. He's one of the few deities who left our realm to help the refugees—he's a hero in Sparklafex."

"There was a war in the spirit world?" Izzy asked, sensing a familiar pull at her soul that she couldn't quite place.

A mournful expression settled on Dax's face as he replied. "Yes. We lost a lot of good souls to the demons. Whole families were captured."

Before Izzy could pose another question, a dense, black smoke filled the air before them. Words appeared within the smoke, written in swirling gold flames.

Meet me at Ancient Grounds—Maddy.

The smoke dissipated, leaving behind the lingering scent of charred wood. "Well," Dax said, rising from the bench, "that's our cue to leave."

"I wish we could stay and explore more," Izzy said, her gaze lingering on the courtyard. "But I really don't want Priscilla to erase my memories of all this . . . of you," she added, with a shy glance at Dax. "The further we get from her, the better."

They crossed the street to Ancient Grounds, where Maddy awaited them. As they approached, she rose, handing Dax a slip of paper. "Here. One of Sarah's descendants has the Bloodstone now."

Maddy then reached over, wrapping her arms around her brother tightly. "I still think this is a bad idea," she said, narrowing her eyes as she glanced at Izzy. After a moment, she stepped back, her voice tinged with urgency. "I can help you reschedule your incarnation appointment. I'm sure they would understand why you didn't show up."

Laughing, Dax playfully ruffled Maddy's hair. "I'll be fine, Maddy. Don't worry." As he drew away, he produced a Meli coin from his jacket. "I'll touch base with you when I get back." He then turned, flicking the coin in the air and said, "*Pasporta Dorasalite!*"

Instantly, a swirling vortex of green light erupted from the coin, hovering in the air beside them. Dax grasped Izzy's hand and led her to the portal. As they stepped through, an emerald mist surrounded them. The last sight of Maddy's disapproving figure faded away—and then, just as swiftly, they stepped out of the fog into a neatly manicured yard.

Izzy let go of Dax's hand, moving toward a familiar gazebo beside a stone fountain. Her fingers traced the weathered wood, her hand sinking into it, reminding her of her ethereal state.

"My dad built this gazebo shortly before he died . . . Why are we at my mother's house?"

Dax shrugged, his gaze lifting to the two-storey house before them. "Your soul was probably drawn here because it's familiar to you." He strode toward the back deck, making his way to the stairs.

"What are you doing?"

"Don't you want to check it out? Besides, we need to find an electrical outlet."

"An electrical outlet?" As she climbed the stairs after him, something darted past her feet. With a yelp of surprise, she lost her balance and stumbled into Dax.

"A freaking raccoon," Izzy burst out laughing. She pointed at a compost bin where a plump raccoon was rummaging around the lid. "My mom will lose her mind over this in the morning!"

Sidestepping the creature, Izzy continued through the sliding glass doors into the house.

The kitchen they stepped into was immaculate, opening up into a generous-sized family room. Above the fireplace, Izzy's eyes were drawn to a framed photograph. It showed a handsome couple comfortably settled between their three grown children.

"That's the last photo we took together before Dad died."

"You all look happy."

"We were," She replied, her words catching in her throat. "Dad was the glue that held us together . . ." She moved past Dax and approached the open archway, ascending the staircase.

"You'll see him again soon, Iz."

Not soon enough, she thought, an ache rising in her chest as she reached the landing. She paused before a closed door, her hand lingering above the firm wood.

"This is Kate's room," she murmured. Memories of her last visit with her older sister threatened to overwhelm her. Izzy caught her lower lip between her teeth, biting back the tears that pooled in her eyes.

Yet, despite her efforts, a solitary tear escaped, carving a wet trail down her face. "She hates me, Dax." Her voice broke as she turned to look at her soulmate.

"Why would you think that?" Dax's voice was soft as he came to stand next to her.

"It's my fault my dad died. If I hadn't drunk so much alcohol, I wouldn't have been nauseous. Dad would never have looked away from the road. . ."

Dax wrapped his arms around Izzy, pulling her into a hug. "You can't think like that," he said, smoothing her hair. "It was an accident. It's not your responsibility to bear."

Gently, he pulled back to look into her eyes. "Don't listen to your sister. She'll realize she's taking her grief out on you . . . and if she doesn't, well, Kate will when she returns home to Orbistia and goes through her life review."

Izzy absorbed Dax's words, nodding slowly. She had shouldered her father's death for a year, her guilt a constant companion. The conversation with her sister had sharpened that pain. Now, an urge to reconnect with

Kate swelled within her. Perhaps, with Kate sleeping peacefully, Izzy could stand before her and imagine, if only for a moment, that her sister didn't blame her for their father's death.

She moved away from Dax and into Kate's dark room. A sliver of moonlight slipped through the blinds, casting a beam on the polished floor. As she glanced around, Dax stepped into the room after her.

Her gaze landed on Kate's bed, expecting to see her sister. Instead, a monstrous figure loomed, its black, slimy appendage connecting its gaping mouth to Kate's neck. White orbs flowed through the cord into the creature.

Dax brushed past her, his spirit weapon forming in his grip. He positioned himself between Izzy and the demon as its red eyes snapped toward them. The monster hissed, a sound that froze Izzy in place. Around them, shadows seemed to stir as if anticipating the unfolding drama.

CHAPTER TWENTY-SEVEN

ANAM CARA

Izzy's pulse quickened. Dax sprang into action, his boomerang slicing through the air toward the creature. The demon reacted with terrifying speed, its talons flashing out. A gasp escaped Izzy as the boomerang was deflected, spiralling out of control and crashing against the wall.

The demon backed away from Kate, its tongue slipping from her neck, leaving a trail of black ichor dripping onto the floor. It reeled in its appendage, only to whip it out again, sending Dax hurtling into the far corner of the room. It then rotated its misshapen head to fixate on Izzy.

"*Advo . . . Telbum?*" Her voice wavered as she called forth her spirit weapon. A high-pitched laugh burst from the creature as Izzy gazed down at her empty hand. It thrust its tongue at her, smacking against the side of her arm as she jumped to the side, leaving a thick coat of slime on her arm.

The demon turned toward her soulmate, dismissing Izzy as a threat. With each attempt Dax made to stand, the creature batted him down again.

Izzy's hands clenched into fists, her mind racing as she struggled to remember the words of the incantation. A scream redirected her attention to Dax—He was pinned under the demon, its black tongue pressed against his face. As he struggled to free himself, a ghostly stream of energy siphoned from him into the creature.

A strange calmness washed over Izzy. Eyes closed, she pictured the Viking sword's hilt, its leather handle cool in her palm. The blade emerged in her mind's eye—cold, gleaming steel, Norse etchings—posed in her hand, ready for battle. "*Advo Telum,*" she murmured.

As Izzy opened her eyes, a luminous glow filled the room. In her hand, the Viking sword shone, its light casting shadows on the walls. With newfound confidence, she advanced on the demon. Her blade struck its head, and the creature burst into a shower of purple sparks. They danced in the air, slowly floating away. A stunned silence filled the room.

Bending down, Izzy helped Dax rise to his feet. "What was that?" she asked, supporting him as he sagged into her, his eyes closing.

"Psychic vampire. Disgusting things latch onto carnies, causing negative emotions and feeding off the energy they produce. It explains why your sister is so miserable and cruel."

Izzy glanced at Kate, taking in her pale, strained features. "Is she going to be all right?"

"She should be, as long as that thing doesn't return."

"Why wouldn't her spirit guides have helped her? That . . . thing must have been attached to her for at least a year!"

"Psychic vampires don't show up on the monitors. It probably took off whenever her guides were around," Dax murmured, his voice trailing off.

"Still, they should have noticed a change in her personality," Izzy said, her voice holding an edge of anger.

When he didn't respond, Izzy's stomach twisted in a knot of worry. "Dax?"

"Just tired," he whispered, his eyes briefly meeting hers. "The demon sapped a lot of my strength."

"How can I help?"

"Could you . . . share your energy?"

Izzy nodded, and Dax lifted his hand and placed it on her cheek. Warmth spread from his touch, and when he pulled back, his eyes sparkled with renewed energy. Yawning, Izzy stretched and rested her head against his shoulder.

"Did I take too much?" His eyes widened as he looked at her.

"I don't think so," Izzy said, smiling at him. She reached out, her fingers weaving through his hair. "I feel perfectly fine."

"Thank you," he murmured, pulling her closer. "You were incredible, you know. Facing that demon on your own!"

"Incredible, huh? That thing was literally trying to eat your face. There's no way you saw much of the fight."

Dax laughed. "Fair point. But having watched you in action before, I know firsthand how incredible you are."

Warmth blossomed in Izzy's belly at his compliment. She rose onto her tiptoes, her lips brushing against his. The moment was cut short by a sudden tugging on her shoulder blades. Breaking the kiss, she turned away, her hands seeking the source of discomfort at her back.

"What's wrong?"

"I don't know . . . there was this weird tugging at my back," Izzy said, her brow furrowing in discomfort as the pull grew stronger.

Understanding flickered across Dax's features. "Your body's stirring. You're going to wake up soon." He grasped her hand, leading her toward the wall. "We should be near your body . . . it won't feel as uncomfortable if you're close to it when you're pulled back in."

Izzy's eyebrows arched upward as he crouched by the electrical outlet. "Um, you're not supposed to touch those."

He looked up, his eyes meeting hers with a bittersweet smile. "One last adventure," he said. As his fingers brushed the outlet, Izzy's world became a blur of dark, twisting tunnels. A warm current buzzed through her, leaving her skin humming. Seconds later, they were standing in her bedroom.

Izzy's hand flew to her hair, patting down the wild strands. "What was that?"

"The Electricity Network. It's a way for spirits to travel around on Earth. Pretty cool, huh?"

"Yeah . . . sure." Her gaze was drawn to her physical form across the room, which was beginning to stir. "Will I even remember any of this?" The question hung heavily in the air.

"Yeah. Priscilla wasn't able to perform the memory spell on you."

"I wish we had more time," Izzy murmured, her lip caught between her teeth as tears welled up in her eyes. "I don't want to go back just yet . . . I don't want to leave you."

Dax's voice took on a tender tone. "We might see each other again soon. Some carnies get really good at astral projecting . . . And if we don't, I'll be here, waiting for you when you finally return home."

A cool sensation encircled Izzy's wrist, and she looked down to find a delicate silver bracelet. Its centrepiece gleamed with a red ruby. Holding it closer, her eyes caught an inscription within. "*Anam Cara*," she read. "What does that mean?"

"It means soul friend. A sacred connection with someone . . . I like to think that it means our souls flow together." He bent down to rest his forehead against hers. "The bracelet is an amulet. It will heat up when danger is near. It can also travel with you to the physical world."

His lips brushed hers lightly. "Think of it as a part of me with you, helping to keep you safe."

Tears cascaded down her face as she reached for another kiss. But the kiss never came. A strange vibration thrummed through her, causing her to recoil in surprise. Her eyes fell on Dax, and then, as though swept away by an unseen current, she was plunged back into her sleeping form. As her awareness ebbed away, she was swallowed by a deep, dreamless sleep.

CHAPTER TWENTY-EIGHT

New Beginnings

The morning sun slipped through a gap in the blinds, casting a warm beam onto Izzy's pillow. Beneath the sheets, she stirred, the mattress emitting a soft creak as she turned onto her side. She yawned and curled up, burying her face into the pillow. Abruptly, the shrill buzz of her alarm pierced the quiet, prompting her to grit her teeth in irritation. With a groan, Izzy extended her arm, groping for her cell phone. Her fingers found the familiar device, and she squinted through half-closed eyes, swiping the screen to shut off the alarm.

As she propped herself into a sitting position, the quilted blanket slid down to her waist. Another yawn escaped her as she rubbed the remnants of sleep from the corner of her eyes. While running her hands through her tousled hair, something solid brushed against her forehead. She paused and brought her hand down, her breath hitching at the sight of the bracelet encircling her wrist.

She gazed intently at the ruby embedded in the bracelet. "*Anam Cara*," she murmured, fingertips grazing the gem.

A rush of realization flowed through her—her dream was real. Her eyes flickered around the room, searching for her soulmate. But the room was quiet, empty of him. A weight of disappointment sank into her chest. Even if Dax was close, she had no way of sensing him. Her expression wavered, and a tear fell down her face.

Swiftly, Izzy brushed the tear aside. He wouldn't want her to cry. She closed her eyes, imagining Dax's hands gently holding her face. For a moment, it felt so real, as if he were really there. But as she opened her eyes, the sensation faded. She sighed and then threw back her covers. Swinging her legs over the edge of the bed, she stood up.

The alarm blared once more. Izzy exhaled sharply and grabbed her phone. A reminder flashed on the screen, capturing her attention. She groaned and dropped it back onto her bed. Today was the day of her mother's charity event.

Her gaze shifted to her duffle bag, and for a moment, she considered skipping the gala. But the prospect of her mother's disapproving look pushed that idea away. Izzy sighed again, grabbed her bag and started packing for Toronto.

A sharp knock at the door interrupted her, and she paused, the bag lying half-forgotten on the bed. She took a deep breath to steady herself. Memories of last night's encounter with Melanie and Kyler replayed in her mind. Her grip on the doorknob tightened, her knuckles going white.

"Yo, Izzy. Rise and shine, Goldilocks." Arlo's playful voice came through the door.

Izzy yanked the bedroom door open and crossed her arms, feigning annoyance. "Seriously, Arlo. It's seven o'clock in the morning."

Arlo grinned, his dishevelled hair making him look impish. "Exactly. Bright sun, clear skies. Today's gonna be gorgeous."

"Aren't you a real Pollyanna this morning."

Clutching at his stomach dramatically, Arlo groaned. "I'm starving!"

"You're twenty minutes early," Izzy pointed out, biting back a smile.

"I know," Arlo said, straightening up. "But I really am hungry. Can we go now?"

"Alright, alright!" She laughed and then rubbed at her stomach as it gave a low grumble. "Just give me a few minutes to get ready, okay?"

Nodding, Arlo walked away, his cheerful whistle filling the air.

Izzy let the door click shut and quickly dressed, pulling on jogging pants and a sweater. She swiftly ran her fingers through her hair, snatched up her coat, and joined Arlo in the common area. Aside from Emily—who cast Izzy a venomous glance on her way to the bathroom—the room was empty.

An hour later, having satisfied her appetite with pancakes, she returned to her room, the duffle bag slung over her shoulder. Just as she was about to leave, her cell phone rang. Placing the bag down, Izzy rifled through her belongings until her fingers closed around her phone. A weight settled on her shoulders as she caught sight of her sister's name on the caller ID.

"Hi, Kate," she answered, her voice unsteady.

"Isab . . . Izzy," Kate corrected. Her voice sounded high-pitched. "Izzy, I . . . I'm relieved you picked up."

"Why wouldn't I?"

"After our last conversation . . . I wouldn't have blamed you if you didn't," Kate said, pausing as a heavy silence settled between them. "Izzy, I'm so sorry. I should never have spoken to you like that. I . . . I don't know what came over me."

"It's okay, Kate." Izzy clenched her eyes shut. It had been a year since her sister had spoken to her with anything but coldness, let alone extended an apology. A spark of hope filled her chest as she thought of the monster that had been manipulating Kate. Now that it was gone, maybe their relationship could be repaired. Maybe she could have her big sister back.

"It's not okay! I've been terrible to you—blaming you for things that aren't your fault; I'm so sorry!" Kate's voice cracked as she started to cry.

"I can't make sense of it. Every morning, I woke up filled with this rage. . . It clouded my vision. But this morning . . ." Kate paused, stifling a sob. "This morning, it felt like a fog had cleared, and I can think clearly again. My first thought was of you, of our last conversation—Izzy, I didn't mean anything I said!"

Izzy blinked back tears, her vision blurring. Retreating from the door, she collapsed onto her bed and clutched her pillow to her chest. Anger surged within her as she thought of the demon that had preyed on her sister. It had exploited Kate's vulnerability—almost succeeding in driving a permanent wedge between the two women.

"Okay," Izzy said at last. "Honestly, Kate, let's just put this behind us."

"Izzy, about university—"

"I'm applying, Kate. I know you don't want me to, but—"

"I do want you to apply. It's your life, Izzy. You should do what makes you happy. Eddie and I can manage the family business. And don't worry about Mother; she'll understand."

"I doubt that."

"I'll talk to her, Iz. It will be okay." There was a short pause before she added, "And about Mother's charity event tonight, you don't need to attend."

"Um, yes, Kate, I do. Mom made it explicitly clear that I have to be there."

"I already spoke with her earlier this morning. I told her it would be good publicity for the business if you attended your fundraiser for the food bank instead."

"And she agreed?"

"She did."

Izzy's breath steadied, the tension in her shoulders easing. "Thanks, Kate," she said, the corners of her mouth lifting into a smile.

"Anyways, I should head off," Kate said. "I hope your event goes well."

"Thanks!"

"I love you, Iz." Kate's voice came through, heavy with emotion.

"Love you too."

After ending the call, Izzy held the phone against her chest, marvelling at the change in Kate. The world appeared to right itself, and for the first time in what felt like forever, she felt a connection with her sister.

A sharp knock on the door pulled Izzy back to the present. The persistent rapping continued as she walked to the door, anticipating Arlo's usual grin. Instead, Melanie's presence greeted her. Heat rushed through Izzy's body as she clenched the doorknob. A surge of irritation rose within her, and she fought the impulse to slam the door shut.

"Melanie," she said coolly.

"Morning, Iz."

Melanie shifted uncomfortably in the doorway. "I just wanted to check in on you," she began. "I'm sorry I forgot to last night." The fatigue etched in Melanie's eyes spoke of a night without rest, likely in Kyler's company.

"Want to grab some breakfast before you head back to Toronto?"

"I've already eaten," Izzy said, her tone clipped. Yet, observing Melanie, a fresh idea started to take shape. She softened her voice and said, "I'm not going to Toronto anymore."

"You're not? What about your mom's thing tonight?"

"I don't have to go now—Anyway, I have to prepare for the food bank fundraiser, but how about we meet for dinner afterward? Michelangelo's at seven?"

Melanie's eyebrows lifted. "Michelangelo's? That place is fancy. What's the special occasion?"

"It's a surprise. Now, I really have to get ready." She shut the door before Melanie could respond.

Moving to her bed, Izzy grabbed her phone and texted a quick message to Mrs. Lake, confirming her attendance at the fundraiser. She then sent Kyler a text as well. Her lips curved into a smirk as she plotted the evening out in her mind.

The day passed in a blur, with all the pieces falling into place nicely. The fundraiser was a success, drawing a large crowd from the city and coverage from local radio stations. While organizing the charity run and collecting donations, Izzy managed to reserve a table at Michelangelo's. Rhylynn even helped out by running an errand for her. It turned out she had had a similar experience with Melanie the previous year.

Later that evening, as the setting sun draped the restaurant in a warm glow, Izzy connected with Rhylynn in the parking lot. "Thanks, Rhy Rhy," she said, taking the bouquet of red flowers from her friend.

Rhylynn smiled as a cool breeze teased her hair. Drawing her green shawl tighter, she shivered slightly. "I'm glad to help. Melanie had this coming."

The soft clinking of silverware and murmured conversations greeted them as they approached the reservation desk. Izzy smiled at the hostess, her hand resting on the smooth surface of the counter. "I have a table reserved under *Adams*." As the hostess consulted the black book before her, Izzy added, "The reservation is actually for two of my friends. They'll be here soon. We're just here to decorate," she explained, gesturing to the bouquet of roses.

"Oh, how sweet! Engagement or anniversary?"

"Just a special celebration."

"Very well, Adams, party of two. Please follow me." She picked up two menus and gestured for Izzy and Rhylynn to follow her. They were shown to a table by a window—the scene outside was beautiful, the bay's waters reflecting the last whispers of sunset.

"The server will attend to you once your friends arrive," the hostess said, placing the menus on the table before departing.

Izzy and Rhylynn set to work immediately, scattering rose petals across the tablecloth. Next, they placed the remaining flowers in a vase at the table's centre.

"It looks great," Rhylynn said, offering Izzy a thumbs-up.

"Let's head to the bar—we can watch them arrive from there," Izzy suggested, hooking her arm through Rhylynn's. They moved through the crowd toward the bar, their jeans setting them apart amid the dressed-up crowd.

Moments later, they watched Kyler saunter in, shamelessly flirting with the hostess as she led him to the table. He halted, his eyebrows drawing together at the sight of the rose petals, but then eased into his chair and picked up the menu.

The sight of Kyler brought thoughts of Dax to Izzy's mind, causing a knot of emotion to tighten in her chest. She found herself wishing he was there with her. Rhylynn, perceptive as ever, gave her arm a comforting squeeze. "You got this!"

Five minutes later, Melanie appeared, her hair styled into a side knot, highlighting her bare shoulders. Clad in a form-fitting blue dress, she made an impressive entrance. Izzy's eyes darkened, casting a sharp, frosty look at Melanie.

Kyler looked up from the menu as Melanie was shown to the table. "Why are you here?" he asked, his eyes narrowing at her.

Melanie shifted uncomfortably. "Izzy invited me."

"You mean she invited you on our date? Why would she do that?"

Sharing a brief look with Rhylynn, Izzy took a deep breath and strode to the table. "I thought I'd make a reservation for the two of you," she began. "After all, since I'm no longer in the way, you're free to enjoy each other's company without hiding."

Kyler's eyebrows knit together as he looked at her. "What are you talking about?"

"I mean," Izzy began, her voice loud enough to carry across to the other tables, "that we're done. I'm breaking up with you." She turned her attention to Melanie. "And you, Melanie, need to find a new friend."

Melanie's voice quivered. "How did you find out?"

"Shut up," Kyler said sharply, shooting her a warning look. He rose quickly, his palms outstretched in a placating gesture. "Babe, whatever you've heard is not true. I would never betray you." He closed the distance between them, reaching out to place a hand on her shoulder.

Izzy flinched away. "Don't touch me," she said. "You're a narcissistic bigot, and I'm done with you."

She fixed Melanie with a steady look. "He's all yours. I hope he was worth it." Then, without a backward glance, she made her way to the exit.

"Izzy, wait!" Melanie's voice cut through the restaurant din. She rushed after Izzy, grasping at her arm. Izzy swung around, her eyes cold, daring Melanie to continue.

"I . . . I don't even know what to say."

"Nothing you say matters now," Izzy retorted, pulling her arm away. She passed through the restaurant's glass doors into the brisk night air. Reaching her car quickly, she got in and closed the door.

A moment later, Rhylynn tapped on her window. With a shaky smile, Izzy rolled it down, grateful that Melanie hadn't followed her outside.

"How do you feel?"

"Aside from feeling like I'm buzzing with nerves, there's a sense of relief. I've said all I needed to them."

Rhylynn nodded, her llama earrings clicking against her neck. She adjusted her glasses and smiled at Izzy. "Good," she said, hugging herself against another gust of wind. "I'm heading home. Call if you need to talk, all right?"

"Yup. Thanks, Rhylynn. I really appreciate all your help."

"All I did was bring roses."

"And support. It made confronting them easier, knowing you were in my corner."

"I'll always be in your corner, Iz," Rhylynn replied, her expression turning solemn. She waved and walked away to her car.

Izzy smiled and rolled up the window, grateful to have found a friend in Rhylynn. A shiver passed through her as the engine hummed to life in her Honda. Driving along the waterfront moments later, Izzy watched the sun's final rays dance across the water, and a serene calm washed over her.

In the span of twenty-four hours, Izzy's life had veered toward a brighter path. For the first time in a year, the horizon glowed with promise, and the weight on her shoulders felt lighter. A warm, tingling sensation wrapped around her hand resting on the armrest, akin to the touch of another's hand atop her own. Her gaze settled on the bracelet adorning her wrist, its stone glinting in the fading light. "Souls that flow together," she murmured, knowing that Dax was with her, always and forever.

COMING SOON

Bound By Darkness

About the Author

Jessica Lee Sheppard lives in rural Ontario with her husband and four children. Her debut novel, *The Adventures of Izzy Adams: Descending into Darkness*, draws inspiration from her daughters, Izzy and Rhylynn. Jessica graduated with a degree in Psychology from York University, a Social Services Worker diploma from Loyalist College, and a Master's degree in Social Work from Windsor University. Her diverse experiences spanning mental health, child welfare, and education infuse her stories with depth and understanding.

When she's not writing, Jessica enjoys gardening, reading, and serial-watching television shows she puts off to write. Aside from establishing a successful writing career, Jessica dreams of watching her children grow into happy adults and of one day travelling to Greece.

Sign up for Jessica's newsletter for exclusive offers, insider content, and updates on new releases.

JOIN THE COMMUNITY!

Dive deeper into the "Adventures of Izzy Adams" series. Connect with Jessica on social media for discussions, giveaways, sneak peeks, and more!

- Facebook
- Twitter
- TikTok
- Instagram
- YouTube
- Linkedin
- Goodreads

For updates and exclusives, visit jessicaleesheppard.com

Manufactured by Amazon.ca
Bolton, ON

41640504R00127